BEAUTIFUL

Massimo Cuomo

BEAUTIFUL

*Translated from the Italian
by Will Schutt*

Europa
editions

Europa Editions
214 West 29th Street
New York, N.Y. 10001
www.europaeditions.com
info@europaeditions.com

Copyright © 2017 by Edizioni e/o
First Publication 2020 by Europa Editions

Translation by Will Schutt
Original title: *Bellissimo*
Translation copyright © 2020 by Europa Editions

Library of Congress Cataloging in Publication Data is available
ISBN 978-1-60945-581-1

Cuomo, Massimo
Beautiful

Book design by Emanuele Ragnisco
www.mekkanografici.com

Illustration at page 269 by Eva Ferri

Cover illustration by Alessandro Gottardo

Prepress by Grafica Punto Print – Rome

Printed and bound in Great Britain by Clays Ltd, Elcograf S.p.A.

CONTENTS

For Claudia and Alberto,
my sister and brother

BEAUTIFUL

THE DIVINE CHILD
Mérida, Mexico, 1976

El nacimiento
BIRTH

On one side of the glass was the face of Miguel—day zero.

On the other side of the glass was the face of Santiago—year five.

The glass reflected back his look of astonishment and the mole on his right cheek. Like the button of a blouse. Like the point of a question mark. And there was only one question on Santiago's mind as he observed his little brother in the crib on the other side of the glass: "Why is he so beautiful?"

Everyone, in fact, thought he was beautiful in a special way. The grown-ups hovering over Santiago kept saying so out loud, like a lullaby. Everyone who passed through the hospital corridor and paused before the glass would, at a certain point, say so.

"He's beautiful," they'd say. He was beautiful compared to the seven other newborns, five boys and two girls, some of whom were quite ugly, each of whom was beautiful to their own mother. But Miguel was beautiful to everyone, beyond a shadow of a doubt. While they were looking at him, he turned over and—where he found the strength was anyone's guess—rolled onto his side as if he might pick up and leave. His backside peeked out from underneath the pale blue blanket to reveal a small mole on his buttock. Like the point of an exclamation point.

A nurse entered the room and spotted the boy on his side among the other babies. But when she went to set him on his back, she couldn't help herself: she took him in her arms, held him to her bosom, squeezed him, and kissed his forehead. For a moment, she stole him. Or maybe he was the one abducting her, carrying her off. That was how Santiago witnessed Miguel make his first conquest, a few hours after the boy had taken his first breath, consummated without a word, not even a look; it was as if Santiago were watching a TV show on the other side of the glass.

When the nurse recalled that Miguel's brother—addled by unanswered questions—and other people were watching on the opposite side of the glass, she placed her hand under the baby's thighs and lifted him in the air like a trophy. Miguel took a breath and contemplated things from on high, from the perspective that he would have all his life, scanning the first slice of the world in front of him. Then, as if to grab hold of it, he reached out his arms and half closed his minuscule fingers, and his lips formed what actually appeared to be a smile, the first of a million, which emerged out of nowhere, like the sun when it rains.

"Why is he so beautiful?" asked Santiago again.

"He's so beautiful," someone repeated out loud, then began clapping. A round of applause erupted, which broke the silence and made Santiago's knees shake. It shook the peeling blue walls, the waxed floor, the foundations of the Hospital Regional, the dusty road, the white houses of Mérida, the Paseo de Montejo and the Cathedral of San Ildefonso, the sandy dunes that stretch skyward—the whole sky shook. The universe trembled before Miguel's beauty. All at once the other children in the room, roused by the commotion, began to cry.

Those with prostate or lung cancer, or with bone, liver, and brain metastases, were sleeping on the floor below. On the floor above, wizened old people lay dying on mattresses that reeked of urine. On the floor in between them sunshine poured through the windows to bless this celebration of Miguel.

The nurse walked out with the newborn and, amid the applause, handed him to Vicente Moya. The man hesitated before taking the child tentatively by his underarms, struggling to find a grip. Stone-faced, proud, the man himself was very handsome. Miguel and his father regarded one another for the first time, under the watch of a handful of relatives and onlookers who had gathered on the landing. It was a sacred scene; the applause faded. No one was breathing now. Vicente Moya didn't smile because he never smiled. He looked at his son as if he were expecting Miguel to speak first. Miguel ran his fingers through the man's thick moustache, tugged them—tickling him a little in the process—and, instead of tearing at his moustache, tore from his father a smile. A splendid, extremely rare, precious smile.

They say that was the only time Vicente Moya ever smiled. They natter on about how, had he smiled that way a little more in life, crowds of *mujeres calientes* would have jockeyed to replace the plain woman he'd taken for a wife. Others suspect that he never even smiled that morning at the Hospital Regional, just grit his teeth and grimaced. But the truth is that Vicente Moya lifted baby Miguel and, after flashing a smile, managed to string together a complete sentence.

"¡Miren que guapo!" he shouted with a hint of surprise.

"Look at how handsome he is!" he repeated with deep satisfaction.

In response, another intense round of applause erupted, and Hermenegildo Serrano, the baby's elderly grandfather, a dancer who hailed from the state of Jalisco, switched on the battery-operated tape deck he carried with him everywhere, which always played "Jarabe Tapatío," and began to hop about on his spindly legs in the folk style of the land of his birth. The happy music flooded the ward, and while Vicente Moya began wiggling his hips and Miguel rocked to the rhythm, everyone clapped and swayed as they formed a procession to bring Maria Serrano the *guapo* son she had just given birth to—the son now held in the air like the baby Jesus.

Between the floors of the dying, a dozen people were celebrating as if there were nothing in life but life, beauty, Miguel's smile, the cheerful sun, cheerfulness itself, mariachi music, a new and brighter future, as if his birth gave rise to hope, as if on the upper and lower floors a miracle might occur.

At the end of that procession headed up by Vicente Moya, with Grandpa Hermenegildo and his tape deck just behind him, followed by a few neighbors, the nurse, and others who just happened to be passing by and were now laughing, dancing, and singing with joy, stood little Santiago—forgotten. He listened to his grandpa's favorite song, which had become his favorite song, and followed a foot behind the procession with his head down.

In Room 6 of the second floor of the Hospital Regional, Maria Serrano was waiting for Miguel. She heard the music in the hall drawing closer. She had seen her son for just a minute, just as he came into the light. The doctor had held him upside down by his ankles and spanked him, and Miguel had let out a burst of breath.

"He's got a small mole on his tush," said the doctor.

Then he turned him right side up to get a look at his face.

"He's beautiful," he added, and handed him over to the nurse.

Until then that was all the mother knew about Miguel, that and an upside-down glance that she'd managed to get as she craned her neck from the bed of the delivery room. The music from Grandpa Hermenegildo's tape deck was now three steps from the door, now two, one more. In came the heavy tread of Vicente Moya carrying wispy Miguel, who floated in the air

like a dark-haired angel. When he appeared in Room 6, soaring to "Jarabe Tapatío," the women lying on the cots next to
Maria Serrano all melted and sighed in unison. But she held
her breath and, with all the strength she had left in her body,
extended her arms to receive what was rightfully hers.

Maria Serrano had never been beautiful. That fact had been
more apparent ever since she'd married Vicente Moya. She'd
become the ugly wife of a handsome husband—that was that.
Likewise, as soon as Miguel had finally landed on top of her, it
was immediately clear that from then on, this woman—pale
and exhausted after giving birth—would also be the ugly
mother of a handsome son. Had someone handed her a mirror,
had someone shown her a picture of her first embrace with her
newborn, perhaps she would have come to the same conclu-
sion. Then again, perhaps not; there were some things Maria
Serrano seemed incapable of seeing. In her white gown on the
steps of the church, she had simply smiled, the way she was
smiling now, the way she had smiled five years ago when little
Santiago had landed in her arms.

Ah, yes, Santiago, who was entering Room 6 behind the
others, beneath the action, noticed by no one. No one except
Maria Serrano, that is, who seemed incapable of seeing certain
things yet always saw them.

"Es hermosa adentro," they said about her. "She's beautiful
on the inside."

So, while all eyes were on Miguel, Maria Serrano lifted her
own and found Santiago behind the crowd. Felt him, more
than anything.

"Santiago," she whispered, holding Miguel tightly.

"Santiago!" she said again, louder this time, so that he'd
hear her.

But she was drowned out by the shouts and music. So
Hermenegildo Serrano pressed the off button with his withered finger and stopped the music cold. As the music died, so

did the shouts. A hush fell over the room, the kind that reigned over the other two floors of the hospital.

"Santiago," Maria Serrano whispered sweetly.

The crowd parted, made way for the contracted body of Santiago, his fists clenched, his eyes solitary and wounded as he looked at the intruder in her arms.

"Come here," Maria Serrano commanded.

Santiago finally screwed up the courage to approach his mother. His brother. He ran to the edge of the bed, placed his hands on the sheets, and breathed in Miguel; the baby, he thought, smelled like cookies.

"What do you think?" the woman murmured.

Santiago didn't know how to unscramble his thoughts.

"He's beautiful," he repeated mechanically.

Maria Serrano looked closely at him; her eyes penetrated deep inside him.

"You are too," she said softly in his ear.

W hen he needed to, Vicente Moya spared no expense, and he always dressed elegantly on account of his line of work. Guayabera salesman.

"Tu trabajo tienes que llevarlo contigo," he believed. You must carry your work with you.

Every day he wore the shirts he sold. Even in the rain, even at funerals. They fell straight down his massive back. In his untucked white shirt, Vicente Moya was always the tallest salesman. He didn't smile in the shop either, yet he knew how to sell guayaberas because he lived in them. They looked perfect on him, eye-catching, worth more than they were: you wound up buying one without even wanting to.

The truth is he liked his uniform. He knew it the day he first donned one, as a boy, on the occasion of his second cousin's wedding. The following morning he turned up at the Casa de Guayaberas in a guayabera and asked to be hired on a trial basis. The owner of the store wore thick lenses but saw far. Noticing a couple of clients enter, he turned to young Moya.

"Sell three shirts to those two and you're hired."

Vicente Moya puffed out his chest, took a deep breath, and headed over to the pair of strangers who would decide his fate. A step away from them, he held out his arms as if he were going to hook them around their necks.

The store owner looked on from a distance; he couldn't hear a word of what was said. The two clients began to nod, then followed Vicente Moya around the store, where the latter moved as if he'd been born in the racks: he dished out advice, waited outside the fitting room, expertly ran his hand over the cloth, now and then stood in front of the mirror as if to show them a pose or a new style of standing. He returned to the counter with four guayaberas and the two men at his heels.

"I took it upon myself to offer these gentlemen the fourth one on the house," he said. "You can deduct it from my salary, naturally."

The old man took his time to absorb all that had been said, pushed his glasses up on the bridge of his nose, and quickly worked out what had just transpired.

"*Muy bien*," he finally exclaimed, and drew up the bill.

After that, Vicente Moya became the Casita's best salesman, the only one always wearing a guayabera, even on his days off. And when the old owner passed on to the next life and was replaced by his son, Vicente Moya was given a raise. Which is why he managed to save a little something every month, why he was always dressed as if for a wedding, and why, when the situation demanded, he would spare no expense. Like the time he organized the party for Miguel's homecoming.

Maria Serrano carried her baby out of the Hospital Regional a few days after she'd given birth, at the end of a torrid afternoon. Without anyone's having noticed, the maternity ward had lost a ray of light, as if someone had taken down the Christmas decorations. From that moment on, the lights came on in Casa Moya, where it would always be Christmas, or at least for as long as Miguel was there. One continuous party for which Vicente Moya spared no expense—he would no longer spare expenses: *fiestas* and music would follow Miguel forever. Perhaps that was why, unlike his father, the boy never stopped smiling.

In his third-hand Ford which he drove without a license, Grandpa Hermenegildo kept the tape deck blaring, and, when mother and son climbed out of the car together, they were greeted at the door by a dozen musicians dressed like cowboys who rolled out a red carpet of *canciones rancheras* on the Moyas' front yard. Six violins, four trumpets, a *vihuela*, and a *guitarrón* heralded the arrival of Maria Serrano and Miguel. All around them were giant bouquets of paper flowers, long tricolor ribbons, and a stream of friends, relatives, and neighbors who had just arrived or were about to arrive. They came from all over Mérida in groups of ten, a hundred. Word had spread throughout the city that Vicente Moya had had a son, a beautiful baby boy, and that the guayaberas salesmen was offering *papadzules* and *panuchos* to whomever stopped by to shake hands and welcome the newborn.

His shirt open, a small cigar tucked behind his ear and protruding from his hair, smashed on happiness and tequila, Vicente Moya clutched an empty glass that swung in the wind. He looked disheveled, down-at-heel, his beauty even more bewitching than usual, softened by the effects of alcohol and fatherhood. He went out to meet his wife and son, danced a few steps as he had at the Hospital Regional, gathered up Miguel with his free hand, and lifted him in the air while raising his other hand, as if he were offering both son and glass to God.

Then he kissed Maria Serrano, a kiss that the people of Mérida would talk about for years to come, the women especially. A spontaneous, dramatic, photogenic kiss that, had he been more lucid, Vicente Moya may never have agreed to with all those people looking on. Mothers would tell their daughters about that kiss. They'd say that, on that warm May evening, perched on the palm of Vicente Moya, Miguel suddenly looked down—and took his eyes off God—and learned from his father how to kiss a woman. The daughters, on the other hand, would tell their mothers in the years to come that the lesson hadn't been lost on the boy—not in the slightest.

Santiago was still a child, yet somewhere inside him that scene was imprinted on the film of his soul, as it was on the soul of everyone present. He looked on from the arms of one of Maria Serrano's friends, who squeezed him tight but not tight enough. And when the kiss was over, he couldn't hear his father's voice, the voice of Vicente Moya, who had turned away from his wife and was calling him by name, calling out loudly. "Santiago!" he cried, "Santiago!" Despite being drunk, his father sensed an absence of weight in his left hand—in his hand that held the glass all the way up to the arm attached to his heart; something, or someone, was missing. "Santiago!" cried Vicente Moya. But Santiago didn't hear him. His name got lost on the wind as the crowd latched onto three quarters of the Moya family, as a stream of bodies swept them up, engulfed them, to honor the newborn Miguel, embrace their embrace, celebrate beauty and love, and earn the tortillas they'd been offered by the man of the house.

Mar de brazos. Río de lágrimas
SEA OF ARMS, RIVER OF TEARS

B aby Miguel spent his days in the arms of his mother
and—more often—in the arms of his mother's friends,
who stopped in to say hello with greater frequency than
they had before and, once through the front door, would take
him from Maria Serrano in order, so they said, to relieve her.

Vicente Moya didn't notice them. When he returned home,
after hours up to his neck in guayaberas, he was too tired to
notice their lingering vibrations, the perfume that rose like
heat from the places they'd huddled all day: the walls, the
wooden chairs, the dishcloths, Miguel.

Miguel, who never cried. Miguel, who always smiled.
Miguel, who had no incentive to do anything else, because
there was always someone to rock him to sleep, a lullaby in the
background, sweet kisses and sweet smells in the air, long eyelashes that brushed against him, soft bosoms on which to lay
his head. In the Moyas' kitchen, he slipped into the arms of
women like a flower into water, as they entered his house, gathered him up, and rocked him in concentric circles to help him
sleep. By the time the sun went down, the baby had traveled
dozens of miles without ever having left his kitchen, had
breathed in dozens of different women. He was born to float
on love; you knew it by the way he yielded to their embraces,
how he repaid their smiles with his smile.

Maria Serrano, on the other hand, wasn't accustomed to all
that to-ing and fro-ing: in a matter of days something like sea-
sickness welled up in her, as did her fear that the child would

lose sight of her face among all those other faces. Instinctively, she held him as often as possible to her breast, pretended to be tired, shut herself up in her room with him, and locked the door behind her.

"Can anyone tell me where she's going?" one of the women asked.

"She says she's tired," replied another.

"She may be tired, but the baby isn't!" responded yet another.

The kitchen would suddenly turn into a wasteland, and the women would scrutinize one another, barely masking their embarrassment, and try to think up an excuse to stay. Some hurried off. Others lingered in the hopes that the time would pass quickly, and in the interim, frazzled, they traded small talk, which soon gave way to gossip and whispers. When the wait went on too long, a deep-seated dissatisfaction came over them, which they could neither explain with any clarity nor suppress.

"I bet she's ashamed," said one.

"Of what?" they all asked.

"Oh please—of how little milk those puny breasts produce," said the one with the fullest figure in the group, almost exasperated.

"Whatever it is, she's too apprehensive," interjected another woman, slighter and more barren than Maria Serrano, in part to redirect the conversation.

"Yes, too apprehensive," reiterated the first woman. "And so sad. I mean, with a son that handsome, how can you never smile?"

Their frustration gave rise to increasingly shrill and indignant remarks, spiteful conjectures about Maria Serrano, especially about the way she carried herself in the world—with no apparent enthusiasm, not a trace of physical beauty. Her defects jarred with her son, like a bad omen.

Only then would someone turn to look around for Maria Serrano's other son, Santiago. Splayed on the kitchen floor, the five-year-old was drawing on a piece of paper. When they checked to see if he was listening, he seemed in another world. So the women huddled closer together to spin out their litany of insults.

Shortly after, without anyone's noticing, Santiago stood up and, sensing his mother's absence, went barefoot in search of her. He reached the bedroom door and turned the knob to enter. To no effect. Maria Serrano and Miguel were in there, and if Santiago put his ear to the door, all he heard was an oppressive silence. The sheet of paper on the floor showed a small brown cactus with long, dark spines.

Then one day Miguel began to cry.

It happened suddenly, during the least stifling hour of the afternoon, and disrupted all the goings-on and chatter of the past tearless weeks of his life. The cry sent a chill through the house, created confusion, and—as if such were possible— prompted everyone to pay closer attention to the little one who at that moment just happened to be in the lap of the thin, flat woman.

The voluptuous woman leaped to her feet and snatched up the child to sort out the situation, as if the child had already started choosing, as if it was in his nature to refuse mediocrity. Without hesitating, she planted him in her chest, buried Miguel in the hollow between her large, exposed breasts that tasted of sweat and sex. He dove into them with relish, and the medicine did work to distract him; with greater intensity than usual his lungs were filled with the promise of what was to come, the powerful odor of regions in which he'd lose himself when he grew up. Once again, he was given a taste of the future, a whiff of the potential delights that should have restored his good mood. But Miguel began to cry again.

The thin woman let out a dirty, vulgar laugh, and in that instant Maria Serrano appeared in the kitchen holding a bundle of habaneros that she'd picked from the garden in their backyard. She struggled to understand the meaning of that laughter and, more importantly, that crying, which had also caught her off guard after weeks in which Miguel had displayed nothing but smiles and joyful moans. The peppers fell to the floor with a grave, excessively loud thud, and Maria Serrano extended her arms toward the woman holding her son, who, like the woman before her, had now become the culprit of the child's crying. But there were five women in the kitchen and all of them, somehow, felt they were to blame, as if Miguel had actually been wired to never cry.

When the child was back in his mother's lap, the other women swallowed a bitter pill and waited. Were Miguel to have stopped crying then, were he to have welcomed Maria Serrano's embrace with one of his smiles, it would have changed everything. It would have been a choice—for that matter, one in keeping with the natural order of things. An understandable choice, were it any other baby. In short, the right choice, the normal choice, had Miguel not deceived them, had he not yielded to each of them without apparent preference and placed them all on an equal footing, including Maria Serrano.

While his mother held him tight, while she listened to his cry for the first time, for the first time she felt the physical sensation that he was hers, that he needed her, and she wondered what she'd done wrong and when exactly she'd lost her grip on him in the rough river of other women's arms. But she wasn't at fault, even if she couldn't be certain about that just yet, nor would she be in the future. It was in keeping with the natural order of things: Miguel was a piece of the sky, sand in the wind, seawater slipping through one's hands, a burning bush. And that was why the silence that the other women were anxiously and fretfully waiting for, an end to that sudden cry, never came; the mother's lap didn't placate the child either, and the women forming a circle around Maria Serrano took guilty pleasure in this revelation.

A kind of hopelessness set in. Now that Miguel had begun to cry for no apparent reason, it occurred to them that he might never stop crying, that he might flood the kitchen, the house, and all the rest with his tears, till all of Mérida lay underwater. A long, endless storm had begun.

Instead, just as everything seemed doomed, she put her lips on the child's forehead, lightly kissed his skin, and looked up at the women to offer up the one possible explanation, the only one, ultimately, in keeping with the natural order of things.

"He has a fever," said Maria Serrano. "Miguel has a fever."

Medicamentos milagros
MIRACLE DRUGS

S ancho Molina was the Moyas' doctor. He was the son of a shopkeeper who spent a few seasons mixing concoctions with strange herbs and testing them on barnyard animals. In the middle of the night you could hear chickens cawing excruciatingly as if it were dawn, only the last dawn of their lives, and one September evening an old woman swore she found a dozen male rabbits behind Molina's ramshackle laboratory all clustered together attempting to copulate.

Then, one Christmas Eve, Sancho Molina pulled a black hat on over his white tunic and went out into the street to heal people. He quickly became a kind of legend in the neighborhood on account of his powerful lotions that rekindled people's desire. They said he revived an old man on death's door by rubbing his chest with an unguent that smelled, according to those present, like manure. Apparently, on another occasion, he fed twine into the mouth of a little boy with a cough and pulled a live frog out of his stomach.

By the time he arrived at Casa Moya, the stars were out. Miguel was crying on the white sleeves of Vicente Moya's guayabera; the latter had returned home, immediately snatched the child out of Maria Serrano's lap, and, as if to defend the boy, refused to let anyone else hold him.

"Call Molina," he said, and sat down in a chair. Meanwhile the child's temperature had risen again, and his shortness of breath was growing more and more worrisome.

Sancho Molina appraised the situation. He placed his

calloused hand on the head of Miguel, shut his eyes, opened them again. In a corner of the room he noticed Santiago sitting silently.

"Come here," he said.

Santiago's heart pounded. It felt like weeks since anyone had looked at him that way. Which was, in fact, the case.

"Me?" he asked nervously.

"Yes, come here," reiterated Molina.

Vicente Moya and Maria Serrano gazed at their firstborn as if he had just sprung from a crack in the wall and, without knowing why, felt a shallow sense of guilt. Shallow as the breath of Miguel, who nevertheless took all the air out of the room, tamped down every noise and regret. When Santiago stood under Molina's hat, the doctor placed his free hand on his head, just as he'd done with the boy's brother, then closed his eyes again.

Santiago felt the man's fingertips touching his hair, his warm palm on his forehead. In the shadow of Molina's arm, the boy traced the invisible line of the man's wrist, the dark skin buttoned up by the sleeve of his tunic, which, to look at it, was like a tunnel to probe. Black, murky, deep, hypnotic. Santiago had the sensation of being tiny and alone, probing the sleeve of the *curandero* like a cockroach in the sewer pipes of Mérida. The tunnel ended where Molina's other sleeve ended, where Miguel lay; he could see him, almost touch him, breathe in his shallow breath. Then Sancho Molina suddenly lifted both arms, and Santiago found himself standing in the same place he always stood—in the middle of the kitchen.

The doctor removed two bottles from his bag, each containing a different colored liquid, and set them on the table in front of Vicente Moya.

"This is for the little one," he said, pointing to the red vial.

"This is for the other boy," he said, pointing to the transparent bottle.

* * *

They spent days on edge. Casa Moya and the entire neighborhood stood still to listen to Miguel's breathing. The women who had until then thronged the kitchen now practiced restraint, took turns dropping by, used discretion when inquiring after news and reporting back to one another.

Every hour on the hour, Maria Serrano would uncap Sancho Molina's red bottle and pour a few drops on the baby's lips. The baby reacted with imperceptible and erratic progress: at times he seemed better, at times he made a continuous wheeze like a broken dishwasher. After she'd seen to Miguel, she would call Santiago over, and the boy would approach. Now that the baby was coiled up in a basket on the table, his face contorted in pain, he felt closer to that brother whose provenance he didn't understand. Just as he didn't understand why he too was ill, nor what illness ailed him, yet he opened his mouth and swallowed the flavorless medicine that Molina had prescribed. He stared at the liquid in the bottle and compared it to the colored liquid in Miguel's bottle, but he asked no questions.

"Bravo," said Maria Serrano, planting a kiss on his forehead.

Santiago went back to drawing. On his sheet of paper was a yellowish meadow under dark gray clouds. Outside, on the other hand, it was a bright afternoon and the woman went out to the garden to get some fresh air and pick beans while listening at the open window for any noises in the kitchen or change in Miguel's breathing. Shortly after, Santiago looked up, having sensed that something had happened: after weeks of being swarmed with visitors, the house was, for the first time, empty.

He stood up with a blue crayon in his hand. He took the few steps required to reach the table, brought his face close to the baby's face, and sniffed him. Then he touched the baby's nose with his finger. That is how the brothers Moya made their introductions—with no witnesses. And thanks to that contact, Santiago realized that they weren't that different after all. With his blue crayon he drew a small mole on his brother's cheek, and the baby, perhaps tickled, returned to smiling.

In other words, everything would have been in order had the baby not gone back to breathing in that dreadful way. Santiago put his ear to his mouth and barely detected his shallow breathing. He felt moved to do something, driven to the corner of the credenza where Maria Serrano had left the doctor's bottles. He picked up his own, the transparent one, uncapped it, and, as he'd seen his mother do, poured a few drops on Miguel's lips, which slipped past Miguel's mouth, down his throat, into his stomach. Maybe it was the red liquid that didn't work. That's what Santiago thought. But nothing about his brother's breathing changed.

When Maria Serrano came back in with the beans, Santiago barely managed to put back the bottle in time and return to drawing on the floor. She rested her eyes on Miguel, on whose right cheek a blue mole had materialized. Confused, she wetted her thumb with her tongue and ran it over her son's skin: like that, the little mole was gone. Then she turned to look at her firstborn, who, on his sheet of paper, between the meadow and clouds, was coloring in the sky. And in that sky the woman glimpsed what Santiago had done with his blue crayon. Maria Serrano finally got it. She was about to say something but caught herself, since, all things considered, there was nothing to say.

Corriendo desesperadamente
A MAD DASH

Vicente Moya ran. He ran like a madman in the moonlight. He ran breathlessly, without looking back, kicking up dust on the narrow streets of Mérida, through the black night in the white city in the direction of Sancho Molina's shack. He arrived, pounded on the door till he'd almost broken it down, with one heave wrested it open. Inside were heaps of empty cages, rusty knives, dark pitch, blackened glass receptacles, jerry cans, congealed blood, spent candles, silence, dirty rags, and a depressing stink. Only Molina was missing. When Vicente Moya stepped back outside, an old woman, roused by the fracas, appeared in the window across the street. She looked at him as if she were in the habit of being woken up in the middle of the night by people searching desperately for the doctor.

"In the fields," she said, and pointed the way.

Behind the hovels the countryside stretched far and wide, dark as the ocean. Out in the darkness a bonfire crackled. The smell of smoke carried on the wind. The head of the Moya household followed the scent and began to run toward the light. Because after days of waiting they were out of time, Miguel had run out of time, the situation had deteriorated, and Molina's red fluid had had no effect.

When Vicente Moya reached the end of that seabed of plowed earth, his breathing was as labored as his son's as he explained the situation to the *curandero*. Molina was naked in the firelight, kneeling facedown inside a circle of feathers stuck in the soil, whispering prayers for fertile fields under a purple sky.

Vicente Moya had never been that tall, yet in the reflection of the fire he cast a long shadow over the field. The profile of Molina bent over, on the other hand, had never looked so puny. Because Sancho Molina knew that gasp; everyone who came to find him in the middle of the night had it: the windedness, that spent manner of breathing. Confronted with such utter desperation, Molina capitulated; he could never manage to get over it, to trust in his magic or believe in good luck, in the thousand concoctions that he had invented to scratch out a living. Confronted with that panting, Molina was naked, in every sense of the word; he was just like everyone else, only more cunning and impetuous, but not, thank God, to the point of leaving a baby to die. He looked up at Vicente Moya, his eyes flecked with fear, and delivered the one word he used on such occasions, though few people spoke of it and those who had heard it refused to believe their ears.

"Hospital," said Sancho Molina in a broken voice.

"Hospital," he said, his hands shaking.

There was nothing to add. All Vicente Moya could do was go back, retreat to where he'd come from, his sense of guilt kneaded with desperation and sweat on his oppressive race home. So heavy was the weight pressing against his chest that halfway down the field he had to stop and catch his breath. And as he was forced to stop there arose a doubt, an image so vivid it compelled him to turn back toward the *curandero*.

"Molina!" cried Vicente Moya.

The other man felt a shiver down his spine, as if at any moment Vicente Moya might decide to shoot him or pull a machete out and run back to skin him alive.

But Moya merely shouted. "The other bottle . . . What was in it?"

Molina felt he'd dodged a bullet.

"Water," he answered faintly in the distance.

"Whaaattt?" screamed Moya, who either hadn't understood or couldn't believe what he'd heard.

"Waterrrrrr!" repeated Molina with all the voice he had in him, as if he had just discovered water at the far end of the Samalayuca Dunes.

Anxiety set in. Vicente Moya felt the urgent need to get back to Miguel, without thinking. He'd never again mull over Molina's response, the meaning behind that bottle, which the man—a fraud, perhaps, yet keenly perceptive—had prescribed out of a sense of justice, as a way of bestowing attention on the quiet child in the corner of the kitchen.

Grandpa Hermenegildo's bloodred Ford lit out from Casa Moya. The family had assembled inside it. Vicente had passed by his father-in-law's house; hearing the word "hospital" in the same breath as Miguel's name was enough for the man to spring from his rocking chair—where each night he barely caught a few hours of sleep—and rev the old engine of his automobile.

Even less was required to rouse Maria Serrano. The whoosh of dust under those worn-out car tires as they pulled into the drive was all the explanation she needed to figure out what was happening, for deep down the dark arts of Sancho Molina had never really convinced her. She bundled the baby in a blanket and woke up Santiago, who had been asleep in the hammock, and unceremoniously dragged him off.

About his childhood, Santiago would always remember that tempestuous night when his mother tore him from his dreams and shoved him, barefoot and in his underwear, onto the patchy seat of his grandfather's car—his grandfather, whose hands clung to the steering wheel. He'd remember the strain on those thin fingers, the desperate hands of Grandpa Hermenegildo, who didn't say a word, who drove faster than the speed of light, who leaned forward to see the dark road in an air of imminent mourning, his regrets as empty and invisible as Miguel, who already seemed elsewhere.

He drove fast, his grandfather, slowing down just before the tallest speed bumps yet still taking them too fast: at every *tope* the Ford went flying, and the Moya family flew with it, holding their breath same as Miguel. For a few brief instants it seemed as though that flight would carry them off, propel them skyward, save them. Then the car would hit the blacktop with a screech of metal. Each time it seemed as if it would die, it and Miguel, and leave them to their tragic destiny, planted in the earth, on Earth. Which is what, after the tallest *tope*, happened.

The surge was so violent that Santiago, the smallest among them, rose off his seat, his hair touched the torn fabric of the car roof, and for a few seconds he even rose above the torment of that ride and the distressing sense that their fate hung in the balance. A sneaky smile crossed his lips as he delighted in his first whirl on a merry-go-round. But when the wheels found the road again, the family fell back down onto their seats with a soft rusty moan, and the Ford eructed something sour that had taken years to digest: a string of white smoke wormed its way out from the cracks of the beat-up hood and Grandpa Hermenegildo's old car suddenly buckled under the weight of the Moyas, of time, of that overwhelming responsibility.

"Good God!" cried Maria Serrano, wracked with fear and realizing the grave consequences that accident had for their future, for the future of Miguel, who appeared to have stopped breathing.

About his childhood, Santiago would later remember only a few images, photographs that floated on the opaque surfaces of that night. Details more than anything, particulars, as if he had been unable to watch the scene in its entirety, as if, to avoid the explanation in the grown-ups' eyes, he had concentrated elsewhere—on their hands.

In the first photograph, in fact, were the childlike hands of Maria Serrano. There was his mother, stopped in the middle of the road with Miguel bundled against her bosom, illuminated by the yellow headlights of a truck that the woman had, to save her son, at the risk of being mowed down along with her son, decided to flag down, and which eventually stopped. She clasped Miguel as if to keep his soul from escaping.

In the second photograph were the hands of Grandpa Hermenegildo again. There was the exhausted old man beside the smoking hood of his Ford, looking on as they continued their voyage in the open truck bed. He watched them drive off, unsteady, powerless, and found relief the one way he knew how, by fumbling with the tape deck to listen once more to "Jarabe Tapatío." In Santiago's memory that image of his grandfather, his gnarled hands clinging to music to find courage, faded on the horizon, vanished on the notes of that song.

In the third photograph were the large hands of Vicente Moya. And the lugubrious sound of the level crossing that loomed before the truck as the barrier was lowered at that exact moment to announce the arrival of a cargo train in the distance. There was the voice of his father crying to the level-crossing attendant, a bald and diminutive man, to lift the barrier. *"¡Te mato!"* Vicente Moya yelled at the man at the edge of the tracks, who was only doing his job. "I'll kill you!" he yelled, raising a fist that appeared big enough to split the skull of a mule and instead, without throwing a punch, lifted the level crossing before the train arrived. Santiago would never forget that, the closed fist of Vicente Moya, raised in the air for Miguel.

But by the time they finally reached the Mérida Hospital Regional, where Miguel had been born only a few months before, Miguel was dead. Or seemed dead, judging from his anemic face. The family climbing out of the truck was no longer the same either: Grandpa had been left on the side of the road, Maria Serrano had become a Madonna without a child, Vicente Moya had discovered in himself a man that he hadn't known existed, and little Santiago in his underwear had pissed himself from fear. His beautiful brother, whom he hadn't invited into the world, whom he hadn't asked to leave it, may have already gone. But it was too great a thought for him on a night too great, and Santiago wouldn't remember it.

Hours after the night had swallowed up the Mérida Hospital Regional, the doctor walked out into the hall where Santiago was sleeping across the legs of Maria Serrano who rested her head on the shoulder of Vicente Moya who had his back pressed against the wall, his heart on the wall. It was the same doctor who'd taken Miguel in his arms, the same who'd sighed and pronounced, "This baby is dead," who'd dashed off with him, who'd peered into the cavern of Miguel's throat and recognized the shadow of diphtheria. Most importantly, it was the same doctor who, in the end, had saved his life, though the family didn't know it yet.

"Which saint do you pray to?" he asked Vicente Moya.

"To Nuestra Señora de Guadalupe," Vicente Moya replied faintly. Having caught the doctor's drift, he got down on his knees.

"Light a candle. She just performed a miracle."

And Vicente Moya, remaining as he was, not saying a word, embraced the man's waist and pressed his head—exhausted, grateful—against the man's stomach. At that moment Santiago awoke and there, before his drowsy eyes, was his father, kneeling beneath a man in a white shirt, seized by a nervous sob that mounted in his stomach, inflated the veins in his neck and cheeks, escaped his lips in a kind of pained laughter.

Vicente Moya laughed out of a deep-felt, liberating sense of joy—all worry and guilt behind him. He laughed because his beautiful baby wasn't going to die. He laughed because his son's beauty had stolen the heart of Our Lady of Guadalupe, who may have been a virgin and a saint but was still a woman. He laughed as night turned to day, a new day, the dawn of a new life for Miguel, who from then on would be seen as even more beautiful for having been blessed by the pure embrace of the Señora.

Then, as if to do penance, Vicente Moya stood up with his arms still wrapped around the doctor, who now found himself hoisted in the air, like a statue in a holy procession.

"Please put me down!" he cried in vain as Vicente Moya, still laughing, marched him down the quiet hallway of the hospital that was just beginning to wake. Sitting motionlessly, her knees trembling from joy and weariness, Maria Serrano began to pray in silence. Santiago took in the scene, a jumble of sleep and confusion. On an empty road, his headlights fading with the morning light, Grandpa Hermenegildo was listening with his eyes shut to his music drone on. In a room at the Mérida Hospital Regional, Miguel simply breathed.

La fiesta de cumpleaños
THE BIRTHDAY PARTY

Months passed since the night Miguel saw the face of death. Grandpa Hermenegildo's Ford had been ditched in the front yard of the old man's house. He hadn't bothered to repair it, hadn't climbed into it since that evening, merely looked at it askance while rocking in his chair on the porch. Some people speculated it was a form of rejection, that he'd shunned the truck for having betrayed him in a time of need. The truth was, Hermenegildo Serrano was still out on that empty road, shrouded in smoke; in a certain sense he'd remained there, had aged overnight while waiting for daybreak to bring news of Miguel's fate. Secretly, he'd sworn to heaven that, were the baby to live, he'd never drive again.

That night, after he'd hugged the doctor forever, Vicente Moya returned to every station along his journey, like a pilgrim. He stopped by a butcher, ordered the largest turkey stuffed with pork meat, threw the *relleno negro* over his shoulder, presented it to the level-crossing attendant, and held out the same enormous hand he'd previously threatened to kill the man with. After hesitating a moment, out of fear and embarrassment, the man shook it. Then Vicente Moya tracked down the truck driver, inquiring in the cafés or among the people seated on the side streets or standing at their windows. When he reached the house, he was greeted by a woman and her three toddlers—the man was at work. Vicente Moya told them what their father had done, so that his children would know, then went in search of a neighborhood store and ordered a large, sturdy hammock big enough to hold the whole family. Finally, he headed in the direction of Calle 50. Along the way he bought a candle a few feet tall and in the fragrant dark of the Iglesia de Nuestra Señora de Guadalupe he set it down before the altar, lit it, knelt, and prayed for what felt to him like a moment, yet by the time he stood up, the sun had gone down. He returned to the road and ventured as far as Camilo Orioles's bar, which was close enough to home that he could get drunk and not risk getting lost.

"Mezcal para todos," he announced. And one glass after another he emptied an entire bottle of mezcal while people kept patting him on the back and congratulating him, same as they'd done the day Miguel was born.

"That boy will go on to do great things!" predicted a tallish old man.

"Here's to Miguel!" cried another.

"To miracles! To the *Virgen!*" cried others.

Vicente Moya finally drained his last glass, took his time to chew the *gusano*, and, bidding the people at the *posada* goodbye, raised his arm in the air, like a boxing champ, battered but victorious. He stumbled home and fell headfirst into a deep, cathartic sleep.

Yet many months later Vicente Moya still shouldered the fatigue of that night. He happened to dream now and then of the Madonna de Guadalupe holding Miguel in her lap. And when he woke up, he felt a pang of guilt, as though the two-meter long candle hadn't sufficed.

So, one morning, he shook Maria Serrano awake.

"Maria," he whispered.

"What?" she answered, emerging from her torpor.

"We have to throw a big party for Miguel's birthday."

"Sure, Vicente, a big party," Maria Serrano repeated mechanically, still half asleep.

"No, Maria, you don't understand," he kept on, sitting up,

staring at a point in the distance. "The biggest fiesta Mérida's ever seen . . . "

Consequently, twelve months after celebrating the birth of Miguel, Vicente Moya was arranging a *fiesta de cumpleaños*, which quickly took the form of a resurrection celebration. The events of that evening were disseminated, and the baby's recovery morphed into a story of rebirth with all the trimmings, which spread by word of mouth from one day to the next and, sustained by the baby's exceptional beauty, sprouted into the stuff of legend.

"Two days!" they said. "The baby had stopped breathing two days before the miracle!" One theory fed another; they said that Hermenegildo Serrano's Ford had soared at least ten feet off the ground and come crashing down like a meteorite, that the Moya family had walked away from the blast without a scratch. Rumor had it that the day after, the truck driver won the *Lotería Nacional*. That the train had never arrived, had broken down a quarter mile before the level crossing. Many swore that the level-crossing attendant's hair had grown back overnight, and there were murmurs that the doctor at the Hospital Regional had, like Juan Diego on the hill of Tepeyac, beheld the apparition of the Señora. They said that she was there in the room with the dead baby, that she knelt down, blew into his throat, and brought him back to life.

That's what they said. And the anxiety over the *niño resuscitado*'s birthday had grown at the same speed as the legend of his recovery. The neighborhood, the whole city perhaps, planned on attending the event, as if it were the Nochebuena or Natalicio de Benito Juárez. Which is why Vicente Moya found no peace. Night after night he was dogged by more frequent, more intense dreams, ignited by a holy fire, almost as if Miguel's future depended on the success of the party. He wanted to balance the books for good, in a spirit of gratitude, to win back his sleep, and because, although women had always fallen for him, including Maria Serrano, the mestizo Virgin had remained inflexible and proud, granting him the same rigid smile that she granted everyone. The fact hurt his pride, antagonized and riled him, made him burn with a feverish passion.

Maria Serrano humored him but didn't get involved. She limited herself to giving him the answers he wanted to hear, because she knew that the *Virgen morenita* wouldn't steal her husband from her and because, to tell the truth, the issue wasn't up for debate—Vicente would have his way. Moreover, with the pretext that Miguel risked having a relapse and required more attention, she shut herself up in the house and managed to keep the women of the neighborhood at bay. For the first time since they'd been together under the Moya roof, Maria Serrano felt like the mother of her son, the mother of a son who—the more she looked at him the more she was convinced of it—was really uncommonly beautiful. She spent hours watching him sleep in her arms. Inevitably, she was falling more and more in love with him; it went well beyond any love she'd previously known, far beyond the reaches of a feeling that had become malleable. She could never have imagined it reaching such a point. She felt flashes of an unfamiliar fear, felt lost in a foreign land, felt guilty for overstepping her bounds. Having fenced herself in, as if there were no such thing as Mérida, she failed to distinguish the details of the outside world, including the dimensions Vicente Moya's party was taking. She barely grasped his words as she listened to her husband distractedly, confident that it was in his nature to exaggerate, especially given his enthusiasm. Meanwhile the boy's convalescence stretched on for an unacceptable period of time and fueled the slander of her neighbors, who would deprive the Serrano mother of an experience—looking at Miguel, touching Miguel—that, given the otherworldly nature of the baby, they felt was *everyone's* God-given right, a privilege due *everyone*. Like the host, like absolution.

Santiago watched the preparations without asking any questions. He spent most of the day in the courtyard. His father would return from work, rush through dinner, and hustle off to the fields where they were setting up the party. At home what reigned was a silent attendance to Miguel, whom Santiago, to avoid contagion, had been ordered to steer clear of. And as weeks went by, he too, like the neighbors, had to face the facts: Maria Serrano was unreachable, resided somewhere far from Casa Moya. To hold that thought at bay, Santiago retreated outside, blended in with the other kids, played from dusk till dawn, hoping no one would notice him. But the adults' talk pursued him there—in the mouths of the children, who asked questions they'd heard their parents ask, said things they'd heard others say in the lead-up to the party, as people grew increasingly curious to see the object of desire, the *niño divino* about whom the city had been talking for weeks.

For some reason, whenever they played *gato y ratón*, Santiago was always picked to play the cat, the one who had to break the chain of arms and capture the mouse, a child that the others defended by holding hands and narrowing their circle. One versus everyone. Everyone versus one.

"Si su hermano es divino, ¿usted debe ser también, verdad?"

"If your brother is divine, you must be too, right?"

El nino diviño
THE DIVINE CHILD

A saint. That was what little Miguel had become. A miniature saint, to see him in the arms of the life-size statue of the *Señora* where he was placed at the end of a hot day. Mérida had killed time under the whir of fans, waiting for things to cool down in the evening. Out on the streets the afternoon was punctuated by the slow breathing of lizards. The heat and stillness had heightened tensions, and people held their breath as if an explosion were about to alter the landscape.

When Vicente Moya realized that the courtyard wouldn't be large enough for the *fiesta* as he had envisioned it, he went looking for an untended cornfield and, slipping the farmer a stack of pesos that the man couldn't refuse, added the finishing touch: "The Virgen de Guadalupe instructed me."

The farmer crossed himself twice and wedged the money deep in his pocket. Then Vicente Moya loosened his shirt button and made the rounds of the cantinas to talk about the party: eating *botanas*, praying that Saint Cerveza would inspire him, that there'd be a flowering of ideas among the patrons, that word would spread from mouth to mouth until it reached the ears of anyone who might be interested in making a donation—businessmen, politicians, crooks, priests. He was at it for months, savoring that sweet and stimulating period, nursing his project in a cloud of alcohol, in rowdy company, while his wife nursed Miguel in a lucid, all-consuming solitude. Day after day he moiled, putting his body to work:

his big hands to shake hands, his thick calves to stride down the maze of halls at the Palacio Municipal, his long arms to gather signatures, his broad shoulders to bear supplies hither and thither.

So, when the airless afternoon subsided into an evening full of stars, when a multitude of men, women, and children ventured out of their homes and wandered over to the party that Don Moya had willed into being to grace his son, when the door opened, when Maria Serrano appeared with Miguel in her arms, when she set foot out of the house after weeks of being captive to love, she couldn't believe her eyes. Maria Serrano couldn't believe it.

A red carpet stretched from the front door on into the horizon, all the way to the field where the event was being held, at least two miles long and lined by an immense crowd of people decked out for the occasion—the women in *huipil tradicional* and white shoes, the men in panamas, red scarves, leather sandals, and guayaberas that the Casita had marked down especially for the event. A mass of *meridaños* of every social class herded together, united in their devotion to the *Virgen morenita*, their curiosity, their *alegría*. After so much buildup, at the sight of the door opening, of the *niño divino* in his mother's arms, there erupted a jubilant roar and a barrage of fireworks that shook the windowpanes of Casa Moya and the bones of Maria Serrano, pinning her to the pavement, to the miracle. She was suddenly aware that, without having noticed, she must have lost something somewhere, that, more importantly, she was about to lose Miguel.

It happened a moment later. Vicente Moya stepped out of the house just behind them, and the crowd exploded into another deafening round of applause and set off rockets to show their gratitude to the child's father; if the boy really was heaven sent, that made Vicente Moya a god. To the naked eye, the party that he'd launched did, in fact, appear superhuman.

Nothing that size had ever been seen before in Mérida, not even during Holy Week or Carnival.

Vicente Moya stepped onto the red carpet in his white pants, extracted Miguel from Maria Serrano's arms, and gently deposited him in the lap of the Señora de Guadalupe, which had been commissioned from the best sculptor in Mérida, so that the child sat comfortably in those wooden arms. After months of being attached to his mother, in the time it takes to crack a smile, Miguelito accepted the other woman's embrace. His smile enflamed the crowd even more, especially when the platform carrying the Madonna and child was lifted in the air to get the procession underway.

A saint. That was what little Miguel had become. And that was what Maria Serrano thought when Vicente Moya unceremoniously tugged her down the carpet and into the procession, amid the cheers of the people, toward the party that had just begun.

"Now what?" she blurted, looking at her husband. He didn't even hear her. What would come of this party? What would come of their lives?

"Merida became so consumed by Vicente Moya's idea that inch by inch the city sank, tumbled, swooned to the relentless beat of a *güiro*, as if an earthquake had split the ground open and there was no chance of escape." No neighborhood was spared, no inhabitant saved. The carpet that stretched from the front door of Casa Moya was an obscene red tongue in a vulgarly laughing mouth set on a massive, monstrous body that had lost control of its arteries and orifices. From the epicenter of the party to its outer fringes, anything could happen, was happening, had already happened. The tequila served by the man of the house oiled the gears, causing the party to blow past the speed limit. To Vicente Moya's mind, there shouldn't have been a speed limit anyway, and amid the chaos what was going on around him escaped his notice. There was too much noise, too much anxious *jarana* dancing, too many tacos devoured, *bombas* recited, tequila quaffed. There was too much everything, mixed with the inebriating sensation of taking part in something that would be remembered, with the presentiment that time was slipping away, as it did in life. *Vaquerías* typically go on for days; here, everything lasted the span of an evening and therefore was to be relished rather than reflected on, squeezed to its last drop—tomorrow was another day.

"The biggest fiesta Mérida has ever seen . . . "

That was the gist of Vicente Moya's dream. It even exceeded expectations. Certainly Maria Serrano's expectations. Then more than ever she appeared to be the one person bewildered by what was happening, the only one who didn't drink. She rested her sober, distant gaze on the drunk people dancing around her, dancing on her head, in her head, an entire population suddenly devoted to the cult of Miguel, like the Israelites and the golden calf. Hot, overcome by boredom, the city seemed to have been waiting for the cool evening air, that easy excuse to abandon themselves to a collective religious delirium with the blessing of the Virgen de Guadalupe.

Hundreds of street performers trucked in from all over lit up the most far-flung corners of Mérida, in the smoke from food carts selling roast chicken and beans, and music drifted into one neighborhood after another, spilled into the streets, played by dozens of *charangas* that Vicente Moya had set up in each plaza, so that everywhere a joyful beat thrummed, you could dance and eat, and there was always a *cerveza* or tequila kiosk serving refreshments for the weary, fuel for the emotional. Essentially it was a network of unavoidable routes that ran from every part of the city toward the field, a funnel conveying energy to the heart of the merrymaking. They washed up there, the *meridaños*; even those who didn't want to wound up unwittingly on that fallow stretch of land that shook with life and would bear the scars of that *fiesta* for years. They swayed in groups, vibrating to the vibrations of drunken music, and coiled around the place where the carpet that stretched from the front door of Casa Moya terminated—at the edge of a stage in the middle of the field where dancers from the Ballet Folklórico de Mérida were bathed in sweat.

On the tip of the red tongue, at the end of that miles-long carpet, the wooden catafalque was wobbling the last few feet forward, carried by strong, willing young men. In front of them a handful of penitents were crawling on their knees, bearing roses full of thorns between their teeth. The wooden Señora looked happy, while, hovering above her, above everyone, Miguel looked on, caught up in the excitement, oblivious to what was happening, and yet by smiling spontaneously he gave the impression that he was possessed of *joie de vivre* and worldliness—characteristics that would be borne out when he grew up.

As they had at the start of the procession, Vicente Moya and Maria Serrano brought up the rear. Beleaguered by all those onlookers, Maria Serrano had shut her eyes halfway there and now continued to walk without looking, gripping the arm of her husband, who was busy smiling back and nodding at the crowd, relishing the applause, intently focused on performing a gesture he had planned in advance: occasionally he would raise his hand and flick his wrist, as if to say, "What, this? No big deal!" His show of modesty was calculated to make the event appear even more extraordinary than it was. That was how Miguel's night became Vicente's night. He savored the spotlight as much as Maria Serrano despised it. She clung to her husband's arm to stop him from breaking away from her rather than the other way around. Despite their proximity, on that carpet the Moya couple drifted apart, cut off all contact.

Then the procession came to a halt, the catafalque was

hoisted onto the stage at the center of the anthill. Vicente Moya left both wife and carpet, climbed onstage, spoke a few words into the microphone, and wrapped his arm around the neck of the Señora de Guadalupe that was cradling Miguel. When Maria Serrano opened her eyes again, she knew at once that she'd been wrong, that the mestizo Virgin had robbed her of her husband, or at least kindled a desire in him, while Miguel looked like the son of another mother, like the son of the Madonna herself. She saw it; everyone saw it. The beauty on stage was so pervasive and crystalline that before Vicente Moya could say a word the crowds spontaneously honored this impromptu holy family by erupting into applause, thousands of hands began clapping all at once, and the noise, mingled with the background music, sent a shiver through the crowd as another round of fireworks cut across the starry sky.

As the clamor died down, Maria felt something tugging her dress. It was Santiago.

"Mama," said the boy staring up at her, "can we go home?"

THE TIME FOR KISSING

Juntos
SIDE BY SIDE

Santiago and Miguel slept in the same room ever since the younger boy had to be moved out of his parents' room: Vicente snored like a hog, the baby got no sleep, and Maria Serrano was left with no other choice. So the two Moya children lay a foot apart, and each time the sun rose Miguel was larger, more alert. At night Santiago examined him—his hands two small eggs, his breathing easy, his proportions that of a tiny man—and wondered how much that tangle of flesh and hair would change or had already changed his life. He looked like a spider's nest quietly dangling in the room; in a minute, a week, or a month he would split open and release thousands of monstrous—or marvelous—creatures that would devour him. That was why, as much as possible, he kept his distance, and when the moon was in the sky and space became, by necessity, narrower, he held his breath. Until one ordinary afternoon—Miguel was walking by then—Maria Serrano decided that the time had come for them to go outside together.

"Coffee, rice, bananas," she told Santiago. And as she handed him the money, she added, "Take your brother with you."

Santiago thought he had misheard her. He looked up at his mother.

"Hold on to his hand and never let go," said the woman.

Santiago and Miguel wound up together under the late afternoon sun, the child's fingers in the little boy's hand. The contact scorched Santiago's skin, and here he'd thought that he could somehow keep his distance forever. Instead, his brother walked beside him and gripped his hand as if his future depended on it, as if *their* future depended on it. They moved through the dust at a fast clip. Santiago instinctively felt like hurrying up, like shirking that nuisance before anybody saw them together. He didn't know how to justify it—not even to himself. But as soon as they entered Anita Soler's store, the presence of the *niño divino* was immediately remarked upon. Ever since his first birthday party, the neighborhood had looked at Miguel as if he were the incarnation of the Holy Spirit. A pair of women snatched him away from Santiago, fought over who would hold him, stroked his head as if he were a lucky charm.

"Coffee, rice, bananas," Santiago told thin-lipped Anita Soler, who, like the other woman, was training her blue eyes on Miguel. When she heard his order, she seemed to wake from a dream. Still smiling, she stuffed the goods into paper bags, handed them to Miguel, and, when he held out the pesos to pay, gestured to him to keep it.

"Keep it," she whispered, turning to look at Miguel again.

Santiago was surprised, puzzled; the woman had always taken the money. Then he put it back in his pocket, turned around, mustered all the voice he had in him.

"Miss, we have to go," he said, staring at the middle-aged woman in heavy makeup who'd abducted his brother. His voice sounded unnatural, unkind. The woman put Miguel down peevishly, fingering the child's head one last time.

On their way back Santiago held the bags in one hand and his brother in the other, the money in his pocket, and on his chest a weight he couldn't take the measure of, which grew heavier with every step, bore down on his heart and shoulders and down his arms to his wrists, his hands, until all at once he opened them and let go of Miguel and the grocery bags, which fell to the ground and hemorrhaged grains of rice and coffee in the middle of the empty *calle*. Miguel, a step behind, examined the contents on the ground as if he were trying to make sense of them. Now that they were detached, Santiago felt he could leave him, rid himself of his brother the way he had rid himself of the bags, abandon him there. He turned and walked away. But after a few steps he heard Miguel behind him.

"Go away!" he shouted, picking up the pace. Shortly after, he turned and found Miguel still there, anxiously trying not to lose him.

"What are you doing here?" screamed Santiago, breaking his stride.

Miguel stopped in his tracks. He seemed unable to understand, to translate Santiago's screams, flight, rejection. He stood still and stared at him with a kind of calm, which was really only uncertainty, and served to further aggravate the other, who now regarded his brother as an emotionless tick determined to survive.

"What are you doing here?" Santiago repeated, meaning in that alley, meaning on that planet. His sudden vexation caused him to twitch; he reached out his hand and brought it down hard on Miguel's head, on the very same spot the ladies at the store had been petting.

A moment of silence followed. They were alone, close, the Moya brothers, as close as they were when Miguel was in the cradle and couldn't breathe, just as he couldn't breathe now, and Santiago poured a drop of water on his lips to cure him. Then the moment passed. Miguel caught his breath and exploded into a noisy cry, the cry of surprise at being hit for the first time. Santiago, on the other hand, felt the weight on his chest lift, leaving room for feelings which he suddenly managed to measure clearly: guilt for having hit his brother, astonishment at his brother's unexpected frailty, embarrassment about that crying, anxiety over the punishment that awaited him, fear that he wouldn't be able to put things right.

"Sorry, sorry, sorry," he repeated mechanically, to no effect. It seemed impossible to stop Miguel's tears. So he put his hands on his brother's sides and pinched him a little, tickled him, which shocked the boy almost as much as being struck. Slowly his tears transformed into hiccoughs, hiccoughs into hiccups, and finally hiccups into mild, then uncontrollable laughter. Miguel laughed, his tear-streaked face already a distant memory, and wriggled happily to escape the tickling. When Santiago felt he'd done it, he laughed too—relieved. He grabbed him, pulled him toward him, and hugged him as if his brother had just saved him from utter disgrace.

"Sorry," he repeated softly, still holding him tight. He wiped away his tears, laughed, hugged him again. Then he turned back around, took a banana from the paper bag, split it in two, held one end out to him, gathered up the scattered grains of rice and coffee beans, blew on them one by one, and then put everything back as it had been.

They returned home hand in hand, as if nothing had happened.

"Anita Soler didn't give you any change?" asked Maria Serrano as Santiago handed her the grocery bags.

"No," said Santiago. It was the first time he'd told a lie.

From that day on, going out for groceries became the boys' routine. Maria Serrano sent them to Anita Soler's store on little errands. She understood that the two brothers needed to be close to one another and that something had happened, was happening, along that stretch of road between home and the store. Depending on her mood, Anita Soler might refuse to take his money, as if she were making a down payment on a slope of Paradise. Santiago was no longer disturbed when the pesos remained in his hand. When he got home he hid them under a bench in his room. Over time he'd accumulated a small fortune. Meanwhile, he never failed to keep his appointment with Miguel—in the same place, he'd hit him the same as he had the first time.

"What are you doing here?" he'd say to Miguel, as if it were a game, a ritual for pure fun. After which he would hit him on the head or punch him in the stomach or smack him. And before it was too late he'd tickle him to stop his crying. That was how he vented his deep-seated resentment, which had shades of his youthful doodles and was his way of reacting to a presence that had glommed onto his life, an injustice he couldn't account for, like the mole on his face that was his alone, that no one could explain. Violence wasn't in his nature but emerged from someplace, clouded his mind with dark thoughts, burst in electric discharges that struck Miguel, like lightning.

He followed a strict routine, Santiago. In a certain way, he was experimenting to see if the process changed things. At the same time, without realizing it, he was training his brother to withstand pain, to endure suffering. At the same time, more importantly, the situation was drawing them closer together, since Santiago wound up sharing with Miguel an experience, involving him in a ritual, an emotion, a memory. More than holding hands, more than spending time together, more than traversing the same ground with different-sized feet, more than anything else what reconciled them was that moment when they stood face-to-face and settled their differences. Because, by being repeated, the act slowly lost momentum, the lightning died down, the clouds lifted, Santiago's hard feelings diminished every time he hit Miguel, and he grew more intent on the next stage of the process: restoring Miguel's smile, making him laugh till he cried, helping him forget, hugging him tight. The place became the site where no one saw them, the secret place where the Moya brothers met. And in time his blows became less convincing, his tickling more intense, his embrace more intimate. Until one afternoon, leaning against the alley wall, Miguel looked at Santiago, turned his beautiful smile toward him, and spoke first: "What am I doing here?"

Los días del perro
DOG DAYS

M iguel's voice entered Santiago's life. His brother's words were constantly in the background, his questions sounded like the questions that Santiago would have liked to ask and didn't or had asked only at a time he now remembered nothing about. When they were together, often among adults, Miguel would imitate Santiago, repeat Santiago's sentences, superimpose his own gestures onto Santiago's gestures, yet in a style that others perceived as different, that seemed unique and melted hearts. Looking at Miguel, Santiago saw a beautiful copy of himself: he possessed a curiosity and courage that Santiago did not, an audacity emboldened by the way in which everyone—women, men, and animals—reacted to his exaggerated beauty, succumbed to their attraction to him. That was always the case, without exception.

One day, while they were out walking, a stray dog planted itself in their path. It looked vigilant, rabid. Its pupils betrayed a violent instinct—which was survival instinct. It had caught a whiff of the bread in the bag Santiago was carrying, just the thing it had been waiting for after days on an empty stomach. It was ready, if necessary, to flash its teeth. At that moment, when a justifiably scared Santiago stood stiff, Miguel let go of his hand and ran toward the dog, approached it with a breeziness befitting his age and temperament, and petted the animal's head, running his fingers over its coarse brown coat. His courage trumped nature and immediately subdued the stray.

By the time Santiago reached his brother, the dog had calmed down, but the smell of bread caused it to let out a whimper that could only have meant one thing. Santiago broke off a morsel and tossed it at the mutt. The animal pounced. Then he worked up the courage to pet it, and the dog sat back on its hind legs. Santiago took another piece of bread, threw it. The dog smelled it, swallowed it, drew a little nearer until the two were very close, nuzzled the back of Santiago's hand, and clamped down on the bread until it had finished the whole bag.

"Well, goodbye," said Santiago, dragging Miguel behind him. But the dog followed. Every so often they turned around to see if it was still there, and it was. Even on the last stretch leading to Casa Moya, to the front yard, the house itself, there it was. They entered without looking back for fear of what they'd find there, until they were in the kitchen where Maria Serrano was frying up onions.

"A dog?" she exclaimed as soon as she saw them enter.

"Our dog!" said Santiago, turning around, discovering he really was there, in the house. Miguel ran to him as if he had just seen him for the first time, petted him again, repeated the phrase he'd just picked up from Santiago.

"Our dog!" he repeated. And Maria Serrano couldn't suppress her smile.

"Does he have a name?" the mother asked her older son while looking at her younger.

"Pan" was the first name that came to Santiago's mind. Bread.

"If you're going to convince your father to keep him, you'll have to give him a bath," concluded Maria Serrano, and she turned around to tend the burners.

Pan had the wits of a dog born and raised in the streets with his nose in the trash and the diffidence of one who bears the marks of men on his skin, marks where he'd been kicked, scars where he'd been beaten for no good reason. Whatever his meeting with Miguel and Santiago had unleashed had no scientific explanation, was a secret tucked underneath the animal's coat, like a tick. No more than an impulse, no different from a kid's: a feral fascination with the one and a resemblance to the other, which Santiago had sensed too. The same empathic frequency that kept him there, the mutt up to his ears in water in a washtub, the little boy soaping him, scratching him, washing away the dirt of a life in the dust. He dried in the last rays of sunlight, running after Santiago in the front yard of Casa Moya while Miguel, unable to catch up, looked on and shouted out of excitement, out of, for the first time, jealousy: the other two were too fast, even for the beautiful child who blew past every milestone, who was growing up rapidly, who captivated everyone who laid eyes on him. So he stuck to looking on from a distance, irked, beating the ground with a wooden spoon that he'd stolen from his mother.

A moment later a pair of strong arms lifted him in the air, and, having caught the scent of Vicente Moya back from work, Miguel beamed his trademark smile. The man stared unenthusiastically at the mutt chasing after his older son in his yard. The boy didn't seem himself. Vicente struggled to recognize him, perhaps because that kind of energy wasn't in the boy's nature.

"Any news?" he asked Maria Serrano as he entered the kitchen.

"None besides the dog," the woman answered.

"What dog?" asked Vicente as if he hadn't noticed. He was still holding Miguel in his arms. But when he turned around, the dog and Santiago were standing at attention side by side like foot soldiers waiting to be grilled by the enemy general.

"Where'd you find him?" asked Vicente Moya.

"On the street," replied Santiago.

"He's a stray. He's dangerous."

"He's very good," said Santiago.

"He's very good," repeated Miguel, brushing his father's chin with his pale fingers, rubbing his head against the head of Vicente Moya, who feigned disinterest yet actually let himself be distracted, be swayed by his son's gesture.

"Are you going to be the one who looks after him?" he asked Santiago, not knowing why.

"Yes," said Santiago.

Just like that, the business was settled. The general capitulated, set Miguel back down on the floor as if he'd been betrayed, retreated to the kitchen, and sat down for dinner having failed to notice that there was nothing on the table, not even a slice of bread.

Santiago followed suit, took his place too. Maria Serrano picked up Miguel and set him in his wooden high chair, then placed a steaming pot in the middle of the table and, with a completely natural, motherly gesture, put a bowl on the floor for Pan.

"Let's eat," concluded Vicente Moya, reaching for the pot to show that he was still the one who called the shots. Santiago betrayed no emotion, as if a movement, an errant breath, could bring everything crashing down, could compromise everything. He was just over seven years old that day and had never before felt what you might call happiness.

At the end of the day Santiago and Miguel withdrew to their rooms and the dog followed them just as he had through the streets of Mérida. But when each climbed into his hammock, Pan stood still between the two brothers. On one side there was the oldest, who had fed him and washed him and played with him. On the other was the youngest, who had petted him. Only Santiago realized what was about to happen, the gravity of the dog's decision to climb into one hammock rather than another. In the end Pan leaped into Miguel's hammock. The boy emitted a moony cry of surprise, petted the dog again, and a minute later was asleep. But Santiago couldn't sleep; he kept thinking about the dog lying beside his brother, feeling a pain hitherto unknown to him, which he wound up confronting in his sleep, in complicated dreams from which he emerged sweating and bone-tired yet intent on fighting to get what he wanted.

So, as soon as the sun came up, he stole a slice of *pan dulce* that Maria Serrano had made for breakfast, held it out for Pan to devour, and lured the dog away by parceling out small doses of the flat bread. They walked out of the house together and headed for school while the other children looked on with a mix of surprise, admiration, and envy. Santiago feigned indifference, yet his heart beat fast. He wasn't used to being the center of attention. When he entered the school, the dog waited outside—rules were rules—and spent the morning with his nose to the ground waiting for bread and perhaps for Santiago too, who peeked out of the window to see if he was still there.

"Is he going to wait for you all day?" asked little Teresa Rodríguez, looking up from her geography textbook. She occupied the desk next to his.

"I think so," Santiago replied.

As soon as the teacher announced that the lesson was over and class was dismissed, Santiago bolted for the door. He was the first one to make it outside, where the dog sat waiting for him, alerted by the noises of people leaving the building, ready to tackle Santiago the moment he stepped outside. The dog threw the little boy off balance, laid him flat on the ground, and stood over him, licking his face, slobbering over his cheeks, forcing the boy to defend himself, to shout for joy, to give him more *pan dulce*.

They spent the rest of the day together. Pan accompanied

Santiago down the backstreets of the city, and the city limits expanded. Mérida became a labyrinth to explore, a fretwork of paths on which to seek adventure. Together they disappeared, far from the kitchen where Maria Serrano tended to Miguel, who now lay on the floor where Santiago used to draw and was drawing a shimmering yellow sun that—surprise, surprise—illuminated the profile of a dog. The dog that had gone off with his brother, nobody knew where to or why, until that evening, when the dark descended, when the two boys lay in their hammocks, and the dog had to pick a side. After following Santiago all day, Pan leaped in the same direction as he had the evening before. He jumped into the arms of Miguel, who squeezed the dog like a doll.

Santiago had another bad night's sleep, but the next day he woke angrier and more determined. He stole another piece of flat bread to lure away the mutt, to have him for himself for as long as possible, and over the following days he did it again and again, conquering Pan's heart, right up until it was time to go to bed, when, despite their separation during the day, the dog went back to being Miguel's.

Santiago had never felt so lonely at night, not even when he'd slept in the room alone, before Miguel was born. But one random night, in the middle of a particularly bad dream, he was startled awake, and there was Pan, nestled between his legs and stomach. Santiago sighed; a miracle.

"You and me forever, right?" he whispered to the dog in the pitch-black room, squeezed together to form a single body in the hammock. Pan's silence, his loyal, expressive gaze, was all the yes he needed. The contact made his stomach warm, and he took pleasure in breathing in the dog's scent, which, as he shut his eyes, carried him off to the forest, to meadows, under the earth, down to the depths of the sea, and up into the clouds.

El aire en el patio
THE BREEZE IN THE COURTYARD

Once again Maria Serrano was alone with Miguel, just as when the child had been convalescing. Vicente Moya went to work, Santiago disappeared with Pan from morning to evening, and ever since the *fiesta de cumpleaños* the women in the neighborhood were more circumspect about coming over and kept the kind of distance usually reserved for priests and nuns. Maria Serrano may not have been beautiful but neither was she stupid, and she was afraid of lapsing into an exclusive relationship with her younger son again. It wouldn't do him any good, it wouldn't do her any good, and there was also the risk of waking to find herself on another red carpet that stretched on for miles. These thoughts were constantly running in the back of her mind when, one bright morning, she heard the voices of other children in the yard. In reality, they'd always been there, but Miguel was considered first too frail and then too precious to be let out on his own. Or maybe he was just too small. But Maria Serrano looked at him and realized with a thread of surprise that he had grown several inches in height and had put meat on his bones and appeared more than ever touched by angels. She looked him over and realized he was ready for the world. So, holding the door open, she asked him an easy question.

"Miguel, do you want to go outside and play?"

He didn't think twice; it was as if he'd been waiting all along for her to ask. He dashed out into the light with the fury of someone released on parole. He looked out at the yard, cleared the space separating him from the heap of dust-caked children playing in the sun, and was greeted with natural curiosity. That was how Miguel began his social life; in no time, despite being the smallest and last to arrive, he foisted his personality on others, went from observing to acting, from imitating others to infecting them. As a consequence, talk of him picked up again, since the *niño divino's* presence out of doors didn't go unnoticed, the news traveled from the mouths of the children to the ears of the adults, made the rounds of houses, fueled a growing interest, restored feelings that the women in the neighborhood had drowned in a sea of tears when the child had been diagnosed with diphtheria. One by one they turned up at Casa Moya. Only this time they didn't enter. They poked their heads in the window and invited Maria Serrano to come out for a breath of fresh air, lingered there and made eyes at Miguel as the boy darted about with the other kids in the plaza, emanating his aura. Until late one afternoon one of the bolder women showed up at the Moyas' door carrying a chair and planted herself in the shade out front. Her name was Clarabella Sanchez. She had a large backside and a daughter Miguel's age who was also playing in the courtyard.

"What are you doing here?" asked Maria Serrano.

"The shade's nice," replied the woman.

"A nice shade?"

"Yes, yes. And there's a cool breeze, don't you feel it?"

Word of the coolest spot in the neighborhood spread, and, armed with this excuse, other women turned up carrying chairs, set up camp, and took advantage of the shade, they said, to keep an eye on the children. The thicket of chairs in front of Casa Moya expanded, as did the noisy chatter that carried through the neighborhood. Maria Serrano ultimately gave in, abandoning her domestic chores to sit with the others and enjoy that unexpected company. As their ranks swelled, the women tended to prolong their get-togethers, which robbed them of time to get anything else done and perilously skirted the hour in which their husbands came back from work.

"What's going on here?" Vicente Moya asked one evening, having returned home to find them gathered around his front door. The group fell silent. No one had the courage to speak up. In the end it was Maria Serrano who stood, walked over to her husband, and responded nonchalantly, "Don't you feel the cool breeze?"

Everyone who stopped by, even just by chance, wound up returning. They couldn't help it. For every woman who left, three more popped up. They arrived dragging chairs behind them, as if a chair were their ticket to enter the special neighborhood hangout. Some came from other parts of town, damaging the alleys they passed through on their way over. It looked as if a herd of mysterious animals had trampled over them: two parallel furrows in the dust crisscrossing other identical furrows. The trail of chairs and chair legs all converged on the same spot, in front of Casa Moya, where chairs and chair owners extended as far as the eye could see.

Friendships were forged, discussions became increasingly intense, women invited new friends and the new friends invited their friends and Maria Serrano purchased an extra set of mugs at the market and got in the habit of keeping at least a couple of coffee machines going on the stovetop. The atmosphere turned lively and getting together became a daily routine that few turned down. They put off other duties so as not to miss out or, if they had to, brought their chores with them. Some peeled potatoes, others embroidered, but between one conversation and the next they all trained their eyes on the open space where Miguel, with his pitch-black hair, had become the de facto leader of the gang, towing behind him a mob of children that, like the mob of mothers, grew larger every day.

At a certain point the row of chairs stretched all the way around the corner of Casa Moya and separated the latest arrivals from the heart of the scene. So that it made sense for them to stay, with feigned indifference the newcomers planted their chairs near the door, in front of the women who had congregated there first, blocking Clarabella Sanchez's view of Miguel, whom she hoped to see close to her daughter Soledad.

"What do you think you're doing?" she huffed, rising to her feet.

"What? Do you own the courtyard now?" one of the usurpers shot back.

There followed a tense moment that short-circuited the seamless murmur of gossip that had gone on for days, a moment when even the children stopped playing, having sensed in that silence that the magic of the square might be broken on account of the adults, a long moment when Clarabella Sanchez considered kicking in the legs of the chair in front of her and putting it out of commission.

"The ones who came last could sit behind you."

It was the voice of Soledad, who had approached to ask her mother for a Kleenex and was watching the scene unfold. She looked like a country mouse, which drove a wedge, physically speaking, between her and Miguel, yet she had a lively wit, a good head on her shoulders.

The woman in front of Clarabella Sanchez stared at Soledad Sanchez. The girl reminded her of one of those withered weeds that sprouts in the concrete. But she knew the child was right and sighed.

"If you all form a row we'll get behind you," she said to the girl's mother.

Clarabella Sanchez took a second to make the decision seem momentous, as if the idea had been her own. Then she lifted her chair with a dramatic flourish and set it down a few inches in front of her. The others did the same, making room for a second row between themselves and the wall.

"*Champurrado*, anyone?" interrupted Maria Serrano, who, having run out of coffee, had warmed up a large pot of chocolate milk. Suddenly the tension lifted, Clarabella Sanchez set her large buttocks back down on the chair, and the women, relaxed, picked up the thread of their gossip. Little Soledad Sanchez blew her nose.

The flow of people to the Casa Moya yard showed no sign of letting up. Three rows became four, four became five, and at that point the women in the first row refused to scoot up any further lest they be driven out of the shade. So the chairs of new arrivals extended cornerwise, forming a blockade around the children. Then, to shield themselves from the sun, which didn't set until the evening, the women procured brightly-colored umbrellas which they tied to their chairs. The others, despite being in the shade, imitated them, as if having an umbrella over your head could improve one's social status in that impromptu community of women.

Were a tourist flying over Mérida to look down at the Moyas' courtyard, he'd see a cloud of gnats and a rainbow in the dust. And once the women had decided that moving their chairs and umbrellas every God-given day was a hassle, the installation became permanent: they left everything where it was with the added bonus of saving the place each had staked out for herself.

Generally, Vicente Moya would return home and find them there, but he let them be because he was tired and besides, ever since she'd gotten involved in managing that congregation, Maria Serrano was happier and at night would surrender to him with an alacrity that she had lost on the carpet at Miguel's party. Then, one evening after dinner, he went out to the courtyard to smoke a cigar, and that sweep of empty chairs and umbrellas open in the moonlight triggered a thought.

"What do you guys drink all day?" he asked his wife.

"*Champurrado* and coffee," she answered.

Two days later, as if by magic, a pushcart selling cold drinks and fresh-squeezed juice appeared. Vicente Moya took a cut of the profits. The pushcart was parked on the edge of the clearing, near the children, because Vicente knew that in order to attract the mothers, you had to attract their children first. The women drank deeply, and the mood of the afternoon was sweetened by the sugar in the lemonade and mango and pineapple juice.

"What do you say we have dinner here?" said a woman one night. She was kidding, sort of.

Enough money was collected to buy wine, meat, cheese, tortillas. The men arranged large open-pit fires on the edge of the plaza, extending the rainbow and closing the magic circle where smoke and the smell of tacos and quesadillas wafted. Families were reunited: along with husbands came other relatives, young and old, depriving their houses of more chairs and tables. Some even brought instruments and began to play. Music mingled with the chirping of the women and the shouts of the children, whose circle became smaller and smaller. So as not to cede their ground entirely, they decided to play *chácara*, a perfect game for establishing boundaries. They made the widest *chácara* court possible: the starting line grazed the chairs in the first row, the lateral rectangles were drawn a step away from the grills, the last rectangle was beside the drink stand. Then they'd toss the marker, hop on one leg, fall, laugh . . . They captured the attention of the adults, who cheered whenever their kid was up. Then, as luck would have it, Miguel's turn came just as a heartbreaking song was reaching its final crescendo. In the silence that followed the song,

Miguel, in a tank top, his eyes shimmering, threw the marker. It landed in the very last rectangle and, given the state of affairs—the effect of the music fading out, the applause, the joy, the wine, the expert throw, the violet sunset, and, naturally, that boy's flawless beauty, that beauty that had lured everyone to that place—given the whole state of affairs, it appeared as if the boy were about to pull off an exceptional feat. Which is why, when he began, when he launched into the first rectangle on one leg, everyone held their breath, as if the game were being played on the edge of a cliff, as if the boy might fall into the abyss.

More or less at that moment, Santiago appeared in the little plaza, back from a day spent with Pan. He arrived and was startled by the throng of people and the total hush that had come over the courtyard; he thought perhaps there was a funeral, or an accident had occurred outside his house. And for some reason he thought specifically of Miguel, for some reason he imagined his lifeless body prone on the ground, annihilated, in that mournful calm. With his dog by his side, he elbowed his way through, penetrated the crowd of men and women, the young and the old silently surrounding the plaza, and once he'd managed to get past them, he found his brother at the center of it all, alive, hopping around on one leg in the final rectangle of a giant *chácara* from which he'd started out and to which he'd returned. He landed inches from the first row of chairs and flourished the winning stone in his fist. The cheers that rang out swept away the smoke in the air and brought down a few umbrellas, as if Mexico had just scored a goal in the World Cup, and the musicians began to play again, more energetic and joyful than before, and Clarabella Sanchez stood, snatched Miguel on the fly, and went in search of her daughter to give her to him as a prize.

But Soledad was on the other side of the courtyard and appeared to be the only one not interested in Miguel. She stood there, rapt, enchanted by the lost eyes of the little boy with the dog who had emerged from the crowd and was looking at Miguel without an ounce of joy, who was looking at Miguel as if he had just died.

The days of Pan and Santiago blew by, far from everyone. Caught up playing, caught by surprise, they ran under the sun, sprawled out in fields to catch their breath, darted down the narrow streets of Mérida, slept on top of one another in the hammock, enmeshed in a feeling they had no words for. The stray and the quiet boy became one and the same; where one went, the other followed. And with Pan next to him, Santiago gained a sense of security. The child who had himself been a shadow now had a shadow that trailed after him wherever he went: on his chest as he rested, against his legs as he sat or walked, a foot behind him as he ran. Pan had picked Santiago. He never left his side, and his proximity to the boy changed his temperament; used to twitching at the slightest noise, taking flight, snarling, sniffing the air for danger, in the arms of Santiago he found peace. In return, he offered his total devotion.

For Santiago, the love he felt for Pan and the love he received in return was precious, rare. It gave rise to a new sensation: the fear of losing someone. At its most acute, he felt a kind of nervy dread, a feeling of joy that rose in his throat as he petted him, as he hollered happily while being chased by the dog or when the mutt nudged his foot under the table to remind him he wasn't alone. In those instances, he perceived, just beneath that frizzy brown coat, the stray pulse of Pan's heart. His response was to wash him, scrub him clean at least once a week, so that his neighbors and Maria Serrano and especially Vicente Moya would see that he was good, beautiful. Yet he could never really wash away his fear. He found himself petting Pan with desperate frenzy, with the premonition that his effort was hopeless.

So, in the child's mind, the span of time between the afternoon in which he'd fed Pan that first piece of bread to satisfy his hunger and the evening in which that hunger had suddenly returned, together with the dark soul of the stray, became for Santiago the natural outline of a picture of happiness that came with an expiration date attached. The picture took on the shade of those sheets of paper that he had scattered on the floor as a young boy, the shade of all the days before the dog turned up in his life and gave it color.

It happened around dinnertime, when Vicente Moya was home from work, Maria Serrano was preparing *poc chuc*, and the kitchen was saturated with the smell of sour orange chicken. Lured by the aroma, hungry, Miguel reached out, tugged at his mother's skirt and asked for a bite. She sliced a piece and delicately held it out to him. Then it happened. Just as their fingers touched. Pan jumped up and bit Miguel's wrist, Miguel dropped the meat, and Maria Serrano broke the silence with her screams. A drop of blood dripped down from the child's skin and splattered across the brightly colored sheets of paper that, like living organisms, populated the floor. There were no traces left of Santiago's drawings; it was as if they had been sucked into the bowels of the earth. The drop of blood spilled over a blue sky and spread out to form a dark rivulet while, coupled with the scream of his mother, Miguel let out a cry, more from fear than pain.

Animal hunger. Nature versus reason. Or maybe it was a natural response to a mother distractedly feeding one son and ignoring another—a way, therefore, of putting things back in order the only way a dog knew how. He didn't even eat the scrap of meat but instead stared up at Santiago, who was staring up helplessly at Vicente Moya, who had leaped from the table and was holding his arms out toward Miguel. And in the manic anguish in his father's eyes, the nervous way he reached out to his son to save him, Santiago discerned the end of life with Pan, the end of that happiness that had the faint color of his childhood drawings, which is to say, the end of everything for him.

The next day Vicente Moya strapped a leash around Pan's neck. They boarded a bus headed for the beaches of Progreso, more than twenty miles north of Mérida. The mutt followed Santiago's father as if he were Santiago himself, having sensed that his fate was in the man's hands. In the country Vicente Moya entered the first *posada* he came across. He quenched his thirst and made inquiries, pointing at Pan, who looked him up and down without making a sound. Then he walked over to a building site where, they told him, the superintendent could probably use a guard dog. Vicente Moya met the man outside a shack abutting a villa under construction. In a few words he explained the deal, got the okay he was looking for, shook the weather-beaten hand in which he deposited the leash tied to Pan, and went on his way, back to where he'd come from, without ever looking back.

Back home he didn't say a word. Neither did Santiago, who collapsed in his hammock, believing the pain might make him melt, might reduce him to a puddle on the floor. For days he spoke only when speaking was indispensable, tenaciously withdrew into silence. He quit speaking up at school and stuck to staring out the window at the place where Pan used to lie on his stomach and wait for him. As if by looking, by looking constantly, he could make the dog reappear.

And one day, when he took his eyes off the blackboard and for the millionth time aimed them out the window, Pan did appear. In his same old spot, in his same old position. Santiago struggled to believe it, to suppress his joy. Like a bubble expanding in his veins, the words he'd been holding back climbed all the way up his throat and burst out of his mouth. And as if the morning were over, as his teacher shouted after him indistinctly in the background and his classmates laughed, he ran, crying out Pan's name till he'd made it outside and found him—flesh, bones, brown coat—wrapped his arms around his neck, kissed him, threw himself on top of him, crushed him, as the dog groaned and wagged his tail for joy, licking his face, his neck, his ears.

They ran all day and when they reached the edge of the city, Santiago thought about running away, about never turning back. But then he convinced himself that Vicente Moya would see what a miracle it was and agree to keep the animal. So he returned home. His father was there, as was Maria Serrano, who had been informed by his teacher what had happened at school and had been waiting for him. Whatever path Pan had taken to get back to Mérida was a mystery Vicente Moya didn't care to know or didn't want to appear to care to know in front of the sweaty, ecstatic boy and his mutt who looked like they'd weathered a bad storm. One terse sentence was all he greeted them with.

"Tomorrow I'm getting rid of him," he said.

Santiago skipped dinner and retreated to his room with Pan. He petted the dog and hatched escape plans to put into action that night, but, worn out by hunger, by too much excitement, he hugged the animal and crashed. When he woke up, Pan was gone. At dawn Vicente Moya had put his leash back on and returned to the bus station. He zeroed in on a guy with a large suitcase who looked trustworthy and ascertained that the guy was headed two hundred miles away, to Cancún. He offered him a few pesos to take the dog and set him free at the last station.

A half hour after Pan had left for Cancún, it began to rain

in Mérida. The rain resembled the heavens weeping as Santiago wept. The weeping went on for days. That much rain hadn't fallen in years. Miguel watched his brother grieve with the same helplessness with which he watched the rain falling outside the window.

One afternoon Santiago slipped out of the house, retread, in solitude, the streets that he had first discovered with Pan, dipped his feet in the wet earth while a cascade of water pasted his hair to his forehead and mixed with his tears. He wasn't outside for an hour but it was long enough for him to catch a touch of fever and declare he was sick. Miguel, who had pressed his nose against the window, was the first to see him emerge from the storm when he came in. Santiago tracked mud all over the hall and shivered as Maria Serrano toweled him off and wrapped him in a blanket from which the boy's infrequent hiccups escaped amid the sound of the squall bombarding the house, the whole city. Every so often sleep robbed him of his tears while the streets of Mérida morphed into rivers of mud and large dark puddles over which, one Sunday afternoon, the clouds finally broke and the sun shone again, as if emerging victorious from a battle. An hour later Miguel and the other children and the ladies and their chairs returned to the courtyard of Casa Moya, gathered on the grounds as the water evaporated in a thin steam.

Just before nightfall, Pan, too, returned to the courtyard of Casa Moya.

Haggard, sopping wet, weakened, but alive, but there. Maria Serrano noticed him by chance and put a hand to her mouth from fright, since the dog looked like a ghost of his former self. She called to her son; the knot in her throat signaled to Santiago what had happened, and he ran out into the muddy courtyard with no tears left in him to shed. The women crowded around the courtyard, silent as monks, scrutinized him as he ran up to Pan and gently patted the dog on the head, as if to make sure it was really him. Only then did the mutt feel that he had made it home. He lay down and put up his paws after days of walking under the rains of Quintana Roo and Yucatán. Santiago gathered him up in his arms. To see him carrying the animal to the house with that mournful calm about him was to see a grown boy, a boy who had become a man.

At the door Vicente Moya scrutinized them too, an astonished look on his face, a hint of thinly-concealed admiration for the dog's wherewithal, for the feeling that existed between the boy and the beast. Which is why he didn't take a position, acted as if nothing had happened. He let the days slip by while Santiago concentrated on nursing Pan back to life, treating his wounds, feeding him, and Miguel kept his distance, same as he had when the animal had become his brother's dog—end of discussion.

Pan recovered and the two went back to being the pair they'd been before. Until Vicente Moya, having returned from work more tired than usual, saw in the brown mutt the stray that had assaulted Miguel, and decided then and there that he had to disappear for good. He phoned an old friend who had enlisted in the army. Two days later a van pulled up in front of Casa Moya. Out came a soldier with a thick moustache and a pistol who kneeled in front of Miguel to ask him a question and then marched toward the house.

Santiago would never forget that moustache and pistol, because Pan vanished behind them, this time never to return, to become the property of the barracks in Vallodolid. Or at least that was what the man in uniform said to console the sobbing boy before carrying the dog away. After that, the van rounded the bend at the end of the block, kicking up dust, which paved the streets of Mérida again, and Santiago could think of one thing only: that Miguel had been the one to win the dog's affection first. That Miguel had been the one who, with one note, had convinced Maria Serrano to keep him. That

Miguel had been the one who had turned Vicente Moya with a single caress. In the end it was Miguel who had stripped him of his dog when his blood spilled on the ground and all over a piece of meat that he didn't deserve, no more than the dog or Santiago himself deserved it. Santiago's thought, hopelessly cast on the horizon, was that his brother was to blame for all of it: the bitterness, the solitude, the pain crushing his chest. It was all Miguel's fault. Meanwhile the boy played mindlessly, luminously, nestled in his oblivious life, trouble free.

El tiempo de los besos
THE TIME FOR KISSING

Miguel hit the jackpot, chanced upon the one-in-a-million combination of tiny details that it was his destiny to steal from Vicente Moya and, to a lesser degree, Maria Serrano, inherited the best of both and fished the rest from the bodies of his distant ancestors, bearers of a single ideal feature: large eyes, prominent lips, a fine face, high cheekbones. First prize in the genetic lottery, a concentration of luck and chance that had appeared promising when he was a newborn and now was beyond question. In particular on the school grounds, in the generic uniform—a row of white and blue stripes from which only faces emerged—there more than ever, Miguel's was the face of beauty. He was six years old, perfectly proportioned, and he strode through the schoolyard during the mid-morning free period, when boys and girls, normally separated, gathered and mixed hormonal urges they didn't know existed but had begun to press against their eyeballs, under the smooth skin of their growing bodies, in their vague thoughts and muddled questions. Miguel moved around, already turning the girls' heads, eliciting giggles, sparking desires. As he walked by, inaudible whispers placed him above the other children, made him a little taller than the rest.

Then, like clockwork, the time for kissing came.

He planted his first on the lips of Rosita Romero, who was in the third grade for girls and was unanimously voted the prettiest girl in school by the fourth and fifth grade boys. A kiss fit for a Prince Charming who had yet to appear, for whom she had been waiting, and over whose absence she had been beginning to despair. When Miguel showed up in the schoolyard, her classmates dubbed him "Rosita Romero's future husband," and she felt her heart pounding, breathed a sigh of relief, and shrugged off their difference in age as a minor detail. Which turned out to be the case. A few days later, she and Miguel found themselves alone in a corner of the schoolyard under the shade of an agave tree, a shelter from prying eyes, and the child didn't hold back but with the curiosity that came naturally to him yielded to her strange request and discovered the sensation of physical contact that would alter his entire worldview. However minor their kiss was, however on-tiptoe, it possessed the power of novelty, the awe of discovery, of trespassing on forbidden territory—territory reserved for adults. Further, it was a meeting of two perfect blossoming creatures seeking each other out: they locked lips. The landing was perfectly planned, perfectly executed.

"Will you marry me?" Rosita Romero asked afterward.

In the face of such an abstract concept, Miguel hesitated.

"Yes," he finally replied, realizing that "yes" was the formula to unlock Rosita Romero's lips again, and again a hundred times over in the days that followed. The girl smiled and sprang from behind the agave plant, her cheeks burning with that kiss and Miguel's promise.

Her classmates, clustered around the window, understood that Rosita Romero's Prince Charming really had arrived, and they were helpless to stop their feelings toward her from subtly changing; she was no longer the unlucky and misunderstood girl but the embodiment of luck itself. The astonishing beauty of Miguel paired with the beauty of Rosita Romero may have appeared to add up to happiness, yet the outside world counted it as a loss, as if the two had stolen something from everyone else. Fortunately, the carefreeness of children tempered certain feelings, though it was true that behind the agave Rosita and Miguel had chosen one another to the exclusion of everyone else, as is natural, especially for those who embody perfection. But neither Rosita Romero nor nature had reckoned on Miguel, who seemed exempt from the laws of creation.

For him, the first days of school were spent waiting to press his lips against Rosita Romero's in a firm bond that made the girl think of scenes in some movie she'd seen. Miguel was willing yet still too young to take the initiative, and at Casa Moya they didn't have a TV, so he simply let it wash over him, following her lead day after day. Until one morning when he found her best friend Florencia Medina behind the agave.

"Rosita has the flu," she told him with feigned regret. "She told me to tell you she'll be back tomorrow," she added.

Miguel absorbed the news with mild surprise.

"O.K.," he said, shrugging his shoulders and taking a step forward, closing the narrow gap between himself and the thin lips of Florencia Medina. To him, the girl was a substitute kisser. To her, who had never kissed anyone before, it was like being catapulted into a movie, launched into forbidden territory—extra forbidden given she was betraying her best friend, which fact left a bitter taste in her mouth. But the shock, the thrill, the levity of her eight years, and the sense that she was getting back at life kept her from refusing, bound her to that act, which was Miguel's first act as a man. Moreover, Florencia Medina was more inclined to physical contact than Rosita Romero, and though her lips remained statically glued to his, she placed her hands on Miguel's shoulders, which gave the kiss an added warmth.

"Will you marry me?" Florencia Medina asked afterward.

"Yes," said Miguel instinctively.

And when she sprang from behind the agave plant, her cheeks burning with that kiss and Miguel's promise, her classmates, clustered around the window, discovered that Prince

Charming hadn't only chosen Rosita Romero. And when Florencia Medina reached them, they first forced her to tell them what happened and then forced her to agree that Miguel wasn't her Prince Charming either. He was everyone's prince—and they'd take turns with him in an orderly fashion.

So when Rosita Romero recovered from the flu and returned to school, at the start of recess a few of the girls found a way to coax her into the bathroom and then locked her inside. And behind the agave plant went Eugenia Gallego, the next lucky girl up, who presented the ideal occasion to test how willing Miguel's mouth was, given the girl's awkward physique: she was fat. Gallego was aware of her shortcomings compared to Rosita Romero and delicate Florencia Medina. Which explained her embarrassment when she stood in front of Miguel and asked the question that might change her future.

"Will you kiss me too?" she asked.

Miguel looked at her cagily; Eugenia Gallego might have eaten the last two girls, he thought to himself, she might even eat me. He reacted by looking down at the girl's mouth, at the two fleshy, protruding, blossoming lips, red as roses.

"Why not?" he replied with a smirk. "But," he added to be safe, "I'm not going to marry you . . . "

El tiempo de las bofetadas
THE TIME FOR TUSSLING

The kissing assignations helped brighten Miguel's school life and prompted him to apply himself. His teacher, who struggled to suppress her slight preference for him, pressed her pen down hard whenever she gave him a good grade—which is to say, more and more frequently. And with equal diligence he would arrive behind the agave on time: he kissed one schoolgirl a day with the perfunctory precision of an assembly line worker and the ardor of a craftsman perfecting his trade. He became more practiced, more confident, more grown-up every time he emerged from behind the plant, while also learning that a kiss comes in all flavors and every mouth speaks a language of its own. The *niño divino* acquired a new nickname: *el pequeño besador*. That's what he was called by the older girls who, despite their age, added their names to the secret list of schoolyard kisses.

The morning that Miguel found Rosita Romero behind the agave, he realized he had kissed them all. After having avoided him for weeks in the halls, she reappeared same as the last time they had met, before the flu and her classmates had taken him away from her. She stared at him with her eyes full of rage and a desire to pelt him with curse words that she'd picked up from adults. But her insults were meaningless, insufficient, and she raised her arm, let her hand soar, and slapped him. After ninety-seven different kisses, he received this affront with the same surprise with which he had received his first kiss from

Rosita Romero's mouth. The concept of jealousy, like marriage, was beyond him.

Miguel stared at Rosita Romero with his cheek burning and the look of innocence with which he he'd kissed them all, and the girl let herself be swept up by a force more powerful than jealousy; she moved closer to him again, pressed her lips against his, and got back to kissing. Only in place of the child she found a man. Or a little man at least: *el pequeño besador*. Miguel suavely pulled her close, placed his left hand on her side and his right on her neck, and dug his delicate fingers into her hive of hair. In the end, following what he had learned from the girls in the fifth grade, he slipped the tip of his tongue between her lips and grazed Rosita Romero's bright white teeth. Stunned, the girl pulled back, slapped him again, only twice as hard this time, looked at him speechlessly, and ran off with her cheeks redder than when she had fled from their first encounter.

Miguel didn't feel pain; he was used to being smacked by Santiago. What worried him was that Rosita Romero had authored the epilogue of the process she herself had set in motion almost three months earlier. He had the misgiving that this kissing business may have ended just like that. He went back to class and took an unusually keen interest in his teacher. That afternoon and evening he had the sensation of having misplaced something. Instead, the morning after, he found Florencia Medina waiting for him behind the agave, all smiles, and realized that the second round had begun

"Here we are again," said Florencia, pretending to be shy.

The little kisser got back to kissing.

Then came a day of gray clouds, wind in the ears. The schoolyard was empty, yet Miguel had the high wind of mid-morning kisses at his back, and moved swiftly, curious to find out if he'd find Rosita Romero, Florencia Medina, Eugenia

Gallego, or someone else behind the agave. Instead waiting for him was an older boy with a scar that ran down his cheek like a tear: the permanent record of the time his father, so they said, had hurled him through a window when he was three years old. His name was Alfonsino Ruiz.

"This is my turf," he said to Miguel.

"Since when?" replied the other.

In reality Alfonsino Ruiz spent more time in the hallway than the classroom, usually being ejected from the latter by his teacher for some impertinence, and by dint of loitering around the school he'd become a little despot of the place. Or so he felt. The coming and going behind the agave hadn't escaped his notice, nor had the girls' whispers about Miguel, and naturally he felt bitter about that parade of kisses. He'd received a handful in all, kisses that is, and each time he had gripped the wrist of the other party to make her stay.

"Get lost," he ordered, and shoved Miguel.

The other boy lost his balance and retreated a few steps backward beyond the plant. From the windows the girls looked on, apprehensive about what might happen to him, and Miguel could sense their eyes on him. He charged forward, was struck harder than before, and flew backward again, only this time he flew a foot off the ground and fell like deadweight. But he was still alive and ready to fight. He got back up and rushed at Alfonsino Ruiz, who was taken aback by the kid's fury, by the helpless rage with which he attacked someone twice his size. Miguel managed to land a blow to his side—his first and last of the match—then clawed at him with his nails. But after hesitating a moment, Alfonsino Ruiz freed himself, threw Miguel down, and kicked him so hard he knocked the wind out of him.

"You want this spot? You can have it," he said. "I'll make it my pissing spot."

He unbuttoned his trousers and emptied his bladder on

Miguel, who instinctively covered his head with his hands, defeated. More than being struck, it was that warm liquid trickling over his ears, neck, and clothes that made him surrender. Miguel discovered that violence can be mild and stink of piss; Santiago may have inured him to punches and smacks, but he hadn't been ready for that kind of provocation. He was subjected to every last drop before Alfonsino Ruiz walked away from the agave. At that point he launched into a long, silent sob. Then he dried his tears and mustered the strength to pick himself up and leave, much to the relief of the girls at the windows who were afraid he'd been killed back there. He returned to class, avoiding the eyes and nose of the teacher, and waited for the morning to end, neither thinking nor making a move. And when the bell rang, he bolted outside to meet Santiago, who was in the habit of stopping by the gate on his way from middle school to pick him up.

It was a melancholy period for Santiago, whose solitary brooding had, over time, become part of his character. "That's just the way he is" was the explanation whenever someone asked. Miguel's life, on the other hand, was painless, shielded by the halo that had hovered over him ever since his recovery from diphtheria and the big party in celebration of his rebirth, shielded by beauty. But on that windy morning Miguel discovered that beauty could bring pain too, and, walking down the street side by side, the two really did look like brothers—in the way they carried themselves, by their mood. Santiago would never have noticed something was amiss had the smell not reached his nostrils.

"Did you piss your pants?" he asked.

Miguel had no intention of answering him. Santiago stopped him, took a knee, smelled the urine on his brother's skin, in his hair. When he lifted his chin, he noticed the bruise under his eye.

"Who did this?" he asked through gritted teeth. His brother said nothing and hung his head again.

"Tell me who did this or I'm going to tell Papa," Santiago threatened, grabbing him by his uniform. Miguel took a breath and recovered a wisp of his voice.

"Ruiz," he confessed.

That was all Santiago needed to know. He took Miguel by the hand and dragged him to the house where Alfonsino Ruiz lived with a mother that was never there. They found him in the woodshed beside his house. Alfonsino Ruiz recognized Santiago, the shy kid who'd been in elementary the year before, realized he was Miguel's brother, and as he sized him up—Santiago was shorter and smaller than him—he nevertheless knew that he couldn't take him. He knew it by Santiago's purposeful clip, the clear rage that shone in his eyes, the confidence in his stride, his trembling wrists and clenched fists ready to strike. Alfonsino Ruiz understood that Santiago was there to avenge much more than a brother, was there to give vent to an anger that came from someplace else, which had nothing to do with him, the same anger with which his father had hurled him through a window though he hadn't made a sound. Maybe that unsolicited memory explained why Alfonsino Ruiz knew what was about to happen and had lost all hope before Santiago even pounced on him, before he struck him with a closed fist, hard as a rock, drove him to the ground, leaped on him, and hit him again. Alfonsino Ruiz knew there was no way around it and resigned himself to his fate as if he had nothing to lose. But at a certain point the scene took such a vicious turn that Miguel jumped on top of Santiago to stop the violence that had gotten out of control.

"That's enough, Santiago," he said. But his brother didn't hear him and continued to hit Alfonsino Ruiz as if he'd been training for that battle all his life.

"That's enough, Santiago, enough," Miguel implored, his voice breaking.

Only then did Santiago come to his senses. Underneath him, Alfonsino Ruiz was a coiled-up body, routed by a violence that the boy may have been expecting, a violence to settle the score for good, that he could look in the face and know that life was what it was: a war where everyone loses and no one wins, so why not avert your eyes and let yourself be struck to get the full measure of how much it hurts. Santiago finally stopped, took a breath, and gently patted Alfonsino Ruiz's head with the grace of a pugilist hugging his punching bag.

Down the groove of Alfonsino Ruiz's tear-shaped scar ran a tear. He knew that it was over and from under his arms he stared up at Santiago. He had the sensation he was staring into a mirror. Between them stood Miguel, the very reason for their clash, whose only wrongdoing had been being there, being born, being who he was—and as a consequence making them feel misbegotten.

Santiago looked at Miguel, his hands shaking.

"I'll never hit another person for as long as I live," he said.

LOST THINGS

Hamacas
HAMMOCKS

That was it for school, at least for Santiago. Now came time to work. Vicente Moya found him a job that he'd keep for years. It came courtesy of Belisario Lopez, owner of the Sueño Yucateo, a man missing three fingers from his left hand who never wiped the toothy grin off his face and wore floral silk shirts. He turned up one night in November from god knows where, bought the old butcher shop in cash, mopped the blood from the floor for five days and five nights, and skewered the enormous rats in the back of the shop. On the sixth day, soon as the sun came up, he stepped outside, a filthy-looking creature, and raised a sign that read SUEÑO YUCATEO FAIR TRADE. On the walls, which he'd painted orange, yellow, and okra, he hung rugs, panama hats, sombreros, *huipiles*, belts, *rebozos,* and, above all, hammocks. Then he put the word out that he was hiring.

When the news reached Vicente Moya (the Sueño was a few blocks from the Casa de Guayaberas) Santiago didn't have chin hairs yet; he wasn't close to being a man. He followed his father in silence and from a distance stared at his back while his father whispered with Belisario Lopez. The two were separated by a marble counter covered in women's blouses and colorful shawls where flies had once swarmed slabs of beef. And as Santiago stood there, completely still, he caught the smell of blood mixed with bleach. Vicente Moya took no notice. He shook Lopez's good hand, turned to his son, patted him on the head—gently, awkwardly—and allocated him the job that

Santiago accepted as his one viable option, in part because he'd never asked himself what he might do when he grew up.

As soon as they were alone, Belisario Lopez briefly explained how the retail business worked, waving the fingers of his mangled hand in the air.

"You earn what you sell," he told him, not one to mince words. "So go out there and don't come back alone."

Santiago put everything into it, all the tenacity and energy stored away in his body. Every morning, in the shade of Plaza Mayor, he would lure clients using a strategy that he'd honed over months.

Today he zeroed in on an Italian couple leafing through a guidebook on a bench. He bought a *marquesita* from a push-cart, pecked at it as he wound his way toward them, sat down on the edge of the bench, and stared off at the sky beyond the foliage. Santiago had learned that you couldn't force the moment; it would come of its own accord. The moment when the client looked up, made eye contact with him as if by chance, and cracked a casual smile. At that point you smiled back, and the lion's share of the work was already done. But your smile had to be honest, genuine, real. That was why, every time he smiled at a tourist, Santiago couldn't help but think of his brother; he'd have been a better fit for that line of work. Santiago devised ways to compensate, dazzling the tourists with jokes he'd memorized, stock phrases he'd customize for each. In Mérida's main square he displayed a side of himself that hadn't existed till then. And even if he was pretending, even if it only lasted the length of a morning, it was during that time that he felt closest to Miguel, physically speaking. He, too, felt beautiful. And, in a way, beautiful is what he became in the eyes of the strangers whose lives intersected with his in the heart of Plaza Mayor. Therefore, after Vicente Moya handed him over to Belisario Lopez, he never pondered the possibility of another job: this one allowed him to be what he wasn't. He conversed with the young Italian couple that he'd latched onto and was talkative, affable, even extroverted.

"So, you must be Juliet? And you're Romeo?" he said, laughing.

He'd picked up the story about the two star-crossed Italian lovers from some travelers passing through. He hadn't understood it, not completely that is, but used it because it worked. Like the words that, over time, he'd memorized.

"Tante piacere! Voi come stai? Molta bene! Segnori andeiamo?"

The couple that morning would never have guessed that he'd called dozens of others Romeo and Juliet nor that they were in possession of everything that mattered to him: a flight that arrived at Mérida International Airport, curiosity, jet lag— i.e., drowsiness—enthusiasm, uncertainty, and pesos. They had pesos. Italians were an easy target. Given their language's resemblance to Spanish, they understood what he said, though Santiago had also picked up words and entire phrases in English, German, French. It was like an outdoor schoolroom underneath the bay trees; he listened for a few minutes to each unwitting teacher come from distant lands, people who lugged behind them bags and stories; each was different, but all Santiago cared about was whether or not he could recycle them. He took his work one day at a time, stuck to learning only the essentials, stole a strip of words here, cut out scraps of lexicon there, and patched together a costume as best he could. Like a mouse in the trap of life, he gathered a few morsels of hope at a time. Every day, more than once a day, he played make-believe with a winning joke, a where-you-from/where-you-going, beautiful Chichen Itza, *tante piacere*, how you do, a traveler's tip or a Mayan joke, news of the city of Montejo, *la noche mexicana*, oh all right, *el Mercado de artesanías*, another joke, eyes on the sky, and, in the end, here it came, the question that seemed to arrive from left field: "You haven't bought a hammock yet?"

In the end, the two Italians entered the Sueño Yucateo. Santiago had steered them there without betraying the fact that he had forced their hand. He told them Mérida was the city of hammocks, the most beautiful hammocks in the state, and, he added, they were woven by natives, and by buying one they'd be supporting local business, and that the shop was just two blocks from the plaza. He mentioned that it was open just three days a week and only in the morning. And—wouldn't you know?—it was open today but closing in less than an hour. He offered to take them there, saying that he'd be more than happy to, that he'd do it to support a fair-trade store, that he'd do it for them.

"*Segnori, andeiamo?*" he concluded, rising to his feet.

The rest was up to Belisario Lopez. When Santiago entered the store with the latest foreign couple, Belisario didn't even need to feign a smile. It came naturally to him, observing how the boy had taken to his job, poured sweat and ingenuity into it, and how every time he stepped into the store and pretended not to know him, the tourists following behind him had already made up their minds to walk out with a hammock.

In the back room, where he escorted the clients, Belisario Lopez had placed a pair of elderly Indios sewing this or that. Above the entrance hung a gilt-framed fair-trade certificate that he had printed himself. Ditto the counterfeit notes on the shop walls, written in every language, tokens of gratitude that appeared to have been left by past patrons: *Thanks, Sueño Yucateo! Belisario ist unser Freund! È meraviglioso aiutare l'artigianato locale! Merci Sueño, vos hamacs sont les plus beaux dans le monde!*

The two Italians studied them enthusiastically while roaming the shop. They would leave with a jute hammock jammed into a plastic bag, having paid ten times what it was worth, and would never know where to hang it. It would end up collecting dust in the basement of a condominium halfway across the globe. And when they paid, when they left the Sueño Yucateo, when they came back out into the light of day with the plastic bag under their arm, they instinctively looked for the boy. But he wasn't there. With one excuse or another, Santiago had quickly waved goodbye, vanished in a flash, was already back in Plaza Mayor, under the bay trees, back on a bench, telling another lie. Telling, telling himself, the same lie.

Los hilos rotos
CUT STRINGS

The rocking chair creaked on the boards of the veranda, marking time like a clock outside Hermenegildo Serrano's house and inside his bald head, which had remained as dark and empty as the road that night. Whatever he looked at, he seemed to be looking elsewhere. Whatever he said, he seemed to be saying something else. Occasionally he'd rise from his chair and amble down the city streets, aimlessly, for miles, following an invisible train of thought, a voice only he could hear. He had watched his grandchildren grow up but seemed not to recognize them, not really. Miguel in particular had remained for him the bundle of sticks that Maria Serrano had desperately cleaved to her lap, illuminated by the head-lights of the van that had taken both of them away and never returned.

Over the house slid dark, low-hanging, silent clouds. The first raindrops pelted the warm dust, the hood of the old Ford that had, like Miguel, died, only it had never come back to life. Hermenegildo Serrano hovered between life and death, a life in which nothing further happened, not even the song "Jarabe Tapatío" could reach him. He'd left the tape deck in a corner, took his post on the veranda, and sat waiting for everything to fade the way his spirit had faded. He sat there for what seemed like forever, enduring, his body wrinkled as a raisin.

It rained all afternoon and suddenly the old man stopped rocking and stared at the space encircled by the rain, which looked to him like a place where one day he might settle. Then the rain stopped, the Mexican terrain drank it up, and the last rays of the sun gave off so much heat it was as if it were trying to set the evening on fire. Hermenegildo Serrano stood up and started out, wiping the window of the Ford with his hand as he passed by. He headed in no particular direction, sometimes down the middle of narrow alleys, sometimes hugging the wall, regarding the sky and the earth with the same bland curiosity, his broken profile reflected in the empty shop windows, wheezing, limping forward.

When he caught the smell of laurel and cheese, he found himself swept up in the joyful commotion of people meeting up after work, children chasing after one another, and the shouts of pushcart vendors in Plaza Mayor. There, where more than anyplace else the heart of the city beat loudly, Hermenegildo Serrano heard the last beat of his own heart. It sounded like the old Ford flying through the air after hitting a tall *tope*, a silence that, regardless of the miles it had traveled up till then, zeroed in on the last foot—go ahead, fall, leave your worries for after. The old man put his hand to his chest, to his heart. Then he collapsed on the ground, a weightless and wizened bag of bones, and the final sound was the shriek of women who understood the meaning of that scene.

At that moment, sitting on a nearby bench, focused on his latest clients, Santiago recognized the wispy profile of his grandfather bent double—his strings cut. He wasn't prepared for that image, not like that, not in that place, not in that way. It left him in the lurch, a trace of a fake smile on his lips midway through his Mayan joke; it caused him unbearable pain. The next moment he was running and holding his grandfather's head in his hands, so that he could look at him one last time, ask him one last question, as if after all those years the man might recognize him.

"Santiago," whispered Hermenegildo Serrano.

"What is it, Grandpa?" Santiago answered, overwhelmed, undone.

"He's dead, isn't he?" the old man managed to say, closing his eyes.

"Who?" asked Santiago, as if everything depended on his answer.

"Who, Grandpa?" Santiago repeated, now screaming, his voice broken. Then someone pushed him aside and ripped open the man's shirt to administer CPR. It was pointless; Hermenegildo Serrano had stopped breathing.

"Who?" Santiago repeated, but no one heard him, and a crowd of strangers closed in and blocked his view of his grandfather. Yet before disappearing behind the crowd, the boy managed to see that on his chest, just above his heart, Hermenegildo Serrrano had a mole. Like a period marking the end of a life.

Maria Serrano took the news with the heartbreaking composure typical of her. In a certain way, she was already prepared for it, having reconciled herself to the idea that on the night she had gained back her son, she had also lost her father. An exchange of souls—that was what people said. That Hermenegildo Serrano had made a pact with God or the Devil on behalf of his grandson, on her behalf, without saying a word to anyone. So, when she was told that her father had died of a heart attack, she spilled what tears she had left, what tears she hadn't cried yet, peeled onions, and thought of him. The next day she prepared the hallway of Casa Moya for the wake, positioning the open casket between two rows of chairs. Air and light entered through the open windows, arrived straight from the courtyard where the number of children and colorful umbrellas continued to grow, and the women stood up now and then to go inside where it was cooler, say a prayer, and recite the rosary. Music drifted around the grandfather in his elegant suit; a mariachi had brought his instrument and strummed the same melody for an hour, then changed places with another man. Finally, flowers, *flores cempasúchil*, placed in glass vases put out a bittersweet fragrance that mingled with incense and painted the house yellow—where they ate, drank, traded memories of Hermenegildo Serrano, or touched on altogether different subjects in hushed tones that grew more audible every time someone arrived bearing more flowers, more food, other questions and stories and prayers.

The funeral of Hermenegildo Serrano brought a new wave of people to Casa Moya over the same path beat roughly ten years earlier for the celebration of Miguel's birth, the procession for his birthday. Old Serrano was well-known in the city, since he used to deliver the mail and made a point of talking to everyone, plus his dramatic departure, in the middle of bustling Plaza Mayor, had been reported in the city paper. Moreover, even if no one dared to mention it, the wake provided many in attendance with an occasion to catch a glimpse of the *niño divino*. Most remembered him as a small promise in the arms of Señora de Guadalupe. They began looking for him as soon as they arrived, yards before reaching the house, and tried to imagine what he might have grown up to be like. With appropriate solemnity, they stood at the door, shook Vicente Moya's hand, kissed or embraced Maria Serrano, respectfully brushed the wood casket where Hermenegildo Serrano seemed to have regained his old geniality. His face was peaceful. Maybe, in the end, he really had settled in the space encircled by the rain. Or maybe, with his last breath, he had found the answer he'd been searching for as he wandered the streets of Mérida. In any case, after going through the motions, everyone turned their attention to the corner of the room where Maria Serrano had told Miguel to sit and pray for his grandfather; more eyes fell on him than on the coffin. He was eleven years old but looked much older. The delicate child had given way to a full-grown, fully-formed man with dazzlingly perfect features—face, shoulders, arms already sculpted. He exceeded all expectations, every dream.

Miguel prayed for the grandfather he never really knew, a man whose spirit had departed this earth when the boy was too young to notice him, so the pain he experienced was an imitation of his mother's pain. To keep him in his chair, she'd told him, "Your grandfather needs you." Miguel didn't understand what she meant but understood Maria Serrano wasn't going to repeat herself. She'd squashed his desire to run out to the yard, where, over time, he had initiated relationships with all of the girls in the neighborhood: the allure of physical contact was increasingly powerful. Shackled to his chair, he tried to understand a feeling—the mourning of a departed relative—that no one had explained to him. He was captivated by the inert profile of the elegantly dressed body in the coffin, and discovered that people, like cockroaches, eventually stop moving and end up flat on their backs.

Otherwise he drew glances and smiles of astonishment, which he answered with his own perfect smile, and thus, without his realizing it, he lightened the mood at the funeral and made the scent of flowers and the smell of the corpse a bit sweeter, occasionally even intoxicating. In fact, that was what Maria Serrano had intended: for Miguel's participation to render the event different, special. The best, the only way to restore to Hermenegildo Serrano what life had ultimately robbed him of—what Miguel himself, in a certain sense, had robbed him of. As always, it worked. The mood changed; instead of death people saw only beauty, the mysterious charm of the turning seasons, of chilling winter giving way to spring, of skies as gray as the wisps of Hermenegildo Serrano's hair that open to reveal a brightness, bright as the teeth of Miguel, bright as the teeth of the living who smile, consoled by the endless drift of things. The musicians, one mariachi after another, also wound up launching into more cheerful songs, providing a backdrop of amusing tales by which to remember the exploits of the deceased; the hilarity that ensued was natural and contagious. Everyone cared a great deal for old Serrano, but none would have ever imagined that they'd be smiling and laughing and laughing some more with such genuine intensity at his deathbed.

The navel of the grandfather became the navel of the world. The neighbors and the neighbors of neighbors gathered around Hermenegildo Serrano's stomach, around his thin fingers interlaced and resting on top of his stiff chest enclosed by the coffin. Casa Moya was like the Paseo de Montejo. Everyone came and lingered there, having found themselves unexpectedly happy. They didn't leave the house until the space in the hallway became too cramped and those who had been there longest were invited to step aside. But many stayed in the courtyard and stood by the windows of Casa Moya so that they could keep listening, laughing, partaking in the scene. Someone eventually fetched a fan and switched it on. The air grew cool, the smell of the flowers wafted over the smell of warm bodies crowded around the cold body of the deceased, above the gleaming tips of his shoes and the aquiline nose peeking out from the wooden casket.

In his room Santiago felt the crowds clamoring at his door, the giggles subsiding here, erupting there. He didn't understand and didn't want to understand. Maria Serrano allowed him to stay in his room after the trauma he'd experienced watching his grandfather die, hearing his last words. Unlike Miguel, Santiago had spent five years on his grandfather's pointy knees, rocking together on his rocking chair or walking hand in hand. That was why he couldn't bear the sight of the old man in a box in the middle of the room, why he couldn't bear the silence that had befallen him at the end of his life. It was a betrayal of sorts, a leave-taking with no warning. He lay in the hammock in the same pose as his grandfather, only sometimes he would lift his fingers to his ears to plug them so that he didn't have to hear the people laughing. What was so funny anyway?

Miguel on the other hand laughed like everyone else and let himself be transported by the general cheer, of which he was the involuntary epicenter. So. Funerals were also, at heart, experiences that gave pleasure. He laughed, shifting his gaze to wherever people were talking, where a voice filled the room with a recollection of Hermenegildo Serrano; having been a man full of spirit, he was the source of dozens of funny stories.

Miguel laughed. Until the moment when, upon the latest rotation of visitors, in walked the Romero family, in particular, bringing up the rear, little Rosita, who was no longer so little. Miguel hadn't seen her in a few years, ever since she'd left elementary school and never looked back. She was as beautiful then as she had been the day they met in the schoolyard, yet she had looked after her figure with the diligence of a knife grinder, patiently waiting for the opportunity to have a rematch. When she noticed Hermenegildo Serrano's inscription hanging on the wall, she smiled—not unkindly—and went off to comb her hair. Her hair had become long, wavy; it framed a face that had been splendid before and now in adolescence had taken on a new light, the light of pollen on a budding flower. And, as was often the case, fortune rewarded her brashness, because the fan hit her the moment Miguel noticed her, the moment they laid eyes on each other for the first time since the slap and kiss with which they'd left off. The breeze rustled her hair and exposed her neckline and for a moment netted the attention of every man in the room. The little lover-in-training had suffered his first defeat. He had discovered that the death of cockroaches and the death of old people can weigh everything or nothing, if in life you found whatever it was he felt coursing through his heart and veins, burning in his stomach, whatever it was he couldn't name but which kept him staring at Rosita Romero from the first to last second that she stood there paying him less regard than everyone else. There was no way to measure the time that the Romero family stood beside the coffin at Casa Moya; it may have been no time at all or all the time in the world. What mattered was that, as soon as it was over, Miguel approached Maria Serrano and asked her permission to get some air.

"Go ahead," his mother said kindly, because Miguel had already done what was asked of him and at the same time the door to Santiago's room swung open and out walked the boy, slovenly, lost, clearly no longer wanting to be alone, hungry perhaps. Miguel had freed his seat, and Maria Serrano signaled to her older son to come take the place next to her. He thought about it before accepting then slipped between the bodies without looking down at the coffin, keeping his head turned away. And there, by pure chance, at the end of the hall by the exit, he caught sight of Miguel snatching up a *cempasúchil* and offering it to a beautiful older girl. Rosita Romero hesitated a minute but eventually accepted, sniffed the flower, and stared at Miguel with a purpose in her eyes that Santiago would never forget. A little later, Miguel took her hand and carried her off, out of the house, as if she belonged to him.

Cosas perdidas
LOST THINGS

As the sun set, a crowd of *meridaños* still occupied the hall and front yard. Many hung back to eat and drink and chat; a second pushcart was now parked next to the fruit-juice cart and sold beer and *tamalitos al vapor*—with the discreet mediation of Vicente Moya. Inside the house the cheerful mood continued to swirl around the body of Hermenegildo Serrano. The laughter and talk died down only when the neighborhood priest came by to bless the coffin and lead all present in a moment of silence to remember the deceased. Then the party in honor of the dearly departed started up again as the heat attenuated and the afternoon slowly slipped into evening. By sunset everyone had paid their respects. Except, that is, for one man, without whom, as a matter of tradition, the casket couldn't be closed.

When Sancho Molina had caught wind of old Serrano's death, he crawled into a dark corner of his ramshackle lab. He knew that sooner or later circumstances would bring him face to face with Vicente Moya. He hadn't forgotten Moya's anxiety and rage that dark night in the field. For the first time in the amateur *curandero*'s career, he felt the weight of the role that he had assumed and which his neighbors had bestowed upon him on account of some stunt he'd managed to pull off. Sancho Molina was afraid. And his fear had remained intact, like a fossil, ever since the men had last crossed paths. Ten years on and Sancho Molina and Vicente Moya still stood in the barren field, hanging in a delicate balance. Ten years on and Molina still had the sensation of having reached an impasse: he no longer felt saved, not even when, a few days later, he got word that a doctor at the hospital had brought the child back to life. After that, he reverted to conducting his experiments on animals rather than on people and largely kept busy concocting teas and infusions.

On the evening of Hermenegildo Serrano's wake, while he sat motionless in the middle of his shack, there came a moment when he fantasized that he'd been forgotten: the sun slid behind the houses, his dark hovel grew darker, and it seemed to him as if the neighborhood had decided to carry on without him this time. But then his elderly neighbor and occasional assistant opened the door and, in the red light that reached the tips of his shoes, he glimpsed the road awaiting him and the color of the blood that he'd spill.

"Everyone's waiting for you, Sancho," whispered the old woman.

Molina stood up, pretending to be more courageous than he was, and put on his white tunic and black sombrero as coolly as he could. He went out to meet his fate. But in the middle of the road, just steps from the house, he stopped, unable to go any farther, and turned back. In the shadow of his hovel he took a milk jar down off the shelf. It was half full of dried mushrooms. He sniffed them; the smell put him at ease. He took one, put it in his mouth, and began to chew. The next thing he knew, he was standing at the Moyas' entrance.

The funeral chamber suddenly got quiet at the sight of him. Molina's pale profile hovered in the entrance, his sombrero fluttered in the whirr of the fan. For some reason he stood still and kept his face hidden. Then it occurred to someone to clap, and the applause encouraged Sancho Molina to doff his sombrero and look Vicente Moya in the eye. They stared at each other from either end of the hall in a mute standoff that no one could interpret, separated by the stiff corpse of Hemernegildo

Serrano. Vicente Moya realized it wasn't the place to take up old battles, that he had to forgive him, if for no other reason than as a sign of respect for his wife and her father. He gave a nod, which Molina had been waiting for, like a sign of deliverance. After which the *curandero* crossed the room to offer Maria Serrano his condolences and more importantly shake hands with Vicente Moya, who whispered in his ear: "Pull any stunts and I'll stick you in the coffin."

Molina felt a shiver down his spine. He chewed the mushroom that had been lodged under his tongue and turned to old Serrano's corpse, placed one hand on his forehead and the other on his heart, closed his eyes, and tried to concentrate on the dead man. Usually at that point he'd improvise. Sometimes he actually did experience a rush of good vibes that bore novel ideas. When nothing came to him, he had a raft of orations at the ready that pleased everyone all the same. But with Hermenegildo Serrano, inspiration struck, thanks in part to the hallucinogenic mushroom that he was chewing so eagerly. He called up an image of the old man in the middle of the road, dancing to his favorite song with the nimbleness and grace that he had possessed in life. He opened one eye and peered into the coffin, then took his hand off his heart, lifted it in the air, and intoned: "*Where* is it?"

Everyone present watched him, rapt.

"Where is it? *Where* is it? *Where* is it?" he repeated, louder each time, his voice rising to a crescendo. And after a pause, at the height of tension, he brought the curtain down: "*Where* is Hermenegildo's tape deck?"

There was only one person who could go searching for the tape deck. And that person was Santiago. It had to be somewhere in his grandfather's house, but Maria Serrano and Vicente Moya couldn't leave the funeral chamber. Yet at that point it was fundamental they find the tape deck, because

Sancho Molina had heard the dead man's last wish, and the casket couldn't be closed without setting what Hermenegildo had asked for in his lap so that he could rest in peace. Maria Serrano really should have thought of it before, but that thing had disappeared years ago when the old man had sat down on the veranda and never emerged from his daze.

"The key is under the vase," she said softly to Santiago.

"I know," he replied, standing up.

He lit out down the road, faster than the fading light, saddled with his responsibility, proud to have been chosen, afraid he might fail to find it.

When he arrived, he lifted the vase by the door, but the key wasn't there. A trickle of surprise, a doubt he'd misunderstood or misremembered. Instinctively he placed his hand on the handle and pressed down, and the door opened. Inside everything was dim, silent, redolent of dust and his grandfather. He thought that perhaps Maria Serrano, busy preparing for the funeral, had come by and forgotten to lock the door. He switched on the light in the middle of the kitchen, the room glowed, and the cabinet towering behind the table immediately struck him as the best place to look. That was where his grandfather kept his most important papers and mementos, arranged in an order Santiago loved. He found everything the same, each item just as Hermenegildo Serrano had left it, bound with twine in the fastidious manner of old people. And placed on top, ready to be switched on at any moment, was the tape deck. Finding it so soon filled Santiago with joy. It was as if he'd found his grandpa again, as if he had understood that man better than anyone else. And he was glad that he was the one to bring him this gift, to give him back that object which he had been so fond of, which he had almost forgotten yet now would take with him wherever it was he was going.

He closed the cabinet, turned back, switched off the light, began to leave. But he was stopped by a noise coming from behind a door that gave onto the hall, the bathroom, the bedroom. More than a noise, it sounded like a voice. Santiago felt the urge to run and did: out the front door, past the veranda, to the Ford parked a few feet from the house. He crouched behind it, breathless, his back against the car, hugging the tape deck to his chest, his heart beating wildly. Breathe. Think. Maybe it was the wood creaking, the house, he thought. Maybe he'd lost his cool when he switched off the light. Maybe. He took another breath, tried to get his bearings. A moment later, he felt better and convinced himself that he'd imagined the whole thing. He decided to go back and close the door; then he'd leave. He stood up and walked back toward the house, keeping his ear out. Nothing. Then something occurred to him: maybe his grandpa was still inside, had something to tell him, had come back to ask him to fetch another object to place in the coffin. The thought prompted him to go back in, gave him a resolve and composure he hadn't expected. He crossed the few feet separating him from the door that led to the other side of the house, opened it in the dark, tiptoed down the hall, and stood warily at the entrance to the room.

And there on top of the bed that Hermenegildo Serrano had once shared with his wife, his wife who'd died too young, engulfed in soft, flickering candlelight, naked and sweaty, was his brother Miguel pounding against the body of Rosita Romero with the rough and impetuous angst of first-timers. Rosita Romero's legs were wrapped around Miguel's buttocks. Her moans were smothered as she embraced him with the pliant surprise of a stranger to pleasure. Miguel's arms were tensed, his hands thrust in Rosita Romero's dark hair spread on the pillow while he thrust into her.

Santiago watched in the dark, didn't move the entire time. An instant, an hour. For a boy who knew nothing about sex or love, the emotion took his breath away. It pierced him just as he'd been pierced when his grandpa had collapsed on the ground and died. Then, when Miguel's body quivered and exploded in joy, Santiago snapped out of his spell, took a step back, and vanished into the same dark from which he'd entered, softly closing the door behind him before speeding off, faster than before, faster than light itself, the light which had faded, which had yielded to the night the way Rosita Romero had yielded to his brother, and yet he felt he must be late, perpetually late to everything, to the flow of existence itself, which ran ahead of him and forever eluded his grasp.

The business about the tape deck, the trembling voice with which Sancho Molina evoked the last wish of Hermenegildo Serrano—that was the topic of conversation in the over-crowded courtyard and was now expected, the latest source of curiosity, a pretext to linger there.

So, when Santiago sprang out of the alley that spit out into the courtyard, running with the tape deck in one hand, a look of dismay on his face, as if his grandpa might depart before he'd gotten back, under the sliver of moon that looked like a gash in the night, the crowd erupted in shouts of joy and applause, and all eyes turned to him. The crowd parted to make way for him, shouted, patted him on the back, whistled, cheered him on as if he were rounding the last bend in an Olympic race, baton in hand. Santiago ran absentmindedly, enjoying neither the moment nor the glory, feeling nothing but the seductive effect of the images he'd chanced upon at the threshold of Hermenegildo Serrano's room, which churned in his stomach and drew him under, far away.

The hallway of Casa Moya glowed with candlelight and smelled of the incense that had been lit to cover the smell of the corpse. Given the clamor preceding the boy, the people leaning against the wall figured his hunt for the tape deck had been a success. Maria Serrano went and kissed him on the head, but not even that made Santiago happy; he was distracted, distant, still hovering in the dark of his grandpa's house where he'd witnessed that astonishing spectacle of nature, of life craving more life, of the vigor of human bodies, beautiful bodies, penetrating one another, and he found inside himself the same desire for life and flesh, a hunger to touch and be touched that had remained buried under a solid block of unconsciousness.

His mother took the tape deck and deposited it in the cold fingers of old Serrano while Sancho Molina chanted with his arms raised and his eyes staring up at the ceiling as if he could see the sky or the dead man's soul departing, drifting away with the tape deck. No one took any more notice of Santiago, who withdrew to his room to think—as if there were something he could do just then, as if it were a matter of resolving a question that had been dangling there, just waiting for the right moment. And that was the moment. He knew it by the way his mind instinctively returned to a place he'd always glimpsed from a distance, about which he'd heard people whisper or make vulgar, ironic jokes. What he knew was that where certain matters were concerned, money was involved. And he had money. Not the pesos from Belisario Lopez's hammocks, nearly all of which Vicente Moya confiscated at the end of each month, but the gold mine he'd amassed over all those years going for groceries with Miguel, which Anita Soler had kindly refused. He took the bills hidden under his bench and went out with his head down, disappeared from Casa Moya, from the deafening courtyard, withdrew to the streets of Mérida, swallowed up by the night, blurred with the shadows. He stopped thinking and gave himself up to a fate that he may have foreseen and desired yet had never admitted to—that was the easiest way to do a difficult deed. He felt no fear, only a need that he intended to indulge. Life craving life. Something like that.

He found the woman outside the trailer at the edge of the fields.

"How old are you?" she asked, waving a fan.

"Old enough," said Santiago, flashing her his roll of pesos.

The woman stood up and shook out her soft, tired thighs. She lit a candle outside the trailer, invited him to enter, then closed the door. And there, behind the plastic door, on a worn mattress stained by others, Santiago became a man. The prostitute, sensing it was his first time, welcomed him sweetly, and Santiago collapsed into the folds of her adult flesh, which he neither recognized nor resembled. He fell into them thanks to the money that, without his asking, Miguel had procured for him, and imitated moves that, without his knowing it, Miguel had taught him, only he added to them his own appetite and anxiety mixed with contempt and insecurity and other fluid emotions that he felt coursing through his stomach, his liver, his testicles, until it was released in a spurt that he'd gone looking for, the meaning of all that grinding, that pursuit, that need, that electrifying agony that had no name since it had taken place in the dark of his grandpa's room, and that electrifying agony that had taken place there, in the trailer on the outskirts of Mérida, on the edge of himself, on the edge of everything. Gently, maternally, the woman ran her fingers through his hair, but Santiago shooed her away in disgust.

"Don't touch me," he said, putting his clothes back on.

At the exact same time, back in Hermenegildo Serrano's house, the candlelight went out. Miguel squeezed Rosita Romero's body and felt a kind of peace. It seemed to him like a place to rest.

In Casa Moya, on the other hand, the last visitors of the night were arriving, a little before the casket was sealed shut. Among them was Clarabella Sanchez, followed by her daughter Soledad, who, as she'd grown up, had retained an effervescent gleam in her big eyes set behind round-framed spectacles. While her mother searched for Miguel, she searched for Santiago. She could never have guessed that, at that very moment, he was encountering pleasure, lying horizontally, like Hermenegildo Serrano in his box, which a few minutes later was closed amid a whisper of litanies. And with the last nail hammered in, they heard—as if by a miracle—music rise from inside the coffin. They heard the chorus of "Jarabe Tapatío."

La belleza del amor
THE BEAUTY OF LOVE

T he hair of Miguel. The eyes of Miguel. The skin of
Miguel. The chin of Miguel. The lips of Miguel. And
Miguel's heart on top of Rosita Romero's naked body.
Miguel withdrew from the world to chart the world beyond
the parted legs of the girl who had let herself go. He took
things as they came and gave no thought to tomorrow. In fact,
there was no tomorrow; there was the present and the blessing
of the flesh, skin touching skin, fingers twined with other fingers, only the soft space between Rosita Romero's lips where
Miguel's tongue licked the air she breathed. And moans blend-
ing with the creaks of the wrought-iron bed that had begged
for passion after all those years of peace. It was their destiny—
they *had* to meet in the semidarkness of the old Serrano house
sooner or later, *had* to wind up there: their names were
engraved on the walls and ceiling, painted on the walkway,
carved into the wood furniture, written in the dust of the
courtyard long before they'd locked lips in the schoolyard,
before Rosita sensed the promise of his arrival, before he died
and was reborn, even before he was born. And, now that the
necessary time had elapsed, everything else belonged either to
the past or the future, and therefore didn't matter. All that
mattered was rubbing up against each other till it hurt, dying
of pleasure, sleeping the bare minimum to recover the energy
to have sex again. Was that love? Miguel couldn't say, had
nothing to compare it to, purely focused on the pursuit of it.
But the feeling about which everyone spoke had to be this

thing here, on which no conditions could be placed: shield her from others, have her anyplace, keep her close, scour her soul, undress her, uncover her every part, listen to her, get inside her mind, kiss her words, desire her again, hold her close, keep his distance so that he felt her absence, and indulge in the luxury of endless promises with words richer than sugar.

"Is this love?" Miguel asked Santiago one night.

"Is what love?" replied Santiago.

"Always having an empty stomach," said Miguel.

"That's hunger," responded Santiago. "There's no such thing as love."

"Then maybe love is hunger."

Days, weeks, months passed. Two years passed in which Miguel grew side by side with Rosita Romero. They escaped Mérida together, hopped on buses without tickets and went exploring neighboring towns hand in hand. They often stayed out all night, sleeping wherever or not sleeping at all and staring at the stars. Whereas she made up excuses to circumvent her parents, Miguel announced their departure over dinner in an adolescent voice with the calm of an adult. For some reason Vicente Moya couldn't bring himself to prohibit his son from anything, and Maria Serrano felt it was pointless to try. Santiago lifted his head from his plate and waited for a refusal that never came. A hush fell over the table, which Miguel tried to climb his way out of by switching the subject to something generally more upbeat, something to lighten the mood. At moments like that, Santiago wondered whether it was his fault for not having the courage to make demands that seemed unthinkable to him. In particular whether he lacked the courage to picture himself hopping on the next bus to go see what went on out there. He always came up with the same answer: perhaps more than anything else it was love itself that he lacked, and therefore love existed and afforded one the strength to do extraordinary things the easy way.

*

Beauty in pursuit of beauty. Having caught Miguel, Rosita Romero had become his prisoner. She supported his needs by making them her own, humored the boy's every inclination—desires that became demands that fueled other desires. For her, picking up and running off, going to get lost in Yucatán, was a consequence of their relationship: she had completely lost control of herself in Miguel's arms that night when they had both given up their virginity. Therefore, the day that yet another bus deposited them near a *cenote*, they felt an intense, intimate echo of the experience that had first undone them; they climbed down into the earth, into a hell painted like Paradise, breached by the rays of the sun that played over a natural freshwater pool, apparently bottomless yet clear, filtered by the soil, populated by tiny fish. They dove into those waters held sacred by the Mayans with the same urge and ingenuity with which they flung their bodies at one another. When they swam to the surface, Rosita Romero picked a flower.

"I never thought there could be so much beauty so close to home," she said, gazing at the *cenote* and sniffing the flower the same way she'd sniffed the *cempasúchil* long before in the hallway of Casa Moya.

Miguel snatched the flower out of her hands and threaded it in her hair.

"Me neither," he said, looking at her.

From then on, whenever they could, they went in search of another *cenote* to explore: Cuzamá, Yokdzonot, Ponderosa, Dos Ojos, Azul, the Grutas de Loltún, Samula. They got into the habit of visiting them when the crowds had thinned. At one point they decided that there wasn't room for anyone else and scaled fences at night, slept in the jungle, and dove into the water at dawn, surrounded by stalactites, rock face, spellbinding grottoes or tropical plants, thick mangrove roots, hummingbirds, and bats. Outside, the sun rose over the sweet chasm where their ancestors spoke to the gods, while they swam in the pit of limestone that had caved in centuries before they'd been born. Vitamin waters, mineral salts, magic algae, balsams, and poultices for the smooth skin of Miguel and Rosita Romero. Their naked bodies inevitably drew close in the middle of the pool, and they kissed. They sought each other there too, unable to resist, penetrating and embracing one another in one soul, lost contact with the surface, stopped breathing, slid toward the bottom of the pit where long ago the Mayans hurled human sacrifices and gold and jade. Eventually they'd come up for air, swim to the top in broad strokes, re-emerge in the sky, and catch their breath before kissing, before making loving again. Miguel couldn't have known it then, but he'd never again taste anything like Rosita Romero's kisses in those water bubbles, in the depths of those *cenotes*, where the proximity to the dark subterranean caves and divinities living down there and the oxygen not reaching their brains gave them a taste of experience that hovered between life and death, where life is closest to reality because it fights to stay alive.

Then one day they reemerged, the rainforest around them harnessed the humidity and arrested time, and Rosita Romero took a deep breath. All of a sudden she was the girl he first met behind the agave plant.

"Will you marry me someday?" she asked him, floating up in the eyes of Miguel, her long wet hair slicked behind her ears, her words and thin fingers trembling on the surface of the water.

"Yes," Miguel answered instinctively, just as he had before, and went back to kissing her furiously. But then, as they sank to the depths of the sacred pit again, he felt the weight of his promise, the urge to swim back up to the surface and catch his breath again.

Llegar a ser grandes
GROWING UP

While Miguel was busy discovering the peculiarities of sex and love, Santiago took refuge in the industry of his career, perfecting his method. Every day of the week he smiled his fake smile, repeated largely artificial expressions. He racked up clients and sales; every bag checked onto planes heading from Mérida for Europe contained a hammock that he had flogged, and because of that, Belisario Lopez had given him a raise. Every month the merchant handed him more money, and Santiago, now that he knew what to do with it, plucked up the courage to confront Vicente Moya. At the table, naturally.

"I earn it, I'm entitled to it," he exclaimed.

"As long as you live here, it belongs to the family," his father shot back.

The next night Santiago relaunched his campaign. Given Miguel's requests, it seemed only reasonable.

"I'll only keep half," he said, brandishing his knife and fork like weapons.

Vicente Moya looked up from his plate and saw that his son was determined to win. He exchanged a look with Maria Serrano, who nodded. The weight of their concessions to Miguel hung in the air.

"Careful what you spend it on," concluded Vicente Moya, and went back to eating.

Santiago masked his feelings so as not to betray his real goal. In his heart he felt the same joyful satisfaction that he'd felt when Vicente Moya agreed to let him keep Pan. It seemed to him that he'd been fighting his entire childhood with his father to gain every inch of ground, to become a grown-up. Then he looked at Miguel sitting across from him; his brother was staring at him with something verging on admiration. And in their look lay the essence of a feeling that they hadn't confessed to one another and yet, despite everything, made them vital to each other's growing up.

Growing up, however differently. Now that he had money, Santiago's one means of learning about love was to withdraw to the trailer on the edge of the city. If you can call that love. He returned a couple of times a month, usually on the weekends, when Miguel left the house to plunge into the *cenotes*. Immersion—that was what Santiago was doing too, sinking into tactile and physical sensations that unhinged him in a way that he was gradually becoming more aware of. The body of the woman who took him in was a reassuring place that made solitude warm; the sharp tang of her mock Chanel, mixed with sweat, was a necessity. Santiago took in the aroma of paid sex with his face thrust between her large breasts, dug his nails into the prostitute's flesh to mount her with his eyes shut, hung over a precipice until finally collapsing with a groan, oblivion having granted him peace, and he lay on top of her, lifeless, like a dirty sheet.

"What's your name?" the woman whispered one night.

"Santiago," he replied, his head on her chest, a little surprised by the sound of her heart beating in her body.

"Do you want to know mine?"

"No."

Growing up differently. For Miguel, that stage in his life had the consistency of water, of Rosita Romero's liquid kisses. The looks other girls gave him ricocheted off his aloof profile. Beauty incarnate had become living, equipped matter, and yet just then a love affair many believed extremely premature rendered him unavailable. The fact made their desire for him spike, thrust Miguel into the private dreams of his peers, placed him at the climax of indecent thoughts that they nurtured while secretly touching themselves; adolescence fueled secret impulses centered on the image of that boy thanks to signals he'd sent unwittingly when he'd fished the key to the door of the Serrano house out from under his grandfather's vase and unlocked sexuality itself.

Rosita Romero was careful to conceal her jealousy, but as soon as she had the chance, she would drag Miguel far away from Mérida; the external pressure of the city had become unbearable. Yet by hemming him in she'd shown him the way out. Without realizing it, she'd handed him over to her worst enemy—*freedom*—which he glimpsed in the vast prospects of Yucatán through the dingy window of a bus. That was the freedom he sought when, through the assertion of survival instincts, he resurfaced from the *cenote* after Rosita Romero asked the question she would be too afraid and intelligent to ever ask again.

For the same reason, it was with indifference that at the last minute she told him about the day she'd been waiting for since she was a little girl.

"Sunday is my fifteenth birthday. Are you going to come?"

Miguel had never been to a *quinceañera*.

"Sure," he asked, not asking what she meant.

The day was a shock for him. At the far end of the church, packed with people, Rosita Romero was married. Married, that is, without a husband. She stood frozen in front of the altar in a pink chiffon dress, her wide skirt concealing her sneakers and her hair sliding straight down her back. She recited prayers for the end of girlhood, for embarking on a new age. In the first row her sharply dressed father struggled to hide his emotion despite his suspicion that his daughter had been a woman for some time. Miguel, on the other hand, stood in the back and had the sensation that he was watching their wedding, hers and his. Only he was absent from it. It seemed like a rotten premonition, a bad omen. He followed the procession out but kept his distance, watching Rosita Romero stride out of the church ahead of her parents, her godparents, seven maids of honor, and their seven escorts, and march to the hall that had been rented out for the occasion.

The smell of *barbacoa*, dug up from the ground and served on plastic plates, wafted in the air, and music brought people to their feet. *Damas* and *chambelanes* performed a group dance and la *quinceañera* Rosita Romero danced a waltz with her father, who was holding her close only to hand her over to whomever she chose, now that she was free to choose. Even if they all knew—including, maybe, Mr. Romero—that Rosita had already chosen, and as soon as he let her go she bounded after Miguel, running toward the girls who may have cornered him, clumsily pressing forward in her dress—cumbersome, a touch too long, its sequins suddenly too flashy—desperately elbowing her guests, who suffocated her with their attention, who lavished her with caresses, who pawed her with their hands, greasy with goat meat, who smothered her at the party she had dreamt of and which she no longer wanted. Several minutes passed that way, amid general confusion, a cat and mouse game of unwanted touches, looks lost in the crowd, beyond the crowd. Then night fell on Mérida and Rosita Romero's fifteenth birthday party. She suddenly quit running, quit hoping and fighting, quit looking for Miguel, struck by the certainty that there was nothing left to pursue, nothing to defend.

That night Santiago woke to someone whispering his name. It was the voice of Miguel, who couldn't sleep, breaking the silence of the room.

"Santiago."

"What is it?" he asked, sitting up in his hammock.

"I need you to loan me some money," said Miguel.

"What for?"

"To fix Grandpa's car."

"His car? To do what?"

"I've got to get out of here."

Miguel didn't know where he was going, only that he needed out. Needed to put a few miles between himself and Mérida, to figure out whether Mérida, whether Rosita Romero, was worth staying for. For Santiago it was revelatory; his brother had begun to distinguish between what worked for him and what didn't, to ask questions and seek answers, to make decisions on a whim that could definitively change his lot. He'd plucked Rosita Romero with a flower. Now he was abandoning her with a car that to Santiago's mind was broken yet which Miguel could imagine carrying him far. His imaginative, bold, slightly reckless, self-confident, and practical ability to make anything possible was something unthinkable to Santiago.

The next day he handed Miguel the money he needed. Then he watched him run off in search of a mechanic and spent the whole day in a daze, waiting to witness a miracle, to see his brother reappear aboard the old Ford, in Hermenegildo Serrano's own seat. By the time it actually happened, he'd thought about it so much he'd exhausted all thought, and it seemed to him a mirage, a hallucination. Miguel turned onto the road around Plaza Mayor with the windows down, his hair blowing in the wind, and a smile that said victory, freedom. The mechanic had shown him how to drive; that it was an automatic helped. As with his grandfather, his license was a photo of the Virgin of Guadalupe on the dashboard and a couple of pesos in case the police pulled him over.

"You did it" was all he managed to say.

"Hop in," said Miguel, "I'll let you drive."

For Santiago it was the miracle of miracles. The last time he'd been in his grandpa's car he was still a little kid, and he felt like a little kid next to his younger brother, who may as well have been his older, having grown as tall as him, having out-paced him in every other respect, accelerating, driving away, turning down an avenue that led out of the city while the view over his shoulder unfolded, his past returned, and new and old feelings mingled in the wind. Miguel pulled into a sandy lot and briefly explained how to handle a car, how to make it do your bidding. He climbed out, stepped around the Ford, opened the door, and goaded him to give it a shot. Santiago reacted with the same brashness—not his by nature—with which he'd strode over to the trailer on the outskirts of Mérida. And here on the same outskirts he was learning to drive, step-ping on the gas, steering, going out to meet the road, to meet life itself, while Miguel hollered and wrapped his arm around his shoulders and urged him to go faster. While the Moya brothers were speeding away together, Vicente Moya was hawking guayaberas; Maria Serrano was hanging clothes on a line; and Hermenegildo Serrano, were he looking down from heaven, was no doubt smiling: his old Ford had been resur-rected and his two grandchildren were tearing off in it, kicking up a cloud of dust.

An hour later Miguel took the wheel and they turned back to the city.

"Can you tell them for me?" he asked his brother.

"I can," answered Santiago. "How long will you be gone?"

"A few days," said Miguel, gazing out at the horizon.

Soon they arrived at a shop off the square.

"Pull over here and wait for me," said Santiago.

He got out, entered a store, and in a few minutes came back out carrying a box. He handed it to Miguel. Inside was a camera that took photos you didn't need to develop. It was called a Polaroid.

"Photograph everything," Santiago asked. "Show me what you see."

Libertad
FREEDOM

M iguel split. Left with no particular destination in the old Ford his grandpa had bought with a tank full of gas paid for by Santiago. Nothing belonged to him but the clothes he had on and his own self.

If Santiago was the one to notify Vicente Moya and Maria Serrano about Miguel's departure, as promised, it was Miguel's absence that notified Rosita Romero. The hours of the evening before, the hours of her first night as a fifteen-year-old, the long morning and afternoon hours while Miguel was repairing the car and learning how to drive—she spent them wide awake in bed, in the pink party dress she didn't have the strength to remove. Every hour burned slow as a match until a frazzled Rosita Romero couldn't restrain herself and ran off to Casa Moya to discover what she already knew. She didn't even get there, didn't need to: along the way she passed Hermenegildo Serrano's house, where she'd first given herself to Miguel, and out of the corner of her eye she noticed something missing in the yard, which intimated something else that was missing. Rosita Romero took a deep breath, prayed she was wrong, then turned her head. In the spot where Hermenegildo Serrano's Ford had for years sat collecting dust, there was now just a shadow; it was enough to erase any lingering hopes she had. She carried herself over to the spot and kneeled, the skirt of her dress billowed in the air, and like a watering can she bathed the ground with tears as clear as the *cenote* waters. You had the feeling a *cempasúchil* might flower there.

Dozens of miles away, Hermenegildo Serrano's red Ford plowed ahead, just as in the old man's dancing days. Miguel felt the thrill of first experiences in his fingers as he gripped the wheel. He didn't know what he was after yet drove on anyway, and the rush of freedom as he cut across the empty roads of Mexico as fast as he could was all the answer he needed. To him, the desire to escape that he'd only just begun to indulge contained the essence of who he was and what he wanted to become, and the presence of Rosita Romero, which he'd once thought necessary, now represented an obstacle. He felt a pang of guilt for having abandoned her with no explanation, yet had he stopped to explain himself, he'd never have left. He'd be back. And when he came back he'd find the words to tell her. And if he did come back for her, then he'd be coming back for good. Yet with every inch of blacktop he devoured, he felt an urge to guzzle more, hungered to discover what was beyond those trees, beyond that house, around the next bend, beyond the road itself, even beyond the horizon. If love really was hunger, as he had said to Santiago, maybe he was already head over heels with this new state of being, with steering toward the beauty of uncertainty, toward anybody's face, any experience, any new sensations waiting to be discovered. He stepped on the gas, neither stopping nor sleeping, not even when the landscape darkened and all that arose from the jungle on either side of the freeway were the noises of howler monkeys and the headlights of the Ford illuminated just a few feet of the road ahead of him, at the end of which, in the dark, Miguel felt his destiny lay. He traveled five hundred miles with barely a breather, only pulling over to piss and let the engine cool. He drove till the new day broke all at once over the top of the hills of San Cristobal de las Casas. And as soon as he saw that patch of colorful houses up there, kissed by the early morning sun, cut off in the woods on the cordillera ridge, he felt he'd arrived at his destination. He stopped the car and took his first photo for Santiago, thinking of his brother, the image emerging on the white film, taking form little by little, just as he himself was. Then he reclined in his car seat and slept the sleep of heroes.

Morning in San Cristobal brought the noises of the marketplace and the smell of roast corn in the open air, meat fried in spicy sauces. Miguel walked to the center of town along a grid of cobblestone streets that gently dipped and rose, giving into the languor within and without, passing through streets lined with bright walls, stopping to sample whatever attracted his attention, a color or smell, in red-roofed *posadas* animated by small talk and music, amid pushcarts selling peppers, papaya, dried beans, and flour. As was his habit, he took the people's smiles in stride, in a flurry of encounters and casual conversations that filled him with the same excitement he'd felt while driving in no particular direction and therefore in every direction imaginable. That was how he discovered among other things the existence of a magical place beyond the hills. San Juan Chamula. A drunk hippie gringo covered in tattoos told him about it over *micheladas* in the shade of a taverna behind the Church of Santo Domingo.

"How do I get there?" asked Miguel impatiently.

"You have to find the woman with an umbrella in Plaza 31 de Marzo."

"A woman with an umbrella?" repeated Miguel.

"What woman?" the other asked.

"You said—"

"I did?"

But Miguel wanted to believe it too much not to check it out. As soon as he reached the plaza, between Palacio Municipal and the mustard-colored cathedral, there was the woman—smiling and holding an umbrella over her head although there wasn't a drop of rain. Her name was Marcelina

Fernández Ortiz, and she drove a shuttle, really a van with no roof, with her arms splayed, her chest forward, all the weight of her body on the gas as they chugged up the Sierra Madre that extended as far as Guatemala.

A half hour later Miguel was sitting in the back of her van behind a dozen Americans in straw hats with enormous cameras who jumped up all at once at the sight of San Juan Chamula above the slope—a heap of mud huts encircling Iglesia del Bautista. He took a photo too.

Marcelina parked at the edge of a graveyard full of white, black, and blue crosses. They made it to the muddy plaza on foot. Men were playing cards and women were selling vegetables beside the whitewashed church with green and blue trimming that stood out against the jungle. They were swarmed by barefoot children who asked them for money—*"Un peso, señor"*—and led them over to the place where the kids' parents had laid their wares out on wicker mats. When they reached the red wooden door of the church, the woman stopped them.

"One thing," she said. "No photos. The Chamula Tzotzil believe they steal your soul. Anyone who breaks the rule will pay dearly."

Once inside, their minds went blank, time stopped. There was a pall of incense in the dark. All around them, candles illuminated wooden shrines to saints holding bits of mirrors to ward off the devil, and the eyes of family members, huddled on a bed of pine needles, twinkled. The worshippers sang, prayed, wept over a *curandero* in a hypnotic trance who was running his hand over the burning wax, touching those around him, picking up bottles of Coca-Cola, blessing them in the fire, drinking from them, and letting out portentous burps.

"Many ethnic groups in Chiapas believe that burping rids the body of evil," whispered Marcelina Fernández Ortiz. "The Chamulas think that acid reflux caused by Posh or Coca-Cola is magic."

The American tourists looked on, paralyzed in a corner of the church crowded with men and women wearing wool clothes and praying on their knees or slowly swaying to chants. Always curious, Miguel clung to every last detail; he had the distinct feeling that the place had been expecting him too. The otherworldly vibrations stirred his subconscious, where the caresses of the Virgen de Guadalupe had settled, the caresses she'd reserved for him on the night of his childhood when they had followed the procession through the streets of Mérida. Anything was possible in places like this, places that for Miguel were becoming the point of entry to the next place, experiences that kept compelling him elsewhere. So when the door flew open, it had to be a sign. The beautiful girl who entered just then was, to him, a message; he'd only seen beauty like that as a kid, in the schoolyard, in the features of young Rosita Romero. This girl was different, smaller and darker, yet she had the proud gait of someone who was used to being looked at. Therefore, in Miguel's eyes, she did resemble Rosita. Maybe that explained why he couldn't work up the courage to approach her, the courage to stop her as she slid through space, stepped delicately over the straw floor, knelt to pray in the candlelight. Maybe that explained why he restrained himself, despite his urge to carry her off to Mérida, to show her to Santiago or compare her image to the image of Rosita Romero in the flesh. Maybe that explained why, spellbound, hypnotized by the beauty that reached the realms of magic, Miguel ignored the rules of the Chamula saints, took his Polaroid out of his shoulder bag, and, undaunted, snapped a photo.

The girl's name was Yaxté. It wasn't until the flash struck her in the darkness that she saw Miguel. But the artificial light struck everyone else too; it was a lightning bolt that shattered the night of devotions in the Iglesia del Bautista and woke all present from the torpor of their religious ritual. Hysteria, shouts, threats—a wave of outrage broke over Miguel's head.

Marcelina Fernández Ortiz tried to save him, explaining in Tzotzil that he hadn't taken a picture, that the flash had merely gone off. But the oldest shaman in the village snatched away the camera, lifted it in the air, and out of his dark throat, through a handful of rotten teeth, uttered his latest proclamation: the saints would decide the truth.

The *curandero* knew, but only Miguel sensed that. To everyone's astonishment, the Polaroid spit a blank picture on the ground, an immaculate spell that prompted people to cross themselves in surprise and launch invectives. The man picked it up, flourished it in the air while invoking San Juan Bautista, and finally showed it to the worshippers who, in unison, bowed to the phenomenon, prostrated themselves before the shiny paper that had been blank and now, by a miracle or curse, clearly showed Yaxté in the foreground praying. It was a grave offense, intensified by the effect of the photograph created by Saint John in the shaman's hand, which had blossomed inside the very walls of the Iglesia.

Miguel was thrown in jail for five days and five nights.

Viajes de papel
TRAVELS ON PAPER

T hat trip changed everything. And not only for those
who stayed.

"Where'd he go?" asked Maria Serrano when she
heard the news.

"He didn't say," said Santiago, betraying no emotion.

Vicente Moya didn't speak. He went out into the courtyard to smoke another cigarette. Maybe he'd given Miguel
too much latitude, maybe he should have established some
rules. Come to think of it, neither the business of his resurrection nor his irreproachable physical attributes had anything to do with it. The truth was his son was just like him.
The truth was Miguel represented what he himself could
have been had he let loose, given vent to the nature he recognized as his own and that, out of insecurity, he had buried
under all sorts of rationales. Vicente Moya smoked and
thought of his son with a sense of pride and a tinge of envy.
Though he'd never admit it out loud, he was proud of his
son's experience with women, young as he was, and how he'd
patched up the car and slid behind the wheel without a
license, without asking anybody's permission, not even
Vicente Moya's. He'd be fine. And when he returned they'd
balance the books their way, like men going about men's
things. Meanwhile he smoked, spit tobacco, meditated on the
fact that he really was worried; if Miguel were gone too long
there was the risk the courtyard would empty out. The seats,
umbrellas, and stalls selling juice and *tamalitos* had become

permanent fixtures there and guaranteed the family an extra income that Vicente Moya kept in a coffee can. It would be a pity to lose that. On the other hand, believing it would last was a pipe dream. He'd have to think up something else.

For Santiago, the time without Miguel was an anomaly. His brother's absence resuscitated feelings he couldn't remember, from when he was an only child and king of his room, of his house. Yet after all those years together, his absence was unsettling; it was as if a part of him had departed with his brother. Half his mind went searching over the horizon of Mérida, where the image of his grandpa's car sallied forth in the clouds. Whereas his other half, the half with its feet on terra firma, recovered a sense of calm that he had lost, an indolence that led him to sleep all morning and by day wander aimlessly through the city streets, as if working, earning the money he'd fought his father for, didn't matter much. He even quit pleasure-seeking in the prostitute's trailer, as if he'd only gone in the first place to even the score with Miguel and without him the experience lost all meaning, all value.

The days were filled with the fact of Miguel's absence and the absence of news of Miguel. The boy's flight became a topic of discussion, gossip laced with suppositions about where'd gone to, when he'd be back, whether or not he had any intention of coming back, whether Rosita Romero had lost her mind—the girl had gone around for days in that pink dress, the hem of her skirt blackened and frayed, as if she'd decided never to take it off, to be fifteen forever. She wasn't the only one to sense Miguel's absence in the empty spot in his grandpa's yard; anyone who passed by noticed the marks in the dust where once there'd been a Ford and thought Hermenegildo Serrano had returned to take it with him to Paradise and had forgotten to let his grandson out.

Therefore, Santiago wasn't the only one to imagine the car flying through the clouds. Many began to sense something surreal about the disappearance of Miguel. Such feelings seemed inevitable where the boy was concerned. The theory gained credence when a gas station attendant claimed he'd spoken to a truck driver who swore the old red Ford had shot by him so fast that an instant later it was gone, like a hallucination. Another day word spread that the car was in the city, that someone had seen it turn down an alley. The news reached the ladies in the courtyard of Casa Moya and held them there, their eyes fixed on the narrow lane, and suddenly a herd of other women came dragging their chairs and leaving mysterious signs in the dust. The story of Miguel was revived by those who knew it by heart and passed on to the less informed, who added their own twists, and those twists eventually became integral parts of the legend. Expectations burned bright, though nothing happened. Yet such frequent thoughts of Miguel brought him closer, and the women were convinced that he would return any minute now, that they would bitterly regret missing the event. Consequently, contrary to Vicente Moya's fears, the courtyard came back to life in the buildup to a finale that mixed hard facts with made-up plotlines.

The head of the household pounced on the prospect: he made the rounds at the market and enlisted more vendors shrewd enough to take him up on the offer to profit from the large, happy, and therefore paying public that had invaded the space in front of his house. The women reacted with enthusiasm. They saw it as an ideal opportunity to do their shopping without having to move and risk missing the prodigal son's return, a chance to be there when the boy came down from the clouds, to receive his blessing, to witness up close how he would make amends with his parents, with Rosita Romero, with the life that had been waiting for him. Ever since Miguel had left home, dozens of pushcarts and hundreds of housewives gathered around the house and waited for his imminent apparition in a supernatural fug. At the end of each night, after collecting his take, Vicente Moya would rub his big hands together. Every so often he slipped somebody a bill to go around to the bars and say he'd seen the red car around the city, this time without a shadow of a doubt.

Santiago's sense of geography was limited to the mental notes he'd taken at school or overheard in other people's conversations. Picturing Miguel was difficult. Whenever he tried, with his arms slung behind a bench in Plaza Mayor, like clockwork he'd end up staring at the sky, that is, in the clouds. And if there were no clouds, he'd squeeze his eyes shut and try to picture him. No luck. His thoughts would turn down a blind alley at the end of which all he could hear was his brother breathing, a sound he'd listened to every night for years. He couldn't have known that on the other side of that darkness was Miguel, who was thinking of him in the empty shadows of prison, where beauty meant nothing, because no one could see it. But for Santiago such premonitions had no shape; he had inherited Vicente Moya's tendency to rationalize. He remained stuck, not knowing what to do, crushed by his brother's energy and the unrivaled power of his endeavors, sapped of the strength to hustle hammocks, to peddle lies to the latest tourist. One day, staring at a foreigner holding a map open, he realized a roadmap like that might be the key to finding Miguel. After days of apathy, he leaped up and ran to the one place he remembered seeing them on display: the Rodríguezes' stationery store, where Teresa Rodríguez, his classmate from elementary school, had replaced her old mother, become a mother in turn, and next to him seemed like an adult—done and dusted.

"He could be anywhere," she said, her finger hovering over Mérida on a map of Mexico spread out on the counter.

"Maybe that way?" said Santiago, pointing at a line running southwest, hugging the coast, toward the middle of Mexico. At one point he ran the tip of his finger over the words San Cristobal de Las Casas, then slid past them, in the direction of the capital, which, because it was the nucleus of a web of roads, captured his attention.

"It's possible," said Teresa Rodríguez.

"What's Mexico City like, Teresa?" Santiago asked her. She was the one person he knew who had her eye on the world. He wanted to gain a sense of a specific place to picture his brother in.

"It's the third largest city on the planet, perhaps the most paradoxical. It contains the best and worst of our country, the glamour and the gutter."

"When were you there?"

"Never been," sighed Teresa Rodríguez.

"Then how do you know?"

The girl pointed over Santiago's shoulder at a shelf stocked with all sorts of novels. On the wall above the shelf was a famous quotation she had painted in her own hand.

La lectura es el viaje de los que no pueden tomar el tren.
"Reading is the journey for those who can't take the train."

The quotation applied to her, since every place she had journeyed lay under a veil of dust in that shop. And now it applied to Santiago, who walked over to the shelf circumspectly and, then and there, discovered literature. He took down a book, leafed through it. He took down another, read the first few lines.

"You're saying I could reach him with these?"

"You'll never know unless you try," said Teresa Rodríguez.

Belisario Lopez immediately sensed something was amiss. Santiago no longer turned up at the shop, which languished, desolate, empty of clients. His growing concern was almost sincere, despite the fact that their relationship was exclusively professional, that he'd never established a personal relationship with the boy Vicente Moya had brought him years ago. He tacked a Be Right Back sign to the door and left to look for him. When he reached the plaza, he was irked to see the boy stretched out on a bench reading; it was as if he had been poached by a competitor. He tiptoed over, grabbed him by the ear with his maimed hand, and tugged so hard he forced the boy to his feet. The book fell to the ground.

"On vacation, are we?" shouted Belisario Lopez.

Santiago took a moment to recover from his surprise, to return from the place he'd gotten lost in. He shrugged Belisario Lopez off and backed up. He had no intention of giving up his journey, the distances he'd traversed in books had already changed him.

"You pay me on commission. I'm free to do as I please."

"Free?" scoffed Belisario Lopez, echoing the boy.

Santiago picked the book off the ground with the care typically reserved for precious things, glared at his employer, turned, and left.

Belisario Lopez watched him walk away and felt impotent, stunned by the boy's newfound strength. Where it came from he didn't know. He felt he could do nothing but hope that the boy changed his mind as he watched him cross the Plaza Mayor, choose another bench, sit down, find his place, and go back to reading. And that is what Santiago did for days to come—read. All he did was read. As soon as he finished one novel, he went back to the Rodríguezes' stationery store, chose another, fled Mérida without taking a train, and went in search of Miguel.

Reading transformed him. He disregarded all else, fell out of touch with reality, and when he returned home, the places he'd been in his imagination, the people he'd met there, seemed to linger, more real than the reality around him. That explained in part why he didn't notice the eyes studying him from behind a tree in the plaza, bright eyes that stared at him with the same intense focus with which they'd watched him in the courtyard when his brother played the little star of the *chá-cara*. The soulful, patient eyes of Soledad Sanchez, a girl with close-cropped hair and palpable desires that had grown with time, who hadn't stopped waiting for the moment to get his attention by subtle means. He, on the other hand, didn't know how to look at a woman. Secretly he assumed that women weren't part of his lot, especially since he'd traded in love for the store-bought emotions of the sex market. He had decided no woman could ever be interested in him and therefore, to avoid suffering in vain, he didn't look at them.

But Soledad was looking at him. She'd been silently watching him ever since realizing that his way of seeming behind and out of place, on the far end of the courtyard, was a way of being. Now, as she watched him read on the bench, an idea took hold of her, suggesting to her the occasion that she'd been waiting for. She crept out of the shadows, drew as close as she could without drawing the attention of Santiago, just close enough to make out the title of the novel. She couldn't believe it; the title sent her into a state of shock, stoked her hopes. It was just the title she'd been waiting for. On the cover of the book was her name.

Cien años de soledad—that's what it said. And it seemed like a promise.

So Soledad ran off, ran with her heart in her throat all the way to the library, checked out the same novel, and shut herself up in her room to read. She read in earnest, devoured each word, read through the night to catch up with Santiago, who had a head start, to reach him in Macondo in the midst of the Buendía family's one hundred years of solitude.

" . . . [T]he search for lost things is hindered by routine habits and that is why it is so difficult to find them," she read.[1]

---

[1] All quotations from *One Hundred Years of Solitude* are translated by Gregory Rabassa (Harper & Row, 1970).

How many hindering routine habits had she placed between herself and Santiago after finding and losing him when she was a girl in the Moyas' yard?

" . . . [H]is confused heart was condemned to uncertainty forever," the novel went on. It was morning when Soledad turned to the last page, and she let out a sigh of satisfaction and weariness. She flew to the plaza where Santiago sat reading. This time she sat down next to him.

"Beautiful," was all Soledad managed to say.

"Who?" asked Santiago, turning away from the book. Now as then, the word made him think of Miguel: it had rung in his ears ever since the day the adults repeated it like a mantra in the glare of the window at the Hospital Regional.

Soledad pointed to the book in Santiago's hands but kept her eyes on Santiago.

"The world was so recent," explained the novel, "that many things lacked names, and in order to indicate them it was necessary to point."

That was how Santiago met Soledad. In the pages of a book, like characters in a story somebody had made up. They talked for hours, discussed its every detail, compared which emotions and scenes had won them over. Santiago still had a few pages to go, so they read them together, studied the end, retraced the route that had brought them line by line to where they were now. The magic lasted as long as the book could sustain it; their reflections on the book exhausted, Santiago had nothing left to say, and Soledad realized she was out of options. She bid him goodbye, returned home, collapsed on her bed, and slept the sleep she'd lost, dreaming of them as if they were still in the story. When she woke up she went back to the plaza where Santiago was reading another book. This one was called *Tienda de los Milagros*, Tent of Miracles. Soledad, who believed in miracles, ran to the library, picked up a copy, read it with the same voracity and enthusiasm with which she'd read the first, in a day and a night, and as soon as she'd finished it, she hurried back to the plaza, sat back down next to him, and started talking about the book to make him talk, to read and wander its pages with him. By the evening they had turned over every facet of the novel, and Santiago lapsed into silence again. Soledad bid him goodbye and left to sleep, her eyes puffy, her throat dry, and the next day returned to racing through another book to find him while he read the same pages and continued his search for Miguel. Now that this girl came around to sit with him, for some reason Santiago felt closer to his brother. As if he had bridged the gap between them. And when, at the end of the day, after the inevitable moment of silence arrived and she departed, Santiago watched her walk away and felt an acute compulsion to follow her, one he didn't have the courage to act on, and he gripped his book as if it were a talisman.

Almas robadas
STOLEN SOULS

I n the dark, without food. It was difficult to keep time. Miguel woke up not knowing whether he was alive or dead. A solitude he hadn't known before made him ill, accustomed as he was to having someone around at all times, and he grew despondent. He sat thinking. He thought about how'd he gotten there, about the meaning of his action, about his flight from Mérida, which suddenly seemed to him like the one safe place in the world. He no longer harbored doubts about Rosita Romero. If he lived through this he'd return for good. Maybe she had been the one he was looking for in that photograph. Then those thoughts fused with the dark, dissolved into a black, shapeless amalgam in which even the memory of Santiago handing him the Polaroid felt ill-starred. He discovered despicable versions of himself, dark sides that frightened him as he caved to them, succumbing to physical agony.

At dawn on the sixth day they set him free. Opened the door and threw him out. Miguel shielded his eyes with his arm to adjust to the light, the life in his veins no more than a trickle. But then, in the landscape slowly coming into focus, the first figure he saw was her. There was the girl, alone. There was Yaxté, waiting for him.

So it had happened—he'd stolen her soul. They didn't speak the same language, but they had nothing important to say. She stared at him nervously, holding the Polaroid that she had managed to rescue. She pointed the camera and through the lens Miguel looked depleted yet alive, no air in his lungs nor spit in his throat yet gilded with a hardened beauty. She took aim, pressed the shutter button, and stole his soul. Then she led him to the jungle, where she'd hidden some food. She plied him with milk, bread, and fruit, and stayed by his side until Miguel recovered his strength. As she watched him eat in silence, she was already, unwittingly, conquered, prone on the bare ground, already begging, already pure emotion and nothing else, nothing but nails digging into Miguel's back. Before sundown that body—born, raised, and suckled for years hundreds of miles from Mérida—found her sense of purpose in the stretch of grass on which she lay under Miguel's firm pressure. It was a kind of waiting, the preparation she'd needed before dying in the arms of this Mexican boy. Or so it seemed now, while what had to happen, what was destined to happen ever since she'd entered the church of Chamula, ever since he'd entered the church in Mérida where Rosita Romero was getting married alone, happened. It occurred naturally: they made love impatiently, shielded in the dark heart of the forest, to hell with Miguel's ties, to hell with Yaxté's traditions, to hell with San Juan Bautista and the flora and fauna that silently looked on while their beautiful bodies were joined, while their moans broke the silence.

Yaxté had thick eyebrows, skin that smelled like honey, muscular legs which she wrapped around Miguel and used to set the pace, taking and expecting more each time they finished, each time they started up again, in a struggle which neither conceded. They clashed furiously, made love as if they had a finite number of minutes, of hours, climaxing, agonizing, crying out together. They could not speak. They only stopped to rest and regain their energy or else engage in a wordless dialogue: looking into each other's eyes, staring at one another in silence, inches apart, to see if there was someone there to know, to recognize. Until Yaxté, who pointed with her long fingers to express her ideas and desires, went in search of what she wanted from the foreign body that had bewitched her, impatiently indulging herself, feeling no regrets.

While he eagerly took her, Miguel made a discovery similar to the one he'd made behind the agave: the method was always the same yet different. The taste of Yaxté's kisses, the feel of her flesh, the mad rush with which they tore at each other's skin, the effect of her scent, her lips on his, was neither better nor worse than his experience with Rosita Romero, merely different. And that instilled in him a new understanding of love, of the hunger that he'd thought could only be filled by dying in the arms of the girl from Mérida. Maybe, had he not spent that dark period in the cell in Chamula, he'd never have betrayed her. But it was precisely that dark rift—when he'd thought he'd recovered her—that provided him the distance he needed to split from her, to collapse in the arms of Yaxté and feel no sense of guilt. His brush with death had brought him closer to life, and once she'd stolen his soul he could do nothing but accept the consequences.

In the years to come they'd say that the flora erupted in the exact spot where Yaxté and Miguel made love. Yet in the days to come Yaxté was shuttling back and forth between the village and the jungle, furtive as a thief, trying to mask her feelings, to not raise eyebrows. As soon as she could, she would hurry off to see him, run breathlessly through the forest, her hunger to be touched growing with every touch, propelled by a visceral force that was a tangle of trees, leaves, and damp earth where she felt like a seed, planted and sprouting up again each time, blossoming in the warm hands of the boy about whom she knew nothing. She'd return to the village with her body quivering and her cheeks flushed and try to hide it. But passion rushes forward imprudently, and the trail it leaves can't escape a mother's gaze; the woman rummaged through her daughter's clothes, extracted a photo of Miguel, figured out what was what, and reported it to the village elders.

The rest was just noise. The noise of jaws, tongues, teeth, voices, rumors afoot, and calls for justice to exact revenge: the Tzotzil forbid mixing with foreign blood.

"Death to the boy!" the people cried. "Death to the boy!"

There was the sound of marching, of a group of men trudging along Chamula turf to flush out the boy, to teach him—with machetes this time—to respect tradition. There was the sound of foliage crumpling underfoot as they cut a path through the forest, in formation, as if they were hunting boar. However faint, there was enough noise to whistle in the ears of Yaxté, who could identify the accents of the jungle and the preludes to peril; enough noise to alert her to trouble as she swayed on top of Miguel with her eyes shut. Under her eyelids she saw him with thirty blades in his back, on the ground, bathed in blood. And therefore, in the end, there was the sound of Miguel escaping, driven off by her, his figure fading in the trees.

When the hunters arrived, they found Yaxté weeping with joy because Miguel was safe and weeping from grief because she knew she would never see him again. At the same time, he ran out onto the road and climbed into a Coca-Cola truck leaving Chamula. He vanished into thin air, same as he'd arrived.

Miguel returned to Mérida at the end of an ordinary afternoon. By then the assorted crowd in the courtyard had lost sight of why they were there in the first place and many had been swept up in what the scene had turned into—a festival, a marketplace—forgetting both its origin and purpose: yesterday his presence, today his advent. Which was why his return burned with the colors of surprise and sunsets, burnishing the old metal Ford, which shone brightly, as if along the journey it had become young again. When he stopped in the middle of the courtyard, in the exact spot where the *chácara* had been drawn years before, there descended the same hush that had prevailed when young Miguel leaped into the rectangle. Only this time a man emerged from the rusty door that creaked open, a teenager who had grown into a man unusually fast, weathered by his two-week journey from home, which felt more like two years given the hole his absence had produced. No one could imagine what he'd discovered out there, but prison had left a mark on his face, a gauntness that made his cheeks more pronounced, a depth in his eyes acquired in his dark cell, in his gait the melodic rhythm with which he'd taken Yaxté, and in his muscles and nerves the strength he'd gained to sleep with her without rest and outrun death barefoot in the jungle. All the women saw it. In particular the girls who had accompanied their mothers day after day, because it stood to reason that Miguel would have to square things with Rosita Romero, that their relationship might be coming to an end, and that the boy come down from the clouds might suddenly become available again. But first he had to deal with the other woman in his life, who was waiting for him with a stern look, arms akimbo. Maria Serrano feigned indignation to hide the relief she felt to see him in the flesh again; she'd prayed for that sight every evening since he'd left. Nothing else mattered at the moment. And were it not for the role she felt forced to play in public, she would have also spared him the slap with which she greeted him now, unconvincing even to Miguel, who had grown taller than her and snatched her wrist and kissed her palm before pulling her toward him to embrace her and ask for forgiveness. A forgiveness benevolently granted him by the public, too, who applauded their embrace, which brought Maria Serrano closer to him than she had been for a long time, perhaps not since the day they had climbed down from the Ford together, in that very courtyard, shortly after she had given birth to him.

"Where have you been?" she asked.

"To see the world," said Miguel.

"How was it?"

"Dirty," he said with a smile. "I need a shower."

Maria Serrano caved. She smiled back.

"Can I fix you something to eat?"

"Thanks," said Miguel, and he turned to the people gathered at his back and waved to thank them too, to signal that everything was fine. Every girl was convinced his gesture was meant for her alone, that Miguel had already decided on whom he'd bestow his next kisses, even if he was looking at everyone and no one in particular, and a moment later he crossed the threshold of his home, and they felt his absence once more. But their joy over his return filled the courtyard with optimism and cheer. The older women thronged the stand for a sweet to feed their appetite, the young women allowed themselves the dizzying luxury of a cold beer to celebrate the end of their waiting, and a passing guitar carried music to the courtyard along with the evening breeze, which appeared to have blown in with Miguel.

But some news travels from quarter to quarter as fast as flies. And in a wingbeat word reached Rosita Romero, who'd been waiting for nothing else, and she ran to Casa Moya with the fury of someone seeking revenge for a second time, her scrap of a skirt trailing in the dust. Her beauty was likewise frazzled, ravaged by the prison of her forced solitude, her hair in knots, her gaunt cheeks streaked with old tears. When she arrived in the middle of the courtyard the music died, everyone fell silent. And the silence alerted Miguel.

The boy stepped out of the house just as he was, his wet hair running down his bare shoulders, a towel around his waist. It was a crushing sight. No one in the city aside from his mother and Rosita Romero had ever seen Miguel shirtless before. The way in which he exposed his body to every girl in town gave Rosita her answer: she'd lost him, he was no longer hers. And then, seeing him in that state, she thought they were his by divine right, she'd been kidding herself—with the brass of a beauty, a real beauty, but—this much was clear now—not beauty enough to keep Miguel all to herself. Miguel cut a path between the chairs, the bright umbrellas, the feverish women who touched him without touching him and were waiting to learn how the story would end. Then they were standing face to face, separated by a brief yet interminable journey from which he'd returned changed; she sensed it in the way he walked, breathed, held his chin up, in his scent, in the leftover traces of another woman's skin that she seemed to perceive with her fingertips. Face to face, he semi-naked, she in the dress in which she'd turned fifteen, an age she'd never forget. Face to face, just as they'd met that day behind the agave, after Miguel had kissed all the others and she'd come back to start over and instead ran away. That time she'd slapped him. And people expected as much now, a slap like the one Maria Serrano had given him, which he would greet with a smile to bend the girl to his will, to get her to forgive him as he had his mother, if that was what he wanted. But Rosita Romero lacked the energy to move a muscle. All she mustered was a desperate cry, a cry to mark the end, which came crashing down on Miguel and forced him to shut his eyes.

"Aaaaaaaahhhhhhhh," shouted Rosita Romero.

Miguel kept his eyes shut. Not out of fear but because he had capitulated. He was prepared to be struck, were that what she wanted. After eluding the men of Chamula's machetes, he was willing to take a knife, on the off chance she was carrying one under her *quinceañera* dress, willing to die without a word. He felt he deserved it for the pain he'd caused her, for having left her with no explanation. On the other hand, had he stopped to explain it to her, he'd never have left, he'd never have discovered what he'd discovered: that he wasn't fit for love. He didn't love anybody. He didn't love Rosita Romero. He didn't even love Yaxté. Barreling across the empty expanses of Mexico in Hermenegildo Serrano's car, he'd realized that, more than anything, he loved freedom. And he was prepared to die for his freedom. Here, now. But when he reopened his eyes there was nothing there, no one in front of him. Just a crowd of people staring mutely at him and the pink shadow of Rosita Romero, already in the distance, gone.

The pages were hot to the touch. Lines, letters, conjunctions wilted. Punctuation evaporated. The rules of the game initiated by Santiago and Soledad had become clear. Reading no longer meant immersion: it meant consumption, destruction of the text, literary combustion, sliding across page and ink to collide after the last word. Santiago would turn up at the Rodríguezes' shop as soon as they opened, return the last book he'd read, *Paradise* or *The House of the Spirits* or *Terra Nostra*, and pick the next, *A Brief Life*, *Pedro Páramo*, *The Lost Steps*, or any other book, since he didn't look while choosing but placed his trust in what the little bookshop had to offer. Then he'd mop up the novel on a bench in Plaza Mayor, occasionally looking up to see if she'd arrived. And she always did arrive. Generally when he was done or nearly done. She came with clear ideas, Soledad Sanchez, and a critical capacity that Santiago thought extraordinary, that made him experience reading as a bridge, a ride, one journey leading to another. Where the book ended, they began. Hardly a word of greeting passed between them before Soledad baptized or knocked a nail into the latest book with a single adjective and only then sat down, so that he wouldn't notice how every day she edged a little closer to him.

"Dreadful," she'd say. Or else "sublime." Or "pointless."

"Boring," she said one day, closing in an inch or two.

"Intense," she submitted as their knees touched.

Santiago took her adjective, disassembled it, molded it to the feelings that the book had left on his soul, and searched for a comparison, a relationship, a point between the lines to join or tangle with her. It was a matter of life and death to uncover the meaning of that reading experience, take its measure, share it, fight for an idea, and, win or lose, battle with verve, walk away from the dispute with bruises on their bodies. Santiago's voice unleashed a string of vowels, consonants, sounds, and phonemes that were unlike him. Santiago spoke. He spoke and listened, and by listening discovered parts of himself that he had ignored, reflected back to him by the characters in the novel that he'd just finished. He forgot about Miguel and, with Soledad Sanchez watching him closely, staring at his lips, inside the books he reached the person furthest from him, the last person he'd ever have imagined meeting: himself. And the moment he found himself, he found Soledad. All of a sudden he found her in front of him, dangerously close, and in her he discovered his desire for a woman, the sensation of mattering to somebody, the hunger for another body that trembled in expectation of him. Santiago finally saw Soledad Sanchez. He saw her after years of her pursuit of him, a pursuit begun in childhood, which culminated on a bench in the middle of Mérida and called for one epilogue only: a kiss. But Santiago wasn't perfect like the heroes in the stories he read. He'd never kissed. He didn't know how to kiss. And therefore he didn't kiss her. He let the moment pass by instead of closing the gap between them with a touch that needed no adjectives, and his self-inflicted regret left a deep scar, which he would return to like a badly written page, with dozens of alternative endings, sentences, actions, each one fitting except the one he'd chosen: to fall silent again and invite her to talk.

"What do you think?" he whispered, referring to the book.

Soledad Sanchez answered without realizing she'd just brushed past the moment she'd been pursuing all her life, since for her that moment was every moment, yet she had decided she couldn't go and pluck that rose too, because if Santiago hadn't the strength to meet her halfway that meant he didn't want her enough. That was one answer. And ultimately, far more than a kiss, what she was after was an answer. If need be she was prepared to read another thousand books, to bide her time for another ten years—she felt capable of that—but she wouldn't steal words he didn't intend to utter nor kisses he didn't want to give. So she humored him, taking a scientific angle, analyzing the least significant detail of the novel in order to seize the opportunity to show him her best side, her mind, to push both of them to the limits of their imperfect bodies, to discover one another in the perfection of words, made-up images, allusions to feelings that eventually materialized. There, as always, Santiago forgot himself, went back to dreaming, wandered inside her, a prisoner to the vocal cords of the girl who didn't squander her words to move him and rub salt in his wounds.

"He doesn't take enough risks," said Soledad. "He's deep, he has a sensitive soul that expresses itself in various ways, but he lacks the courage to become something more . . . "

As he listened to her, daylight faded. At a certain point, Santiago caught sight of his brother over Soledad Sanchez's shoulder, at the end of the road leading to the plaza, bringing the evening with him. The unmistakable figure of Miguel, returned from his journey, more attractive than before, like a soldier home from war. He wasn't prepared for that scene. He'd ceased to think about it once books and Soledad had entered his life. And now that he had something to be happy about, now that he had something to lose, he fretted over the fact that Miguel might rob him of everything, his presence alone left room for no one else, as had been the case with Pan. The acute memory of his feelings for the dog he'd lost deprived him of oxygen, gripped him by the throat, tightened its hold with every step Miguel took. Just when he felt he would choke to death, he coughed up the few words that he figured would solve his problem:

"Go away," Santiago interrupted.

"Sorry?" she asked, confused.

"Please go away," Santiago repeated.

Soledad Sanchez searched Santiago's eyes for a meaning but came up short. She was afraid that she'd made a mistake, that she'd said something she shouldn't have. Plus her fatigue had been mounting for days, years; she now fell silent, fearing she may have wasted all that time on a hopeless endeavor. She slammed the book shut and—mad at herself, at him—split.

Miguel reached the bench a moment later.

"Who was that?" he asked with a smile.

"Nobody," said his big brother.

Seeing as Santiago didn't stand, didn't greet him, didn't ask him anything, Miguel sat down beside him in the very spot Soledad had recently occupied and rested his elbows on his knees.

"I need to ask another favor," he explained, staring at the cloud in front of him.

Santiago turned to look at him without saying a word, waiting.

"I want to come work at the Sueño Yucateo," said Miguel.

La mitad. El doble
HALF, DOUBLE

Vicente Moya was floored to find Miguel seated at his usual place at the table when he got back from work.

"Hey, Pop," said Miguel nonchalantly.

Santiago kept his questions to himself and wondered where his brother found the strength of purpose and maturity to always face his father as an equal.

Vicente Moya searched for the right response, finally deciding that no response might be the most effective. He sat down without comment. Which worked, in effect, leaving Miguel in a state of suspense he was unaccustomed to. Maria Serrano understood and put dinner on the table. She'd made *puchero de tres carnes*, as if it were Sunday, but her husband didn't bat an eye.

They ate in silence, which imbued their gestures with meanings they didn't have, the tension that mounted anticipating a catastrophe. Then, as if nothing were odd, Miguel broke the silence with the one statement that might save him by directing their attention elsewhere, toward the future, and give clear confirmation that he'd recovered his sense of responsibility.

"I start work tomorrow," he announced.

The words compelled Vicente Moya to speak.

"Where?" he shot back in disbelief.

"At the Sueño. Santiago says Lopez will definitely hire me."

Santiago kept silent, but Vicente Moya didn't look to him for confirmation anyway.

"Half of what you earn goes to the family," he said curtly.

"Of course," said Miguel, chewing his food.

That was that, business concluded. In a certain sense, thought Santiago, his brother had just bought Vicente Moya's forgiveness with his first paycheck from Belisario Lopez. Even if, and this Santiago couldn't foresee, that wasn't the real reason Miguel was looking for work. Freedom was the one thing he wanted to purchase; he needed pesos to live far from home on his own, whenever he came of age to depart, for real this time, for the world that he had barely glimpsed yet already planned to conquer. Miguel knew how to elicit a spirit of practicality from his own light touch with a light touch. The pragmatic art of molding materials to meet the needs knocking about inside him, which he impulsively indulged. Just as he'd swiped the keys from under the vase to unlock the door to love, just as he'd fixed the Ford to take his journey, Miguel had chosen a profession, any profession, the same profession foisted on Santiago by his father, in exchange for his emancipation.

Dinner done, Vicente Moya felt as though his son had once again gotten the better of him. Right under his wife's judgmental eyes.

"Come with me," he said, standing up, the air of a hangman about him.

Miguel got up from his chair unafraid. He followed him out of the house, where hundreds of empty chairs and open umbrellas in the courtyard whispered of his power. Vicente Moya lit a cigarette for effect.

"Next time you give me a heads-up. Understood?"

"Understood," replied Miguel.

Then his father signaled to follow him. They went out into the night, the scent of vanilla smoke trailing behind them. They turned down the street to Camilo Orioles's bar. When they arrived, Vicente Moya ordered two shots of tequila.

"I just want to know one thing," he said.

Before finishing he took a last drag of his cigarette.

"Was it worth it?"

Miguel recalled his excitement in Chamula. He recalled Yaxté.

"It was," he exclaimed, staring straight into his father's eyes.

Vicente Moya picked up the shot glass and squeezed it in his palm, slammed it twice on the counter, and downed his tequila.

A moment later Miguel mimicked him.

The next morning Santiago and Miguel turned up at the Sueño Yucateo where Belisario Lopez was lying in a hammock riffling through a magazine.

"Why should I hire you back?" he asked Santiago.

"Because you have no other options," the other replied. "And," he added, "because I brought my brother with me."

Belisario Lopez looked at the boy behind Santiago and was stirred, same as everyone who met Miguel for the first time. He remembered the child he'd been, but he could never have imagined the boy he'd become. One glance and he was counting the coin he stood to make from the deal. He foresaw that, even if he stuttered or were dumb, Miguel would draw a flood of tourists, in particular members of the fairer sex, which was to say, the type with a greater affinity for his goods and more purchasing power. Yet like all shrewd businessmen, Lopez concealed his excitement: he'd learned that the right amount of indifference can occasionally move thousands of pesos.

"You think you can come and go as you please?" he said to Santiago.

Then he scratched his chin with his two fingers as if he were mulling things over.

"Half what I paid you before. Take it or leave it."

Santiago clenched his fists. He didn't want to bargain with Belisario Lopez or return to working for him or, for that matter, return to work at all. The fact was he had taken no stock of his own plans, had let himself be swayed by events, had as usual bowed to external pressures: a combination, maybe, of Miguel's return and desire for a job had driven him to lend a hand just to keep him away from Soledad Sanchez. In the inordinate amount of time it took him to answer Lopez, he pined for those days on the bench, the novels that he'd read and those he had yet to read. More than anything else, he longed for her.

Before Santiago could speak, Miguel stepped in front of him and drew near to Belisario Lopez, who was taken aback by the force of this ambush, by the look of beauty up close. He dropped the magazine he'd been holding in his good hand; several half-naked women littered the floor.

"Double what you paid before. Take it or leave it," said Miguel.

So, the boy didn't stutter and wasn't dumb. On the contrary, his voice was bewitching, the movement of his jaw hypnotic, the whiteness of his teeth blinding. Belisario Lopez heard in his head, as if by magic, the rustling of the bills to come. The sound made him sluggish, and he swung gently in his hammock-for-sale.

"Du-du-double?" he managed. Now he was the one with the stammer.

"Take it or leave it," Miguel repeated firmly.

Belisario Lopez was about to call the deal off but couldn't, held in check by commercial instinct, clinging to the thread of reason of an unscrupulous businessman. How he had wound up on the other side of the bargaining table he couldn't explain, but for the first time inside the Sueño Yucateo he was being out-haggled, maybe because he had never trafficked in goods that precious. Terrified to hear himself speak, he fell silent.

So Miguel did what he had done before without ever having been taught how: he turned around, made to leave, took five steps forward and reached the door of the shop. He was about to walk out.

"*¡Está bien!*" coughed Belisario Lopez just as Miguel was stepping outside and he risked losing him for real. His cry came crashing down on Santiago, who stood between the two, a jumble of contradictions, feeling unprepared, incapable of deciding whether to be happy or sad about what had just transpired.

Belisario Lopez climbed down off the hammock, stretched his legs, and cleared his throat.

"Now go out there and don't come back alone," he ordered, in the voice of a despot, to recover at least an ounce of his authority.

TAKE ALL

Victorias y derrotas
WINS AND LOSSES

There they were, the Moya brothers, in Plaza Grande. For four years they worked side by side, spurred on by a spirit of emulation and rivalry that both united and divided them. They measured their success by how many pesos Belisario Lopez paid them at the end of the month, sums they took to Vicente Moya to tally. Their unspoken war kept them in a constant state of tension, trading wins and losses in a perpetual draw that forced them to press on, to keep improving.

Miguel mastered the art of charming tourists, thanks in part to his natural way with languages, which he rapidly picked up in the field. Santiago had experience, doggedness, the ability to stay focused. He concentrated on recruiting potential hammock buyers with the same dedication he had shown before discovering books—with greater dedication—burying the memories of that holiday of made-up stories and literary heart-to-hearts. He ripped the page with Soledad Sanchez's picture out of the book of his life. He convinced himself that it'd be a struggle to express himself with a girl, put his feelings on view, pinpoint the proper way to receive the kind of attention that in any case could be bought. Therefore, periodically, he'd go back to buy a warm body in the trailer, at the end of a day full of lies and void of thinking. Santiago thought of nothing besides beating his brother, outselling him. Meanwhile he studied him from one bench or another, carrying on the same conversations as his brother did, while begetting interactions that differed. Miguel formed genuine relationships, abuzz with compassion and smiles, with people from all over the world who wound up devotedly buying a hammock almost as if it were a prize, and who felt, furthermore, in his debt.

It would have been no match, in fact, were Miguel to have plied his trade the way Santiago did, resting at the end of the day and waking up at a reasonable hour. But when his older brother returned home or nodded off, the younger stayed out or left again to reap at night the fruits he'd sown by day. He'd find the same clients that he'd charmed and allow them to pay off the debt they felt they owed him however they preferred. He let them pick up his food and drink in Mérida's *posadas*, where the owners welcomed him like a dear friend. He spent intense evenings talking in English or French with tourists of various origins, sprinkled with intoxicated groups who adored him. He emanated gladness like a fluid snaking through twisting plots, formed relationships with every individual in a given group, asked pertinent questions and made exactly the right move each situation called for. He possessed a rare, engaging congeniality that made people listen up, delight in his company, delight in life. He even made other men forget that his beauty was a threat. On the contrary, he convinced them that in the battle for survival they had nothing to lose—and say he were to prevail? At the end of the day he deserved it, objectively speaking, given his obvious superiority. Some nights he spent in the intimate company of lone travelers who flailed their arms and talked under their breath about politics and revolution, life and destiny. Other nights, naturally, he spent naked in the arms of women whose names he didn't know, under the sheets in all types of hotels, or standing half naked against a wall on a dark street in the mouth or between the legs of stupendous and astonished women who came from afar or were born and raised right there in the city and had therefore restrained themselves for years, waiting silently for their chance to be transformed by dirty pleasure, to scream without restraint.

"Where were you last night?" asked Vicente Moya.

"Living, Papa," was Miguel's cocky answer.

The courtyard at Casa Moya felt the effect. The children's playground became a wasp's nest of young women who floated in on the drift of voices. Men too. Without knowing why, they followed their trail, their scent. The gatherings now occurred after dinner, and there was next to no room to sit. They cleared a space to dance and an orchestra played late into the night. Fruit juice was replaced with hard liquor, Maria Serrano's *champurrado* got cold in a pan in the kitchen. Everyone celebrated, and no one knew what they were celebrating, but by then that was the heart of Mérida's nightlife. Those who turned up late and couldn't reach the epicenter were happy to hang out on the fringes, to participate at all, to feel part of an event the source of which you couldn't even see sometimes. When it was over Miguel would return home, or else he wouldn't return at all, but now and then he enjoyed the fiesta, would stay and flourish there, and that was enough to stoke things for the days when he didn't show. In part because, smiling, chatting amid the crowd, nursing his drink, he nearly always locked eyes with someone who caught his attention more than the others. In that flash he'd make up his mind that sooner or later the night would end there, in the languor of those eyes. That was why all the girls knew that the Moya courtyard was, in essence, the place where the contest for his lips, for his body, perhaps even for his heart, was most likely to be won, despite the stiff competition.

On those nights, Santiago usually cut a path to the fields with cash in his pocket and took shelter in the arms of his whore.

* * *

The Moyas' courtyard changed profoundly during those

years. With the money he earned under the table, Vicente had the walls repainted, installed a pair of porta potties, and bankrolled a group of musicians who returned every night. Music made people happier, happiness boosted liquor sales, and liquor sales paid for the music in a kind of perpetually spinning merry-go-round. The afternoon group of gossips changed dress at sundown, apparently spontaneously, and the party came to life, while Vicente Moya strutted around like the lord of the manor, which in effect he was, shaking hands and offering the occasional *cerveza* on the axis of relations that, thus consolidated, reinforced his position of dominance. When the authorities got wind of the event, he forked over a few bills to politicians and policemen to circumvent signatures, licenses, and inspections, at the same time savoring the taste of omnipotence. Years of profound change. After a lifetime of apparently untapped potential, Vicente Moya became more sure of himself, realizing that a part of him, straitjacketed by a guayabera, was perhaps destined for this: PR work, organizing events on top of the organizer's pedestal, in full view. For that reason, one night after many nights, he wound up joining the crowd—something unthinkable not long before—on the edge of the dance floor, overpowered by the energy that he himself had fed. He began to move his hips, elbows raised, swept up by the rhythm. Next, in a concession that seemed inescapable, he accepted an elderly relative's invitation to dance. Finally, fueled by drink and the melody of the *rancheras*, by his sense of superiority over that time and place, shadowed by the long looks of some unmarried woman his own age who had lusted after him since he was about Miguel's age—by, in short, the whole dynamic—Vicente Moya dove onto the dance floor and for every song danced with a different partner. To be fair, he danced at a safe distance, keeping his arms wide and slipping a hint of naïveté into his joyful look in an attempt to kill any talk about there being something mischievous about his dancing. But if you thought about it, there was a flank of housewives devoted to the art of gossip and for them, underneath that swaying and flailing about, only one thing mattered: Vicente Moya was, figuratively speaking, back in the field. And despite the weight he'd gained since he'd first stepped off the floor—having chosen Maria Serrano of all people—he had retained his past allure, the allure that Miguel had inherited, exhibiting a confidence in his footwork and a way with his hips that suddenly made him almost as irresistible to the mothers as his son was to their daughters.

That night Maria Serrano was sitting near the entrance to her house, surrounded by other women, but the murmurs were more powerful than the music for anybody who, from the procession on the red carpet and with the passage of time, had discerned that her husband was traveling someplace where there was no room for her. Day by day, month by month, year by year, Vicente Moya had searched for his own reflection in Miguel. She had expelled her son the moment she'd given birth and never managed to get him back. He, on the other hand, had embraced him, sponged up, even from a distance, those parts of Miguel that had already been his, that he himself had passed on to the boy. Without Miguel, there'd have been no party. Without Miguel, there'd have been no music, no dance floor. Without Miguel, there'd have been no man in a guayabera dancing with perfect strangers. Without Miguel, Maria Serrano's heart wouldn't have broken at the mere thought of that scene being whispered about. The strain kept her from finding the strength to walk over there, to go and see for herself, to grab him by the hair and drag him away as she should have. The strain shattered her when, to discover the answer that she already knew, she stood up on her chair, rose on the tips of her toes, and saw the head of Vicente Moya, just his head, tilting toward the head of another woman, dancing in time to a song that Maria Serrano would carry with her into the next imperfect day and which kept repeating, *"Bésame, Bésame mucho, Como si fuera esta noche la última vez."*

For her it was, in a manner of speaking, the last time, the last night, even if she didn't say so aloud. Without so much as breathing she got down off the chair, went inside, put on her nightgown, and went to sleep, leaving the music and the party going on outside the house, away from her, with all that the party contained. Down the hall Santiago was also struggling to sleep, his ears plugged with wax. While beyond the perimeter of the house Miguel and Vicente, scattered in opposite parts of the courtyard, were the life of the party and its music. Were, most of all, beauty itself. All the beauty of the Moya family.

Tomarselo Todo
TAKE ALL

While Miguel's body moved amid other bodies, quick and warm-blooded, Santiago's body slept the sleep of the dead. By day they worked in the exact same open-air space, piloted clients to the same shop, and, on the nights that Miguel came back, concluded their day in the same room. And yet, like two trains running on parallel tracks, they barely brushed past one another, because Santiago sought to minimize contact with his brother, because the sales race pitted them against one another, and because Miguel was drunk on freedom, on youth that takes all.

Santiago had guessed that things would unravel that way, that the return of Miguel, the end of his relationship with Rosita Romero, and his employment at the Sueño would set in motion an unpredictable and fatal chain of events that would ensnare first him, then Vicente Moya, who overnight had taken to dancing, and finally Maria Serrano, who suffered frequent headaches and had lost her grip on happiness.

Work and sleep were good solutions to distract yourself, to put distance between you and the buzz of the courtyard and the whole city that seemed to quake in a frisson of excitement. But eluding Miguel and the noisy life he ignited around him, the fires that spread in the people and places he touched, wasn't easy. That was how Santiago wound up having to take stock of himself, modify his own actions, alter his state of mind to shoulder the pile on of his brother's needs. Almost without fail, a woman was involved.

That afternoon it was Lucille Renaud, a woman with straight blond hair fifteen years Miguel's senior who spoke unimpeachable Spanish laced with soft French *r*'s. Her husband, François Renaud, thirty years Miguel's senior, watched her talk with him about hammocks, but failed to see him as a potential threat; the boy could have been his son. Which was why, after paying Belisario Lopez, he didn't fret over the fact that his wife had disappeared, was no longer in the shop, nor that the boy who had brought them there had disappeared with her. He stood in the entrance, looked outside with the peace of mind of those lacking in spiritual sensitivity, and lit a cigarette, sure that she would pop out of a side street with a gift for him—cologne, a box of cigars. He smoked and smiled. He finished his cigarette, tossed the butt on the ground, flattened it under his sole, lit another. Now he was no longer smiling. When Santiago arrived, he was on his fourth cigarette, breathing nervously, sitting on the entrance stoop, his elbows on his knees and his face splotchy with doubt.

"Take him for a drink," whispered Belisario Lopez, who had understood everything and wanted to avoid a scene in the shop. He handed him a few pesos from the register. The boy looked at the man and accepted his assignment, not suspecting that there too lurked the shadow of Miguel.

"They serve excellent tequila across the street," he said to the Frenchman, "our treat." François Renaud extinguished his cigarette and followed Santiago—he'd do anything to escape waiting. But a few minutes later in the stifling *posada* a few feet from the Sueño, he folded under the evidence, launched into a vulgar monologue riddled with limp *r*'s, his voice broken by alcohol and jealousy as he cursed the boy who had stolen his partner while he was buying a hammock that he hadn't a clue what to do with. He picked it up and threw it, plastic packaging and all, in the direction of the door, where it landed and bounced a few feet away.

That was all Santiago needed to figure out that the thief was his brother. He slid another glass of tequila to the cuckold and rested a hand on the man's shoulder; he felt he knew the man's pain. Then he took a swig of tequila himself. Just then, Lucille Renaud appeared in the *posada*, all smiles, picked up the hammock, reached them, gave her husband a peck on the lips, and set a box of cigars on the table.

"For you, dear," said Lucille, "I went looking everywhere for them . . . "

François Renaud believed her. He believed what was convenient for him to believe. He squeezed his wife, happy to have recovered what he'd lost, and ordered her a drink. They drank in a different albeit still excessive way for different reasons neither would utter. Santiago left them without saying goodbye. They drank until the man was far gone and the evening had swallowed up the afternoon. Then she opened the box of cigars, lit one, took him by the arm, and walked him back to the hotel.

The Moya brothers were already eating dinner at that hour. They didn't touch the topic, but Santiago sensed Miguel's restlessness.

"Where were you today? I didn't see you all day," he asked.

"A tough client," remarked the other, not looking up from his plate. You could tell he was in a hurry to finish and go back out, which was often the case. But this time Santiago followed after him without being detected.

Miguel sprinted through the streets of Mérida to the French couple's hotel and, as though he had it all planned out, scaled the low wall to the balcony window. He entered the room. Santiago watched him from the shadows but couldn't imagine what was about to happen, couldn't guess what intimate horizon his brother intended to reach, to take what he wanted merely because he wanted it, without a care for anyone or anything. Santiago stood there in a kind of holding pattern, close to the hotel room yet far, very far from the bed on which Lucille Renaud lay waiting for Miguel and with a finger bade him to be quiet and bade him enter the bed where he slipped out of his clothes to slip into her.

Miguel lay on top of Lucille Renaud's naked body, which she undulated expertly—her back arched, her blond hair brushing her buttocks. They had sex on the same mattress where François Renaud was stretched out in an alcohol-induced stupor so deep he couldn't be woken, a blind spectator, deaf to the silent spectacle, which condemned him to mediocrity, like the victim of an unsurprising theft. Santiago suffered the same mediocrity and therefore was incapable of even remotely perceiving the powerful feeling Miguel rubbed up against while rubbing Lucille Renaud's nipples, gripping her sides to thrust harder, edging toward the abyss, in the heart of enemy territory, actually a few inches from the enemy, dangling between fear and recklessness, which makes passion more authentic. Miguel had decided that life lay in the forbidden honeypot. And he had climbed up to the balcony to nick some. Santiago, on the other hand, stood in the middle of the road ignorant of the taste of honey. Ignorant that such a pot existed! Standing still, he felt a deathly, apparently hopeless solitude.

There was a moment, in the middle of the night, when François Renaud gave a start and jerked awake, sat upright for a brief instant and opened his eyes. The two lovers looked at him and froze. Then he fell back asleep, hauling that image with him into his future nightmares, while they laughed, relieved, then shut up and got back to having sex with greater intensity; the taint of their arousal made their veins bulge, and they smashed through the walls of pleasure with a shudder.

There was also a moment, in the middle of the night, when Santiago, back at home, harried by unanswered questions, jerked awake too. At that moment, in the dark of his room, he felt the distinct absence of Soledad Sanchez.

Because if Santiago stopped to consider his brother, if he looked at him, as he was doing now, from the other end of the plaza while he bartered with a couple of young tourists, he saw someone who hunted after answers. His vocation was to solve enigmas, to leave nothing unresolved. Whereas if he considered himself, he saw before all else the constant, reflexive endeavor to bury questions. Over time he had developed and perfected that faculty, had learned how to stifle questions before they came up for air, while they were still incomplete, unclear, and therefore easier to hide. And that was how he saw himself: an undertaker of infant—even embryonic—questions.

Yet he was about to get a taste of hunting too. On a dish served up by Miguel, naturally. From the opposite side of Plaza Mayor he signaled him over. Because Miguel had never before asked for help, it was clear that this was an invitation. This time the prey were two; Miguel was dangling one for him.

"Emma," said one of the girls, and shook his hand.

"Zoe," said the other, and shook his hand more limply.

Their roles were immediately clear. Zoe had delicate features and a slender figure that Miguel regularly leaned into, as if marking his territory. Emma was less attractive but more precocious. In a sensual voice she spouted South American slang. Many words were lost on Santiago, who listened to her and mulled over what she was saying, assuming positions that made him appear more interesting than he felt he was, especially in the matchup of brothers he imagined she was doing in her head: Santiago's full face versus Miguel's lean, oval face; Santiago's knotted birds' nest versus his brother's smooth locks; Santiago's busted nose versus the other's shapely profile; and of course she'd noticed the mole on Santiago's right cheek, while Miguel kept his hidden, only exhibiting it like a battle scar—ironically, heroically—to the women to whom he offered his bare ass. Santiago reacted by turning his face, presenting Emma with practically nothing but his left profile. Then, out of alternatives, he opted for the jokes he'd committed to memory, the ones that worked on English-speaking tourists, hoping to appear lexically dexterous, naturally clever, as if he weren't pawning off counterfeits. His words were directed at Emma alone, since Miguel had cornered Zoe, who had a kind of drum with her which she was trying to teach him to play.

"It's a djembe," she explained, tapping the leather stretched across the top.

Emma didn't appear particularly interested in music and therefore remained in Santiago's fly zone, giving him her attention, even laughing at his stock jokes from time to time. Santiago kept to the comfortable line of shopworn phrases, but he felt Miguel was a step ahead of him. He caught him touching Zoe's fingers with the excuse of learning how to play the djembe. A rhythm filled the air, interrupted the rhythm of Santiago's repartee, broke in on the sound of his hesitant words, trivialized his efforts to talk to Emma about anything in order to avoid standing there in silence, in order not to be left staring at the other two. Which was how, without realizing it, Santiago arrived at the end of his routine, reached the last stop of his daily banter.

"You haven't bought a hammock yet?" he asked just to say something.

Miguel stopped beating the djembe and glared at Santiago as if the latter had just blasphemed. He couldn't understand whether the other really intended to run to the shop, swear off the two Americans, hand them over to Belisario Lopez. For the first time it occurred to him that Santiago could be a virgin, that he might not even be interested in that sort of thing. In effect, they'd never talked about it, but Miguel had always regarded his brother as being uniquely capable of burying his

secrets, of operating on the sly, the way he did with the hammocks. The suspicion arose, but by then it was too late, the
question had been asked, and the only path forward led to the
door of the shop.

They walked the city streets in pairs, each alongside his
lady: Miguel and Zoe ahead, Santiago and Emma behind.
Santiago realized two things thanks to that formation. The
first was that his brother was now taller than him, had out-
grown him by a few inches, having inherited, predictably, his
height from Vicente Moya. The second was that he turned
more heads than a car wreck. He was a little under eighteen
that day, and no woman, young or old, alone or on somebody's arm, could resist—at a certain point they all capitulated. Some from a few feet away. And they didn't take their
eyes off him until they'd passed by. Others appeared to
restrain themselves out of modesty or shyness, but a step
away they all conceded, sought, in a flash, confirmation, or at
least a glimmer of hope. Zoe noticed and so did Emma. The
only one who didn't seem to pay any mind was Miguel, who
perhaps filed it under "facts of life," and returned their looks
and smiles with the lightheartedness of someone playing with
a gun he doesn't think is loaded. At one point, Zoe clasped
his arm, latched onto him so that he wouldn't slip her grasp,
essentially conceding defeat, surrendering herself to him
without his having lifted a finger. On the contrary, Miguel
seemed more interested in the djembe. He kept talking about
it, asking for explanations, his voice filled the streets and
reached Santiago and Emma, who were following behind in
silence. Santiago, for his part, had nothing left to say: all the
English he wielded was useful only for selling hammocks. So,
when they arrived at the Sueño Yucateo, he merely steered
her toward Belisario Lopez, as he had a thousand other
tourists, hoping something would happen, that she might tell
him what to do to cross the threshold into the unknown,

place her faith in him the way Zoe had in Miguel, who hadn't even asked.

Miguel lingered in the doorway with the girl and watched Belisario Lopez go about his smarmy business, glibly quoting her an extortionate price and backing it up with fictitious figures and anecdotes. The scene made him sick. Until then he had only been able to imagine it, since Lopez demanded that at that stage they already be out looking for more clients.

"Best hammock in Mexico, young lady," Lopez concluded.

Emma bit, picked up the hammock and went to the register to pay Belisario the outrageous sum. Santiago was behind her. He hadn't left because he'd decided that one way or another he too was going to hound her with questions, and as he stared at her back, this was his unspoken question: "What's going to happen between us?" And what was about to happen would change everything.

Emma had already set the money on the counter when Miguel came crashing into the store.

"That's a rip-off!" he shouted.

Emma and Santiago and Belisario Lopez looked incredulous.

"You can find the same thing for half the price at the artisanal market," Miguel explained. "And this store isn't fair trade. It's all a fake!"

Belisario Lopez's face turned red. Had he a gun handy he'd have shot him, pulled the trigger with his missing index finger. But Miguel gave him no time to react. He turned his back on him and the Sueño Yucateo, took Zoe by the wrist, and carried her off. She had little idea what had just happened in the shop, but what mattered was that Miguel had finally decided to give her what she wanted. He led her straight to the van she and her friend had driven from the United States, taking turns at the wheel and sleeping on an inflatable mattress in the back where she and Miguel now wasted no time to strip.

Back in the shop, time stopped. During his brother's out-burst, Santiago had caught a whiff of dried blood from the old butcher. He felt disgusted with Belisario Lopez, with Vicente Moya for tethering him to the place, and, above all, with him-self. The Sueño Yucateo was still a butcher shop. Except he was the meat on sale: loin, topside, rump, chuck steak de Santiago. Cuts of Santiago went to the highest bidder, only no bidder came forward. At that point not even Emma. After Miguel's confession, she realized what was what and looked first at Belisario Lopez and then at Santiago with a tinge of contempt. She cursed in American—Santiago understood her perfectly—threw the hammock on the floor, and walked out. She wandered aimlessly for a few blocks, trying to decide what to do. Then, out of a sense of vindictiveness and survival instinct, she went to the one place she could go: to the van parked on a side street far from the center of town in the shade of an old abandoned warehouse.

She forced the doors open, where inside Miguel and Zoe were lying together, resting after sex, before sex. Zoe showered them with words, said something in broad slang that Miguel didn't catch. She sounded like someone defending her terri-tory. Emma stood there, wavering, gazing at Miguel's body with a sense of yearning and envy, undecided as to whether she should back off and accept her friend's rebuff. But Miguel sorted things out. He kissed Zoe, whispered something in her ear that made her giggle, climbed out onto the street naked, and with the sweetness with which he had kissed the other, drew close to Emma's lips and kissed her too. Then he led her by the hand into his, into their love nest.

Ir. Volver
GOING, COMING BACK

Santiago climbed down from that afternoon dizzy and nauseated, as if it were a carousel that spun too fast. He couldn't keep up with Miguel, and while he waited in the dark room for him to return, were he to return, he couldn't help but feel on the wrong end of things. His incapacity to relate to people, his ineptitude with the opposite sex, his job, which suddenly seemed to him a fiction, all a sham. Miguel had, as usual, drawn back the curtain, acted without fear of the consequences. For Santiago, the one right place now lay over there, somewhere beyond his imagination, wherever his brother was taking what he wanted when he pleased. And the worst place to be was there, in the room that he'd fled to, in the space of a heart that had been emptied of sentiments that didn't feel equal to the sentiments that had weighed on him since he was a child. And while he was battling with his thoughts and his insomnia—it was nearly dawn—Miguel reappeared in the room. He had steered through the night and the city half-naked, shirt in hand, bare-chested, his loins tired but proud, on his skin the intense odor of the wild terrain that he had staked out, the women he'd consumed.

"Belisario Lopez wants to talk to you," said Santiago, thinking he might surprise him.

But it seemed normal to Miguel that his brother was still awake and that Lopez had summoned him.

"Does he want to fire me?" he asked, clearly amused, flopping down onto his hammock.

"I don't know," said Santiago, though he did know that if the merchant wanted to see him, it was to try to patch things up; were it anyone else, he'd never have given him a second chance, but his brother was worth a fortune.

"Doesn't matter," said Miguel, "I'm leaving tomorrow."

"Where?" asked Santiago without working out his feelings.

"Somewhere. With the Americans . . . "

In that plural Santiago picked up an image that pertained to reality yet was blurred by his lack of competence in the subject, interspersed with elements gleaned in the prostitute's trailer and elevated to the power of Miguel. He had an image of his brother caressing Emma's head, Zoe's head, feeding both their mouths, eyes shut, swept up in a pleasure that he continued to mistake for omnipotent possession.

Santiago got quiet. He felt robbed of something that wasn't his, that hadn't been his for a second. Silence reigned while the faint early sunlight crept into the room like a burglar. After a few minutes the two brothers crashed practically in tandem, wiped out for different reasons.

Miguel left the next day. He went to the trouble of telling Vicente Moya, as he had promised, and granted Maria Serrano a hug. But he didn't wake Santiago. He watched him sleep a little, then decided to leave without another word between them. He returned to the Americans' van and kissed them both with equal vigor, as if he wanted to make clear that he had no intention of giving up the three-way nature of their relationship. He sat down between them, master of the van and everything in it. He commandeered Zoe's djembe, wedged it between his legs, and tapped away while the wheels skidded down the road and the three of them talked, laughed, sang, shouted, caught up in the excitement of a road trip mixed with the aftereffects of their orgy, the intense smells of pleasure still wafting around the van. Zoe drove languidly toward the

Caribbean, clutching the wheel nervously, now and then resting her palm on Miguel's thigh as Emma kept her arm around his shoulders in search of the heat from the night before.

They hadn't been driving an hour when Zoe said, "You can have it," meaning the djembe.

"Really?" he asked and stopped playing momentarily.

She nodded, took her eyes off the road to look at him, and tried to gauge how much ground she had just gained. Miguel gave her a caress, yet it was only as tender as the way he let Emma run her fingers through his hair, and soon enough he started playing again, with no apparent change in intensity and no comment, as if owning a musical instrument didn't interest him or as if he had already known that at some point it would be his. They drove south of Yucatán toward the forests of Quintana Roo. There was nothing on that ribbon of road but the occasional lone tarantula and miles of jungle all the way to the coast.

By evening they arrived in a fishing village called Mahahual that lay snug against the beach, buffeted by the sea breeze. They were tired from driving but more than anything victims of a desire that had accrued in the van, echoes of the night before that had stirred up their need to repeat the experience; the girls were driven apart and drawn closer by their feral instinct to possess him and their need to share him. So, in an epilogue that had already been written, they walked to the edge of the beach, undressed, slipped into the blue waters of the Caribbean, and became one body, a shivering wet profile that distorted both contours and decorum. Then they crashed onto the shore like wreckage and died on the sand, naturally ending up having sex, in an equilibrium that perfected itself at every stage and, perfecting itself, produced images that would feed their desires in the days to come. They'd last weeks on the beach in peaceful Mahahual, united, hanging in that perfect, precarious balance.

The day Miguel left, Santiago woke up in the late morning and knew from the silent objects, which either had been moved or had vanished, that his brother had gone; knew it, as well, from the muffled noises in the house where Maria Serrano was pacing around around as if she were looking for something she'd lost.

"What are you doing today?" his mother asked to fill the silence.

"Reading," he told Maria Serrano on his way out.

He returned to Teresa Rodríguez's stationery store, asked her for a book about love, distance, brothers, differences, life. Teresa Rodríguez studied the dusty bookshelf that she had scoured from top to bottom, combing through her memories of its contents, then took down the book she'd been searching for and handed it to him. The book was neither better nor worse than the others, or maybe it was, but in any case, it was exactly the story that Santiago had to encounter when he encountered it. And that made the book special.

He carried it to the bench in Plaza Mayor and began reading. Now and then he had the feeling he was inside the story, physically part of it, that he could change it, lead it wherever he wanted, decide the outcome of its plot with no regard to the original plot or to its author. For the first time he felt as if he could correct his own life, using, for example, the book as a lure to flush it out, to capture it, to never let it go. While he reflected on this, it dawned on him that he knew nothing about Soledad Sanchez; he had asked her nothing but literary questions. He didn't know her age or where she lived or where she came from or how to find her. She could be made of the same stuff as the books they had read: a character on a page, a projection of his fantasy wrought by the printed word. Soledad Sanchez might not exist, may never have existed. Maybe she was the ideal construction that Santiago had assembled to avoid being bored in Miguel's absence, and that was the reason she had begun to flood his thoughts now that Miguel was gone again. Yet just as he was about to give up hope, after two hundred slowly-turned pages and two days of waiting in a trance between fiction and reality, just when Santiago had convinced himself that the story had seduced and abandoned him, he was riveted by an image that seemed unreal: Soledad Sanchez stepped out from behind a tree, just as she had the first time, and like the first time, she sat down next to him, as if she had been waiting for him all that time, as if she had passed by the plaza every few days to see if he had come back yet, if he had begun to read again.

"Incredible," she said, meaning the novel in her hands, the same novel that Santiago was reading, that seemed to be about them.

Santiago slowly leaned over and pressed his lips to hers.

La Música en la Sangre
Music in the Blood

This time Miguel's absence from Mérida produced wide-spread panic, left a very real, physical, and hormonal sense of something missing in all those girls who had had the luck of his attention for an evening, perhaps for just an hour. Word that he had left with a couple of *gringas*, without saying whether or when he would be back, felt like a theft, a collective betrayal. With each passing day, the air went out of the evening get-togethers at Casa Moya while they waited dispiritedly. Vicente Moya's profit fell proportionately; he quit dancing, then quit paying the musicians. What remained were the chairs and a couple of pushcarts. What remained were the bright umbrellas and, most of all, the natter of old ladies venting their loss by piecing together the story of the thousand relationships that Miguel had accumulated in recent months. Some came from the vain reports of daughters and grand-daughters who had benefited from his willingness, others from the malicious gossip of those who were left out, the disappointed ones whose wait was eternal, those whose lips were still dry and who took thin consolation by heaping scorn on him. They exploited the fact that the lady of the house, Maria Serrano, rarely hung out in the courtyard, less so now that her husband had stopped dancing. As is the case with all absent parties, she wound up becoming the subject of their talk, the object of their derision, until she'd briefly reappear among the ladies, sense their silence had to do with her, and beat a retreat behind the walls of her house. There was also talk of Rosita

Romero, who had survived her pain, chosen to continue school, enrolled in college, and left for Mexico City in what seemed an understandable escape to save herself. And there was talk of, among other things, the fact that the older Moya boy had also moved on, that many had seen him clinging to the daughter of Clarabella Sanchez in broad daylight. But that last topic was rarely expanded on, since Soledad's mother was a permanent fixture in the courtyard chatter, and she would nip it in the bud with icy replies and glares that betrayed her not inconsiderable frustration that, of the two Moya boys, she'd gotten stuck with the older. Everything, in short, stopped, as if Miguel were the neighborhood's one source of energy. All that remained was tired gossip, suffocating heat, the flutter of fans, and knotty conversations that solidified the legend of the beautiful boy and their profound longing for him.

Maybe that's it, thought Santiago, that's how destiny presents itself. In the novel of his life, the name Soledad Sanchez was already written, it was just a matter of arriving at that page. And on that page the two were linked, like a plain noun and a plain adjective that, together, become colorful, make a formidable pair that affects anyone who sees them hugging and kissing with the curiosity of those discovering kisses for the first time.

One day they joined hands and meandered through the city. Seen with Soledad, Mérida had an appeal Santiago hadn't suspected. As they explored it, he let himself be won over while she told him the secret stories of its buildings, streets, trees, shops, the writing on its walls. He discovered the beauty of walking alongside someone else, swapping stories, making important decisions like which road to take next or whether to choose not to choose. Time flew as they covered miles of streets, talking about things practical and abstract, playfully unpacking questions and answers, or else earnestly, now and then stopping for a kiss, learning to kiss in order to kiss again, extending their journey and anticipation, in no hurry to seal their relationship, that it existed was enough, that it existed was already so much.

"Is this love?" asked Santiago.

"Is what love?" she replied.

"Always having an empty stomach."

"Then yes," said Soledad, and kissed him.

One step at a time, they arrived in the courtyard in front of Casa Moya. The day was so muggy that even slinging gossip was a struggle for the old ladies. Santiago and Soledad Sanchez emerged from a street on the fringe of the courtyard and could have turned around in time for no one to notice them. They stopped, almost amazed to find themselves there, to have landed there drifting along in intense conversation. They had to decide whether to proceed and pass in front of Santiago's house and the firing squad of housewives commanded by Soledad's mother, or else turn back, make a run for it. They had to decide, essentially, whether to publicly announce the feelings that they had only revealed to one another under their breath by borrowing words from books and gently blowing on them, like embers.

"Now what?" said Soledad Sanchez, pushing up her glasses.

Santiago had the reckless courage of a lover.

"We could dance," he said in all earnestness.

Soledad Sanchez stared at him, stunned.

"Do you know how to dance?" she asked.

"No, but how hard can it be?"

"There's no music," insisted Soledad.

Santiago smiled and put his hands behind his back, assuming a pose from a courtship dance he had seen at county fairs. He began humming the song Grandpa Hermenegildo had played for him as a child to put him to sleep, every minute of every hour of every day, drilling that rhythm into his brain. But the impulse to move his hips came from the heart, in the blood, giving Santiago's movements the grace of someone who carried music inside him and didn't know it. It was the other gift Hermenegildo Serrano had passed down to him, besides that mole on his cheek, a gift concealed by his shyness and lack of self-esteem. More importantly, maybe, he had been waiting for a partner he hadn't had until now, this girl stunned to see him singing, floating in the sky with spellbinding agility, courting her with his dance. Soledad Sanchez took up his challenge, accepted his invitation, lifted the hem of her skirt with her fingertips, quietly hummed the tune of "Jarabe Tapatío," and followed Santiago's lead, moving delicately toward and away from him, as the dance called for, holding up her dress ever so slightly. Their bond took care of the rest, the power of their feeling, full of enthusiasm and desire which delineated, in their courtship dance, their courtship underway, amplifying their movements, making them more real, charging them with a natural sensuality and kindness—the moving image took your breath away.

"Isn't that your daughter?" a woman asked Clarabella Sanchez.

The old lady turned to look where the others were looking, and all at once the fans stopped fluttering. After years of prattling on uninterrupted, the band of gossips fell dumb. It hadn't been that quiet since, perhaps, the time Miguel leaped into the *chácara*, or rather the same moment in which Soledad Sanchez saw Santiago for the first time and fell in love with him. Ten years on, those children now found themselves dancing alone in the middle of the courtyard, kicking up a cloud of dust, which made the scene more ethereal; they were united by an energy that came with the hardship of being born in an imperfect body, and the combination of their mutual imperfections was all the more arresting in its pure abandon because it was short on such things as might fade. They danced in silence, itself imperfect, with no music or applause. They danced to tell a story, their story, doing away with words, to show their families and neighbors those feelings that they didn't know how to hold back, to be genuine and unashamed. They danced for the simple taste of dancing, to touch one another, to get closer so as not to risk losing each other again.

As they slowed to a stop and Soledad's skirt ceased twirling, all that was left in the air was a swirl of sand. Seated under their brightly-colored umbrellas, the women looked on, completely still, as if posing for a photo. Then, from way in the back, two hands began clapping. The faint sound filled the hole of that moment. The hands applauding belonged to Maria Serrano, who had been watching from the doorway; it was her way of welcoming Soledad Sanchez into her house and, in a certain way, welcoming her son too. Watching him panting after his dance under the sun, she thought he looked like a butterfly. Hatched from its chrysalis.

After a month and a half Miguel spoke English as if he were a native of New Orleans and played the djembe as if he'd been born in Bamako. He'd robbed the two girls of their skills and, without meaning to, of any ambition they had that didn't concern him personally. They were both innocent victims of a bad spell, so that they breathed the same air he breathed. Their one desire was to continue to bask in Miguel; their one fear to lose him. Therefore, they gave everything they had, more often every day, to surprise him, to satisfy him. For him, they were lovers, friends, sisters, mothers, devoted slaves. And they only stifled their jealousy because they knew Miguel stuck with them for the thrill of having them both. So they formed a tentative alliance while attempting, by any means possible, to emerge on top: Emma by cooking, Zoe by teaching him about music. Naturally, making love also became a bout between bodies driven by a rivalry that none of them mentioned yet which was visible from every angle, in every act, with every movement that kept them tethered to the beach for weeks, always pushing one another a little further. The very idea of a Mexican journey had faded into the background, ceded ground to the bodily journey at the far reaches of erotic experience, which Miguel had christened that day in Mérida. The sickness had spread to their bones.

The time in Mahahual became an almost mystical parenthesis: fish and fruit were Miguel's entire diet. He spent the day staring out at sea, his hands drumming the skin of the djembe. At night those same hands, the calloused hands of a drummer, rubbed Zoe's smooth buttocks and Emma's breasts, exploring their wildly different bodies in the warm light of a bonfire or in the dark of the van from which feverish moans escaped.

Then one day Emma pretended she felt ill so that Zoe would go to the market in town. As soon as they were alone, she ran to Miguel.

"Come with me," she said.

"Where?" asked Miguel.

"Under those palm trees. There's something I want to show you."

"What is it?" he asked, following behind her.

"It's me," she answered, offering herself up with an intensity that she seemed to have been hiding, a residual energy she used to conquer him, steeped in pure acrimony, possessiveness, frustration, lust, and love. Miguel let himself be taken. And for a moment he felt a pang of guilt, not for betraying Zoe, but for having stolen Emma from Santiago. He should have been there in his place. For a moment he thought of his brother, then lost himself in the girl.

When Zoe came back she caught the one inside the other, kissing, as if they were in love, and the reaction that shot through her came from the same ancestral instinct that had driven Emma to act: they were two females fighting to mate with the dominant male; if necessary, they would kill each other for him.

"No!" was the first word that came to Zoe to stop them as fast as she could, then she pounced on her friend/enemy, vomiting insults, disentangling her from Miguel, who watched them fight the way as a boy he had watched Santiago plant his knuckles in the ribs of Alfonsino Ruiz—depleted, terrorized, helpless. He watched as Zoe bit Emma and Emma tore Zoe's hair, as Zoe turned around and dug her nails into Emma's flesh, as Emma cried, bled, spat in her face, grabbed the other by the throat to strangle her. And she would have had Miguel not finally snapped out of it and gotten between them to calm them down. But the anger that assailed them, their desire not to share the boy, was so violent that they pushed him back, once, twice, again, flinging insults from their sand-caked mouths, whipped into a fury of jealousy, which they had suppressed before and now gave free rein.

When, worn out from their skirmish, they gave up, the waves hitting the shore announced that something in Mahahual had been broken irreparably. They took off in opposite directions, far from one another and farther still from Miguel, who suddenly missed everything that he'd left behind.

That night, as soon as the girls had fallen asleep on the beach, far apart and burned out, their bodies scratched and bruised, Miguel slung the djembe over his shoulder and took off down the road leading out of Mahahual. As he penetrated the night, waiting for the sunrise and a ride home, he played a sad music that came from within, from the thought that he had robbed something from Zoe and Emma that didn't belong to him. With every step he put between them, he felt as if he were delivering them from evil.

Día de los muertos
DAY OF THE DEAD

As she did every All Souls' Day, Maria Serrano prepared the house for her father's return. Once again, the scent of *flores cempasúchil* wafted in the air—from the vases on the shelves to the floor to the courtyard, where she had scattered them so Hermenegildo Serrano could find his way home. The yellow path culminated in the hallway where his coffin had sat on the day of his funeral and where there now stood a shrine to him with a heaping portion of *mukbil pollo*, two bottles of beer, and a pillow. He would reappear, her father, he would reappear in their memories, in the conversations of his loved ones, in the legs of his grandchildren who carried his musical DNA in their veins, his rhythm, his talent, his elegance, his harmony.

Miguel too would return, any time now. In fact the yellow path was also for him. He was on board a truck delivering the fleshy flowers of the dead, grouped by the pound, with the bittersweet scent penetrating the air and his nostrils, but all he seemed to smell was the bitterness. Maria Serrano was waiting for him with a mother's anxiety, even if, in the solitude of her house, while the plaza was celebrating, she had worked out an equation in her mind: When Miguel wasn't around, Vicente Moya lost his sense of security and, as a consequence, went back to respecting her with the same devotion as before. Meaning that by gaining her son back she had to lose her husband. No matter how she did the math, she was left with only a fraction of happiness.

Santiago spent the morning searching for a gift for Soledad at the Lucas de Gálvez market. He wended his way through the tortuous labyrinth of stands, breathing in the aromas of fruit, leather, spices, live animals. All Souls' Day was a good day to declare your love. Past the shoe stands, the tables sparkled with jewels, as if to alert him that he'd arrived. He spent a long time examining the precious stones, brooches, necklaces, rings. But in the end he let a pair of vendors choose for him. A *maquech*, they explained, was the perfect gift. They sold it to him for about twenty pesos and placed it in a perforated box, which he hid in a drawer in his room.

In the afternoon the family took their party to the cemetery to celebrate with their dearly departed. Santiago followed Vicente Moya and Maria Serrano, pulled along in the slipstream of people headed in that direction. The graves were covered with tea lights, candles, skulls made of sugar, crosses, plates of salt, *pan de muertos*, and glasses of water or tequila.

While they picnicked on a tablecloth draped over Hermenegildo Serrano's headstone, Santiago caught sight of Soledad and the Sanchez family nearby. Her large mother was laughing about some cheerful memory of a husband who had passed on to the other world many years ago and was staring at them mutely from a photo on his tomb. There was death, it was there around them, but all Santiago seemed to see was Soledad and all he heard was life churning inside him, as well as a desire that he couldn't restrain any longer. A voice that sounded like *papel picado* blowing in the breeze whispered to him, and it seemed like the voice of his grandfather, or maybe it was his brother. A voice that showed him a way, a place and a time, a simple and, for that reason, now that Santiago had understood it, brilliant solution. Santiago left his parents, walked over to the Sanchezes' plot, politely greeted them, and came up with an excuse to borrow Soledad. The minute they were out of the cemetery he kissed her, then kissed her and kissed her again, took her hand and dragged her, faster than death, through the streets of Mérida, flickering with fireworks, to his grandfather's old house. Santiago found the key under the vase, opened the door, closed it behind them, and led Soledad Sanchez into the dark, silent bedroom. For an instant he remembered that he'd forgotten the *maquech*, but then he began to undress her slowly and that was all that mattered.

On their way home Vicente Moya and Maria Serrano heard drumbeats in the distance. The closer they got, the louder the drumming. And when they arrived in the courtyard, now abandoned for the cemetery, there was Miguel, leaning on a chair in the carnival of open umbrellas and yellow flowers strewn across the ground, playing the djembe, his chin up, his eyes shut. The melancholy lullaby sounded like a prayer, almost a plea for forgiveness, and it didn't suit Miguel or his light or the lightness he instilled in everything. But the sands of Mahahual, the days spent playing in that ascetic delirium, the dissolute nights of sex that did nothing to stem his obsessions, the tension, the disquiet of the fight between the American girls, all that, intensified by the scent of the afterlife that hovered in the air, coursed through the litany he kept playing until he heard his parents' footsteps.

"You learned to play?" asked Vicente Moya curiously.

While Maria Serrano, who had read between the notes, asked, "What happened?"

Miguel looked at them and felt happy to see them. He smiled, relieved to know that he'd returned home.

So as not to answer his mother, he answered his father. "Yes," he said, "I learned." Then he went to hug her and squeeze the hand of Vicente Moya, who was staring at the djembe next to the chair as if Miguel had fished it out of a *cenote*.

"Will you play for us later?" he asked his son as they entered the house.

"Sure," said Miguel distractedly. "But now I have to sleep."

Shortly after, he was in his hammock, sound asleep, all the fatigue that had accumulated on his return home had swept over him; he hadn't slept for the entire journey, maybe to be sure that the next time he woke up he'd be far from Mahuahual.

"What are you doing?" Maria Serrano asked Vicente Moya, realizing that her equation had been correct.

"Making a few calls," said Vicente, holding the receiver to his ear. He slipped outside, lit out on the road to the graveyard, soberly approached the families assembled around their gravestones, and curtly broke the news.

"Miguel's back," he announced. "He's putting on a show for us tonight."

It took less time than usual for news to spread. It spread like wildfire; everyone in the cemetery, even the most distant relative, was already warm with mezcal. Word swept over the headstones, magnifying the feeling of joy on that day when the departed are honored with music, and now that music would be provided by Miguel Moya, in person, after his prolonged absence from home. The excitement was so great even the dead were liable to dig themselves out so as not to miss the event. As evening fell, a torrent of people, flocks of women, abandoned the cemetery with one destination in mind. They gathered candles from the tombs to light the road to the Moyas' courtyard, where Vicente had reassembled his army of pushcart vendors.

Miguel was awoken by the racket outside. He went out as he was: bare-chested, barefoot, in a pair of lightweight and low-slung pants, his long hair smelling of the sea. From the dark courtyard only a streak of yellow emerged, lit up by hundreds of candles. Maybe there was a mass, thought Miguel, a consecration, a funeral. He stood on tiptoe to study the multitude of people gathered around the house and in fact noticed a kind of altar erected in the center of the courtyard. But when he strained to look he discovered that it was actually a round platform about five feet tall. And right in the middle of the platform was his djembe. Just as he figured out what was what, a woman spotted him and shouted his name, giving rise to a hysterical roar, an explosion of female voices that rang out in the courtyard. The wave crashed on top of Miguel, physically carried him away, a thousand hands touched him, caressed him, forced him forward, sucked him out into the crowd—there was no way out—compelled him toward the center of the courtyard, and transported him to the platform and to his instrument. From high up onstage, Miguel looked out and apprehended that Mérida was female, that all of her was there, that she adored him, was crazy about him, and had suffered in his absence, had waited impatiently for him ever since he'd decided to leave. And at that point he did what he had to, almost as if it were a social obligation: he picked up the djembe, slung it over his shoulder, closed his eyes, took a breath, and, amid the absolute silence, began to play for her.

El diablo y la cucaracha
THE DEVIL AND THE SCARAB

Silence. There was a pregnant silence in the Moyas' court-yard. Sounds, voices, all manner of noise was stifled, a rhythm that came from afar held sway, a rhythm passed down orally from one musician to another over centuries, from the kit bags of memory to the palms of people's hands, played in theaters, streets, plazas, meadows, and deserts, on moun-taintops and ocean shores, in crowded music schools, lonely huts, and empty rooms. The rhythm had journeyed to Miguel's hands and a neighborhood in Mérida and held the city captive. Around Casa Moya the silence had settled under a veil of high, low, and in-between notes which the boy was stitching together, pounding or pawing the skin of the djembe, as the spirit moved him. Looking at him in the moonlight, the women felt both jealous of that instrument and turned on by the way he treated it; you might say he had established an intimate rap-port with it. The djembe possessed a spirit, and it was Miguel's spirit floating in the air and brushing up against the people. The rhythm was a cycle, a transport. And in that vortex, the living, on the day of the dead, let themselves be carried away, coursed into a place that had nothing to do with the living, a place where Hermenegildo Serrano fell silent and listened to his grandson play, and inside the music was a part of him, Mother Earth, nature, the heartbeat Miguel listened to before being born, Maria Serrano's heartbeat, the beat of his own heart. The lady that venerated him, the Lady Mérida, dreamed of tearing out his heart with her bare hands, scrutinizing it up and down with a thousand amorous eyes as it poured out that ecstatic music that stripped it of humanity and united it with the divine in an atmosphere saturated with the mysticism of the Día de los Muertos, in the dim candlelight that framed it with a surreal aura.

If Miguel's beauty was undeniable, it had reached its apogee right there, shored up as it was by the power of the music that he himself had singlehandedly created, by the dramatic flourish of his strap hanging across his bare, sweaty chest, by the power of his biceps that bulged in the lusty language of the drums. At his feet desires and prayers multiplied in people's mute, open mouths. The melancholy he had brought back with him from Mahahual also played a factor; it may have wiped the smile off his face and lined his brow, yet he looked even more seductive, shadowy. Miguel expressed his melancholy by pounding out musical notes that pierced people's spirits and excited their bodies; a primordial energy coursed through the veins of the earth and seemed to emerge from the ground that quaked beneath them. Till the last pounding of the drum, the last beat. Till the end.

Then all that remained was silence. Silence.

The silence grew out of the crowd's amazement, their astonishment—they felt even applauding would be insufficient. What remained was the candlelight flickering over Miguel's body, the reverberation of his music, and the sinful thoughts that had streamed over him while he played. The meaning of what had happened was lost, there was only the sensation of having witnessed an unrepeatable spectacle; the sensation that, given such moments, on the day of the dead, it was life that counted more than anything else for moments like that, moments that would never return, miracles big and small, after which nothing would be the same: somehow time should stop still and life be lived, hazarded, relished, sung, shouted, touched.

One girl directly below the stage couldn't resist the temptation. She was too close to restrain herself. She furtively stuck out her hand and touched his ankle. That prompted the woman next to her to do the same. She reached out and grabbed Miguel's pants leg and pulled him toward her. Those farther back felt this was their chance, they were inches away, and they began pushing. Someone fell. One man reacted by swinging his arms at random, and whomever he hit, hit back in turn. A fight broke out, escalated into shoving and punching. In the crowd were women who had had Miguel but wanted him again, as well as women who had lived their lives depressed at the thought that they hadn't had him, anxious they might never. The dark energy was simply looking for a pretext to be released. Some fell and were trampled. A husband was restraining his wife from rushing the stage, other women were wrestling on the ground and tearing at each other's clothes, still others were shouting, attempting to elbow their way through the crowd and lap up the body of the divine boy who watched in terror as that inchoate mass writhed underneath him and the religious silence devolved into war cries, insults, screams of pain and violence, out-of-control commotion and open hostility. The earthquake he'd generated cratered the courtyard, produced a hole that swallowed them live. The end of that day was gripped by the feeling that this was the end of days, disquieted by death in the face of life's beauty, of which Miguel was the most radical expression. Enchantment warped into a nightmare, the Moyas' courtyard became a circle of hell. The food stalls were assailed, flipped over, bottles of beer and liquor shattered, sending glass flying and frothing over the sand, the housewives' chairs collapsed under the weight of a monstrous humanity that had lost all sense of decency, umbrellas were trampled by people darting in every direction, seeking safety in the courtyard, fleeing from the crowd that, sick with frustration, had lost its mind and erupted into an abominable wail.

Tomorrow they'd say the devil had been in the courtyard. What other explanation was there? The devil had infected them with his sweet-talking musical notes. And among those who fled was the devil himself. Miguel launched into the melee that, twisting in on itself, had forgotten all about him. He slipped between the bodies and booked it to the edge of the courtyard, reached it in a pant, scathed from his skin to his spirit. At one point he looked around and saw the space boil over into bleak, meaningless violence, into dust and *flores cempasúchil* flying in the air, blows and tears. The courtyard where he'd first arrived swaddled, where he'd grown up, contained the world's most terrible instincts, and he was its fatal epicenter. Above the little stage two women were clawing the skin of the djembe, either to take a piece for themselves or simply to destroy it.

A couple of blocks away in the Serrano house, kisses were being blown. Kisses on the wall. Kisses on the ceiling. Kisses on the floor. Kisses on the naked body of Soledad Sanchez, which for Santiago was home, the place he wanted to live. He was kissing her to give thanks for her having patiently waited for him since the day she first saw him. He was kissing her to relocate, to move inside her, and build a life.

"Was it love at first sight?" he asked her.

"I don't believe in love at first sight."

"Then what was it?"

"A premonition . . . "

Santiago thought that Soledad had seen their destiny, had seen that one day they'd be right where they were. He thought she might even have seen the images engraved in that place, images he wouldn't tell her about, of Miguel discovering love for the first time on the same bed years before.

Soledad's short hair rested on the pillow where Rosita Romero's long hair had once rested; her naked body, ready to receive him, lay where the naked body of his brother's lover had once lain. As he climbed on top of her, he caught a glimpse of the hiding place from which he'd spied Miguel, and felt victorious, as if after a long race he had arrived at the finishing line.

But Soledad froze. "You're not scared?" she asked.

Santiago didn't say anything, and in his silence Soledad Sanchez glimpsed the image he didn't want her to see: the trailer on the edge of Mérida, a place *not* home, *not* love, at a far remove from her, her virginity, her patience. Yet the place existed, and for Santiago it had been a shelter, which Soledad couldn't deny him, had to accept, but which removed from the scene any mutual innocence that she had painted in.

"Do I really know you?" she blurted, but she regretted it immediately. She hugged him without saying anything more. He held her tightly, they intertwined as if they'd just risked losing one another. Sleep carried them off together, outside only the faded echo of some mortar reached them while the moment of physical love evaporated, was tacitly put off to another day, whenever that would be, without their being able to do anything about it. They slept in an embrace awhile and dreamed of embracing.

When Santiago awoke the first thing that popped into his head was the *maquech*—he'd left it in the drawer in his room.

"I have something to give you," he said as soon as Soledad opened her eyes.

"What?" she asked.

"A present. It's in my room . . . "

They dressed in a hurry and took the road all the way to the Moyas' courtyard, which was now lit by the moon and no longer the same. There they found a yellow puddle of trampled flowers, the remains of bottles, bits of wood from broken chairs, open umbrellas with their canopies torn, strewn across an apocalyptic canvas, where the remains of clothes, *huipiles*, sandals, and hair hinted at the battle that had just been waged.

"My god, what happened?" whispered Soledad.

"I have no idea," said Santiago, though it wasn't true. He knew immediately that there could be only one person behind that kind of a catastrophe; his brother was back.

Inside the house, Vicente Moya and Maria Serrano were seated at the kitchen table, he absorbed in thought, she in prayer. At the height of the storm they'd lost sight of Miguel, but clearly, so it seemed, their son had managed to escape the crowd. Vicente Moya crumpled.

"It's my fault," he said, shaking.

"It's not your fault," replied Maria Serrano, taking his hands in hers.

"Too much beauty," he added, gracefully kissing them.

But about this last point, recounting the events of that evening to Soledad Sanchez and Santiago, Maria Serrano naturally didn't say a word. The boy listened unruffled to the entire affair but couldn't manage to feel genuine concern about his brother.

When she was through, he said, "I'll go look for him," for that was what his parents were hoping to hear him say.

"I'll walk Soledad home and then go look for him," he clarified right after, for Soledad's benefit too, as he took her hand and carried her off.

When they were at the end of the hall and about to go out, in a flash of pride Santiago decided Miguel wouldn't rob him of that moment too.

"I'll be right back," he told Soledad, and disappeared into his room.

Miguel ran all the way to Camilo Orioles's bar, one of the few in the city open all hours, the same place Vicente Moya had taught him how to drink and how to forgive. In effect, drink and forgiveness were what he needed, given his guilt, then and now, for the hatred of the Americans, the rage of the women in the courtyard, the torment of Rosita Romero, the broken dreams of all the girls he'd used, the boyfriends and husbands he'd trampled now babbling like collection agents in his head. No more joy, no more happiness. But he walked into Camilo Orioles's *posada*, bare-chested and barefoot, and felt relieved: there were no women there, just a pinch of drinkers and cardplayers, bad lighting, smoke. What was more, for a few pesos the bartender could be counted on to serve up a *jarra* of beer, nachos, and sound advice from behind the bar.

"What happened?" he asked, seeing Miguel half-naked.

Miguel ordered a *cerveza* and drank it in one gulp without taking a breath.

"I hurt people," he said, drying his lips on his arm.

Orioles scratched his head and mulled it over. He picked up a newspaper from behind the bar, flipped to the page he was looking for, filled another *jarra* to the brim, and set both paper and *jarra* down in front of Miguel.

"On the house," he added.

The newspaper pictured a necromancer kneeling on the ground with his arms raised to the sky, bent backward, a fire blazing behind him. Above it the headline announced La Noche de Brujos, All Hallows' Eve. The first Friday of March in the city of Catemaco, in the state of Veracruz.

Miguel drank one beer then another, tore the page out of the paper, and stuck it in his pocket. He felt enough time had passed for him to return home.

He arrived in the same condition he'd left: his hair hanging down past his bare shoulders, his muscles aching, his mind cloudy with beer and emotion. In the doorway he found Soledad Sanchez, but he didn't recognize her with her back turned to him. Besides, he'd only seen her once from very far away on the day he'd returned from Chamula, when Santiago had chased her away to ensure that they never met. He stopped just behind her, thinking she was the last woman left in the courtyard, the most tenacious, the boldest, for having waited till that hour, in his house no less, where what prevailed was an end-of-party, day-after-the-day-of-the-dead air.

She was alone, waiting for Santiago, two steps away from the Moya brothers' room; one step away from the open door and, though she couldn't have known it, from Miguel; and a step away from the shrine to Hermenegildo Serrano. She extracted a *cempasúchil* from the vase on the side table and sniffed it. Perhaps, she thought, Santiago would return from his room with a ring.

Miguel reached out a hand and touched her arm to get her to turn around. Soledad Sanchez turned to face a fate not glimpsed in any of her premonitions. A fate in which Santiago reappeared in the hallway at that exact moment carrying the *maquech*. A fate in which he walked in on a scene that, by all appearances, was the same scene he'd witnessed years before when his grandfather was lying in an open casket and Rosita Romero was holding a *cempasúchil*, and the way Miguel looked at her foretold everything to come, and he dragged her off and slept with her on the bed in Casa Serrano where Santiago hadn't managed to sleep with Soledad Sanchez. And now Soledad was standing half naked in front of Miguel, her hand on Miguel's arm, and in Santiago's eyes she seemed willing to let herself be carried off without a word. None of it was true, but that's all Santiago saw, or managed to make out.

The box Santiago was holding fell to the floor and popped open. The *maquech*, the live beetle coated with pearls and rhinestones, the equivalent of an engagement ring, scooted slowly across the floor. Santiago felt like he'd lost something for good: the way the beetle turned from him symbolized Soledad's turning from him and toward Miguel. It was an event that, somewhere inside him, he'd long regarded as inevitable. Yet he'd hoped, was even convinced, that Soledad would be his alone. In the lingering vibrations in the courtyard, Santiago reacted with pure violence. After pummeling Alfonsino Ruiz, he had sworn to Miguel that he'd never lay a hand on anyone again, but now he narrowed the gap between them with a closed fist and struck Miguel in the face. Miguel took it. He wasn't capable of defending himself against anything or anyone, least of all his brother, nor did he want to; by equivocating, maybe he was finally paying for their life lived at close range, at opposite poles.

The punch was unbelievable; Santiago hit him with all he had.

The blow sent Miguel a mile back, brought him to his knees, split open his cheek, and marred his beauty. Blood flew between the two brothers and splattered across the floor, as when Pan had bitten Miguel either for hunger or vengeance. There were no more sheets of paper on the floor. The bright drawings of the happy boy and the bleak drawings of the sad boy belonged to a time that was long gone, yet it was all there, pierced by the cry of Soledad Sanchez, a discharge of pure feeling, irreparable disappointment. The scream brought Maria Serrano and Vicente Moya from the kitchen; including the photo of Hermenegildo Serrano above his shrine, that meant everyone was there in the hallway when love died and Soledad stared at Santiago and cried, choking back her tears, searching for words between her hiccups.

"Do I really know you?" was all she murmured, once again, before recoiling and running off.

Santiago felt as if he'd ruined everything, lost everything. He looked Miguel up and down, looked at his speechless parents, looked at the cold gaze of his grandpa in the photo. Finally, he raised his foot, brought it down sharply on the *maquech*, and sent rhinestones and beetle guts flying.

Too Much Beauty

Sueño
SLEEP

What remained of that punch was in the conscience of the giver, the receiver, and those who saw it spring from Santiago's fist and land on Miguel's face. Soledad Sanchez shut herself up. Miguel left, departed first thing the next day, puffy face and all. Like Hermenegildo Serrano after the night his car broke down, Santiago let that moment finish him off. He quit working and only left the house to dull his senses at Camilo Orioles's bar. The rest of the time he slept, particularly during the day. At some point he purchased a TV, installed it in his room, and lay down on a recliner where he passed the time devouring junk. He got fat, stopped thinking of Soledad, and lived vicariously through telenovelas divvied up into thousands of episodes. He expected them to tell him how to patch together the bits of his own broken life. In the end, after months of one continual flow of canned scripts and close-ups interrupted only by commercial breaks, he figured there was no way to patch things together. Maybe one day he would wake up just as his grandpa had and go drop dead in Plaza Mayor, the square where in another life he'd turned the pages of a book and dreamed of love. Or maybe he'd expire on the recliner, choke on the food he ate to distract himself.

Catemaco wasn't what Miguel had pictured after seeing the newspaper in Camilo Orioles's bar. It was full of tourists on the hunt for bargain-bin spirituality and pushcart vendors in every corner of a city that petered out at the lakeshore. The morning after Santiago hit him, he climbed aboard a truck transporting cocoa beans and settled into a long sad journey sweetened by the smell of chocolate mixed with gasoline. Six hundred miles from Mérida, from home, from his brother, he felt far enough away to stop, and in that setting were a lake, the White Monkey Hill where the *brujos* gathered once a year, and the city of Catemaco, dozing in the sluggish quiet of the early afternoon. Crossing it by foot, smarting from the blue bruise on his cheek, he got the feeling he didn't like the place, yet he'd stay. His decision was due to exhaustion and the desire to remain, as far as possible, hidden from the world in a hotel room while his scar healed. A nondescript sign advertised the Hotel Josefa. He found himself in a small room with a ceiling fan and a queen-size bed on which he'd pass the time merely waiting for the pain to fade.

Then there was the true story of Belisario Lopez, who resurfaced one afternoon at the end of February when the circus pitched its tent in the city. Clowns and chimpanzees led by a camel and an elephant bringing up the rear paraded through the streets of Mérida. Playing drums and trumpets, distributing paper flowers and flyers, they marched past a swarm of screaming children.

Belisario Lopez recognized that racket, the music. He had once walked in crimson coattails with that menagerie. Before arriving in Mérida, he worked with the circus, a secret he meticulously guarded in order not to tarnish his phony image as a professional hammock salesman. Back then he specialized in conjuring tricks and hoodoo that he'd concocted with the same sick imagination with which, years later, he pulled a fair-trade store out of his hat. The low point of his performance consisted in rolling up his jacket and shirtsleeves and sticking half his arm and a black rabbit into a rigged meat grinder. The

contraption spit out bloody bits of offal amid the crowd's horrified screams while Lopez pretended to writhe in pain. Then
the machine would stop, he'd appear to struggle for another
moment, and in the end, with a flourish, he'd pull the rabbit
out of the meat grinder, brandishing it by the ears, miracu-
lously alive, healthy, and—of all things—white. The crowd
cheered in relief.

The night the machine jammed, clouds of white and black
rabbit hair sailed through the tent, and Belisario Lopez's cry
tore a hole in the sky before he fainted from the pain. He woke
up with three fingers missing and promptly abandoned the circus.

On that February afternoon, when he heard the familiar
brouhaha drawing closer, he was lying in a hammock in the
store, the spot where he now spent most of his time, ever since
he'd been abandoned by the Moya brothers. He looked out at
the street. A clown, approaching with a flyer, recognized him.

"So this is where you wound up?" he asked. The other nodded. "What business you in?"

"Hammocks," answered Lopez. He was about to give him
the spiel about fair-trade practices but then stopped himself.
In effect, he'd been less willing to talk ever since Miguel had
confronted him.

"How's it going?" the clown asked, pointing at his two
remaining fingers.

"Ancient history," Lopez said dismissively, fanning them
under his nose.

The man flashed him the same clownish smile that was
drawn on his face.

"If you feel like coming to see us again," he said, extending
three free tickets.

As soon as they said their goodbyes, Belisario Lopez threw
the tickets in the trash can and lay back down in his hammock.
But then he got an idea—maybe this was the opportunity he'd

been waiting for to relaunch his business. He put on a panama hat, fished the tickets out of the trash, closed the store, and walked across the city. With every step he grew more hopeful.

When he knocked on the door at Casa Moya, Maria Serrano answered. She knew immediately what he was after. She didn't like the man, had never liked the way he employed her children, but she'd even prefer to see Santiago back in the plaza hawking hammocks for Belisario Lopez than in his current daze in front of the TV.

"He's in his room," she said, pointing the way. "Would you care for a coffee?"

"I appreciate the offer, but no," replied Belisario Lopez, doffing his hat and heading for the boy. He found Santiago half asleep in the recliner. He placed a hand on his shoulder, and though Santiago opened his eyes, he hardly reacted. It had been months since he'd last seen Lopez, yet it struck him as almost normal to encounter him in his own house. It was if he'd been expecting him.

"What do you want?" he asked listlessly.

"I brought you these," said the man, holding out the circus tickets.

Santiago didn't deign to look at him. Belisario Lopez set them on top of the TV, which was hot enough to fry an egg on.

"I thought—" Lopez began.

"Not interested," Santiago interrupted.

"I just wanted—"

"I said I'm not interested!" Santiago shot back, raising his voice.

Belisario Lopez sensed it was hopeless. He turned and made for the door. He wanted to rail against Santiago, insult him somehow, but when he turned around again, he merely felt pity for the boy. He returned to the shop in a state of frustration and compassion—for himself too—tinged with wistfulness, also, for his days in the circus, days never to return, just like the days of building his business on the backs of the Moya brothers. And for a moment, as the afflicted man wended his way through the streets and in his thoughts, he seemed to feel again the unbearable pain of the meat grinder in that instant before fainting.

One punch was all it took to pin both brothers to the ground. It had leveled them, made them apathetic, though now they couldn't talk to one another about it. The hotel room in the middle of Catemaco welcomed Miguel, who slept so as not to think, yet ended up the victim of recurring nightmares that carried him back six months and hundreds of miles to the center of the courtyard and the hallway he'd fled from. He relived particular scenes as if they were real and repeatedly woke up covered in sweat and crying out loud. Santiago usually appeared in his dreams, but Miguel never found a way to talk to or touch his brother.

"I hurt people," he kept muttering unconsolably.

One particularly bad night, as a steady drizzle fell outside his window, he suddenly woke up to find himself on the wooden platform in the middle of the Moyas' courtyard, devastated by the inhuman rage of that evening. And in the crowd fighting at his feet—a single, writhing, vomiting body—there stood an old lady a few feet away, immobile, staring at him, her eyes pierced by a rank pain, wearing a pink quinceañera dress.

Miguel stood up and ran to the bathroom mirror to get a look at himself. His hair had grown so long he had to push it back with his hands, a gesture that made him sick of himself and his hair. He grabbed a pair of scissors from the cabinet and began cutting it, calmly at first, then gradually more frenzied. Black tufts of hair fell to the floor at an increasingly feverish, ferocious rate, and the clip-clip echoed in the room as Miguel scissored away, wracked with anxiety, possessed by a self-destructive force. When he was through, his snipped hair on the ground, his head shaved, he let out a triumphant cry, as if he'd fought and slain his enemy. Yet in the fragile and dim evening light the enemy was still there, staring back at him in the mirror, stronger than before, because now that his hair was gone his face came fully into view.

With the gloomy sermon of the rain going on outside, Miguel looked at himself with no expression whatsoever. Then, with the detachment of someone who has lost his soul, he pressed the sharp end of the scissors against his face, above the spot where Santiago's knuckles had opened a gash on his cheek. He tried to disfigure himself, to strip away his beauty, to hurt himself so as not to hurt anyone else. The skin opened, the blood ran from his cheek and down his neck, the neck of the beautiful boy, and, seeing himself, Miguel came to his senses, returned from wherever it was he'd gone, stopped the stroke of the blade before it was too late. He couldn't do it, not like that, not alone. He dropped the scissors on the floor in a fit of terror, realizing in that instant that the solution was to ask for help, for someone to place a hand on his chest and scoop out the heart of whatever evil spirit possessed him—realizing in that instant that there was such a place, such an event, and it had been expecting him ever since he'd left. The place was White Monkey Hill. The event was La Noche de Brujos.

As he did every night, Vicente Moya peered into Santiago's dark room and stared at him, though he never found the courage to confront him. He watched him sleep, the words caught in his throat; that the boy had let himself get fat and weak disgusted him. Most of all, while he watched him he was gripped by a feeling of rage, which mounted a little more every night, at his stupidity for giving up the one girl who had courted him and at the action that had driven Miguel away. To Vicente Moya's mind, it was that punch that had brought an end to the dances, the parties in the courtyard, the days of abandon. He'd decided that the violence that had erupted in the courtyard was not the cause but the effect of Santiago's having hit his brother, that everything had ended as a result of that gratuitous and irrational blow with which the boy had selfishly decided to draw the curtain on the best time of their lives. Essentially, he made Santiago the scapegoat that he needed to accept the change, go back to their previous mediocrity, and bury his own guilt about the slaughterhouse of the courtyard, an event he himself had planned and promoted, which he didn't have the courage to contemplate; it was easier to stare at his son, grumble under his breath, nurse a grievance against a sleeping enemy who had no means of returning fire.

That night Maria Serrano got up to get a drink and found her husband standing at Santiago's door, lost in thought. Vicente Moya fumbled for something to say to defend himself.

"You don't plant trees when a moon is waning," he said under his breath, referring to the night that they'd conceived Santiago.

Maria Serrano didn't think twice about what prompted his words, which had come months after Miguel's departure, a period when her husband had been absorbed with the question of what was or what could have been. She slapped Vicente Moya with an open palm that left him crushed and consumed with rancor, doubt, anxiety, and fear.

"Don't you ever say that again," she muttered, her lips quivering.

Vicente Moya was stunned by his wife's reaction; she'd never laid a hand on him before. He studied her in the dark, disfigured by the tension, and suddenly found her hideous. He took a step back, silently withdrew, went out to smoke a cigarette, completely at a loss as to what had just happened, what was happening, yet he felt the palpable desire to leave, to clear out, like Miguel.

Santiago witnessed the scene. Lying around all day, he

couldn't sleep at night and would lie half awake, observing his father in the doorway while he pretended to sleep. He couldn't make out Vicente Moya's words, but he saw Maria Serrano smack him and figured it was his own fault. Everything was his fault—that's how he saw it. No different from the way his father saw it. And yet, after months of nothing but telenovelas, for some reason Santiago also had the distinct sensation that they had all arrived at the final episode, that they couldn't go on like this, and that he would be the one to put everything right.

The next morning he woke up early and made his parents breakfast.

"I'm taking you to the circus tonight," he said, and set the three tickets down on the table.

Demasiada belleza
TOO MUCH BEAUTY

The big top was hoisted on the same field Vicente Moya had rented for Miguel's first birthday party. After all those years, he could still hear the people of Mérida clapping in his honor as he stood onstage and hugged the Virgen de Guadalupe.

With Belisario Lopez's tickets, they wound up in the front row, a hair's breadth away from the parade of ostriches, little people, horses, trapeze artists, lions, zebras, and clowns, which presented the Moyas—who had never been to the circus before—with an occasion to smile again, to huddle together like a happy family. Next to his parents, Santiago devoured an enormous box of popcorn and felt like a kid again, back before Miguel was born. What a brilliant idea this was, he thought, to bring Maria Serrano and Vicente Moya here; maybe the joy of that evening would carry over into the house, and things would return to normal, as if nothing had happened. He even considered going back to work for Belisario Lopez in a few days—after all, he'd given him a precious gift and was partly responsible for this new lease on life heralded by the blare of trumpets, rings of fire, roars of wild beasts, and pirouettes in the air.

A small basket made of palm leaves was set down in the middle of the tent as a shirtless man played the flute in total silence. Shortly after, there appeared the head of a boa constrictor, big as a fist. The crowd gasped. Once the snake had fully emerged, it seemed impossible that it could have fit inside that basket, which was why the big top shook with cheers when next from the basket emerged a woman in nothing but a skimpy gold costume who unfurled her body, like the snake. She rose to her feet, picked up the boa, and draped it over her shoulders.

The woman's name was Frida Ribeiro, and after taking a bow, she approached the crowd with the reptile still over her shoulders and looked for a participant for the next act. It didn't take long; she'd already picked him out. She'd noticed him as soon as she was out of the basket, his distinctive if slightly faded beauty amid a sea of ugliness, and as she had a hundred times, she went over to collect him in order to savor him close up. As she extended her hand, it struck Vicente Moya as perfectly natural to stand and accept her invitation, to follow her to the center of the ring and welcome the crowd's applause in the very spot where he'd been applauded years before.

Maria Serrano and Santiago remained looking in from outside, just as they had that long-ago night, and the young man stopped shoveling popcorn down his throat, now gripped by the same anxiety he'd felt as a little boy when all he'd wanted was to return home. Vicente Moya, on the other hand, excited to reprise the leading role he'd played in his own courtyard, agreed to the show with levity, displaying a courage rightly attributed to his carelessness and pride yet which appeared to Frida Ribeiro as a fascinating demonstration of bravura. She had led many beautiful men to the target stand and seen them transformed by fear when the first blade grazed them.

"Don't move," she told Vicente Moya once they were aligned with the target and holding one another as if they were about to dance. But he had no intention of moving, in part because the woman, with feigned indifference, had already seized on the chance to press her breasts against him. They smelled nice, stuffed into her costume to make them more pronounced. A moment later the flute player, Ribeiro's lifelong partner, snatched up his knives and began furiously throwing them. They whistled in the air and landed a few inches from the body of the woman, the boa, Vicente Moya. Vicente Moya had guessed what was coming before the first dagger arrived, but by now he was already elsewhere, swept up in the sweet aroma rising from Frida Ribeiro's chest and in the green liquid of her eyes that reached into his soul and down his trousers, kindling a desire that he hadn't felt in a long time.

"Who's getting married?" asked Frida, staring at his guayabera.

And Vicente Moya, who had always been a man of few words, at that moment felt there was only one word that held any meaning.

"Us," he answered firmly, as a knife hit the wall just above his shoulder, an inch from his heart. It was an answer that he seemed to have stolen from Miguel, one he'd never have had the courage to venture under rational circumstances, but it came to him in the spur of the moment, and he didn't feel a trace of guilt. Right after he'd said it, Vicente Moya had convinced himself it was the correct answer and should therefore be stood by. He straightened his shoulders and lifted his chin to throw his profile into relief.

Just like that, after having ducked a thousand knives, Frida Ribeiro let Vicente Moya's voice, word, promise—on top of the statuesque beauty and audacity of this stranger whom she'd plucked out of the crowd in Mérida, whom she'd chosen above everyone else—pierce her skin. She stared at Vicente Moya with an intensity unlike any she'd shown the others, trying to understand whether he really meant it. And he, drunk on the feeling of danger aroused by the knives raining down on them, responded by tightening his grip on her side, as if to prove that he intended to carry her off, then and there, half naked in her gold circus costume. They were being watched by thousands of eyes, grazed by dozens of sharp blades, yet to him this was a deeply erotic, private dance. He'd never felt such energy, like a river of lava under the ground. He felt as though he'd regained the faith he'd lost after Miguel's departure, as though he were returning to the dance floor, and this time he wanted to dance for the rest of his days on earth. Wanted to die dancing.

Maria Serrano connected this image to that of Vicente Moya in the same field when he was in thrall to the Virgen de Guadalupe and little Miguel. Back then she'd believed that it was the Señora who had stolen her husband, but she'd been mistaken. It had been a foreshadowing. In her son's place there was a gigantic snake, which seemed to embody the devil, and in the Virgin's place stood Frida Ribeiro, a professional contortionist, the farthest thing from a virgin.

The same thought crossed the mind of Frida Ribeiro's partner, who for years, each time they put on their show, suffered in secret knowing that she would choose whom she wanted in the hopes of finding the man she'd always been waiting for. He saw her quiver at the stranger's words and in a flash of jealousy wanted to strike back, to hit her square in the head with the next knife and finally have done with his wretched suffering. But at the last instant he came to his senses and with an imperceptible flick of his wrist tilted just enough to send the blade flying elsewhere, or so he hoped, and then shut his eyes.

Instead the crowd's horrified cry told him he'd killed.

When he reopened his eyes, half a minute later, he saw the bloody head of the snake pinned to the target, the rest of its long body writhing in agony. Barely a step away, Frida Ribeiro and Vicente Moya were holding each other even tighter than before. They were indivisible. They held each other the way you do when you've just eluded death.

The first Friday of March, Miguel was standing on top of Cerro Mono Blanco, having climbed there to free himself from the curse of beauty. Shirtless in the firelight. His arms extended in the middle of a Star of David drawn in the dirt. Thousands of candles flickered and as many faithful and curious onlookers huddled together in a circle, their arms raised, goading him on with prayers and chants. There was also a plethora of magi, authorities and amateurs, witch doctors, prophets, and charlatans. Down in the city tolled the church bells of the Basilica of Carmen. That afternoon the grand *Misa Negra* had taken place, the mass to cleanse the black spirit, a purification ritual of the *brujos blancos* to wipe away the stain of sinners. They had carried the sculpture of the Virgen del Volcán here from the church. The virgin was so named because she had turned into a statue after appearing to a fisherman on the day that the Sierra de los Tuxtlas volcano erupted. There she was, right behind Miguel, as she had been on the night of his first birthday. He couldn't remember that night, when his otherworldly beauty was publicly sanctioned— that beauty he was today repudiating—under the gaze of the infatuated people of Mérida, under the afflicted gaze of Maria Serrano and Santiago, who had already sensed the burden of that beauty and the price they would pay for it. In front of Miguel, in the place once occupied by Vicente Moya, stood the master himself—the *Brujo Mayor*. He wasn't going to pass up the opportunity; he had noticed the beautiful boy and approached him, having intuited that such a figure would add luster to the whole ceremony. Asking nothing in return, he offered to perform a *limpia*, a rite of redemption.

That was how everything began and how everything ended, with drumbeats in the background drifting up to the sky while the grand master loomed over the young man like an enormous angel in a sheer white robe with a bushy beard and eyebrows. He placed a hand on his head, invoking el Señor del Encanto and pointing to the energy points around Catemaco: the hill itself, the Sierra de Santa Martha, and the Laguna Encantada, whose waters were moved by wizards. He ran his large dark fingers over Miguel's shaved head and, with swift movements, made to exorcise the evil. Then he drank and spat a jet of water on the boy to cure him, following a ritual of the Olmecs, the ancient inhabitants of those lands who had chiseled the colossal heads into the basalt of the surrounding volcanic belt.

Miguel cleared his mind. In fact, he'd stopped thinking months ago. He was swept up in the witchcraft, in the magic-engendering atmosphere, and his emotional participation intensified the event. He didn't believe in anything, yet he wanted to believe, and the energy that was unleashed from the middle of the Star of David on the summit of Cerro Mono Blanco was so powerful, shook so much that it seemed as if the hill would transform into a volcano, as if it might erupt right under the bare feet of the boy who was expecting to be healed of his beauty or perhaps punished for his presumption. No one could comprehend that burden, that millstone. All that endured was the sensation that White Monkey Hill, which shook with endless drumbeats, might open its mouth of rock, fire, and lava, and swallow the entire sabbath, the master of ceremonies, the multitude of people chanting in a circle around them, and the tents clinging to the slope, studded with totems, amulets, brews, love potions, and tarot cards. The sense of foreboding washed over the more than two hundred *brujos* and *brujas*, chiromancers, fortune-tellers, herbalists, and *curanderos* who, despite traveling to Catemaco once a year, had never felt an energy that profound. It was like a river of lava was under their feet. They looked on in astonishment, aware that they were witnessing a sensational, unprecedented spell, and afraid it might be their last.

But the ritual came to an end. Nothing happened. The hill remained where it was.

The *Brujo Mayor* lifted his arms to deliver one last prayer and liberate Miguel, who ignored the thunderous applause around him and avoided looking at anyone lest he discover the truth in their eyes. He walked with his head down, one step at a time, descending the hill, drifting through the streets of Catemaco to his hotel to return to hiding from the world. Then he fell asleep, same as always, only for the first time in months, perhaps exhausted by the pressure of the event, he slept a long, dreamless sleep. At sunup the next day he gathered his small rucksack, settled up at the hotel, and boarded the first bus out of Catemaco with no particular destination in mind. Miguel got lost in the world, as was his destiny.

Three days later the circus struck the tent in Mérida, churning up a cloud of dust on the edge of the city. Maria Serrano ran out to meet the caravan of cars, trailers, trucks, and cages bearing bored-looking animals.

"Have you seen my husband?" she asked desperately.

Everyone had but no one answered her. They kept moving, pretending not to have understood her question. The knife thrower got out of his van and approached her to say something, but then changed his mind. He simply threw up his arms. A few hours later, word in the city was that Vicente Moya was last seen on the sidewalk outside the bus station just before boarding the coach, his destination unknown, in his loosely buttoned guayabera, a suitcase in hand, and, by his side, a small basket made of palm leaves.

When Maria Serrano arrived home, aggrieved and disoriented, Santiago was sitting at the kitchen table with his head in his hands.

"It's my fault," was all he managed to say to his mother.

What came to Maria Serrano's mind was the same phrase Vicente Moya had uttered the night that Miguel had played in the courtyard and catastrophe had ruined them. That moment, in which the man had admitted his responsibility and fragility, seemed to her the last time she had felt truly close to him.

"It's not your fault," she told her son. Same as she'd told her husband.

"Demasiada belleza," she added in a whisper. "Too much beauty."

A Sentimental Map

Mapa de un sentimento
A SENTIMENTAL MAP

As soon as the envelope arrived, Santiago knew what he'd find inside. A sip of cold beer, the smell of fried chicken wafting in the hallway of his house, his shirt stained with hot salsa, his fingers smearing grease on the crumpled envelope mailed from afar, the faded postal seal from an office that could have been anywhere, that might not even exist. He pictured it: dirty, cramped, a fan hanging from the ceiling above a guy in shirtsleeves groggily stamping a hundred, a thousand letters a day. Or else just one, just this one, just the envelope Miguel had sent him bearing snapshots of his endless, aimless journey—panoramas he'd taken with the plastic camera Santiago had given him, a dozen or so shots of the world, which he mailed a couple of times a year for about three years. Nothing else. Instead, he opened it and found an actual letter in his brother's faint script, a letter that Santiago had been waiting for forever, even if he didn't know it yet.

Every year, twice a year, once he'd studied them, Santiago would tack the photographs from the latest envelope to the walls of the closet, which had become a window on the world. Afterward he would count them from first to last, a task that generally took him a long time. He'd lose count, start over.

He just barely found comfort in that number; as he counted, he crumpled up the one envelope from Miguel that didn't contain images, that weighed less yet more, that bore words he didn't have the courage to look at. There were seventy-six photos tacked to the wall. By the time he got to the last he had gone around the world with him again, if only in his mind, in a relationship that the images intimated while intimating places he had nothing to do with.

On the day Miguel's first letter arrived at Casa Moya, Santiago hadn't even opened it. He'd buried it in the dark chest of drawers in the dark closet—out of sight, out of mind.

On the day the second arrived, six months later, Santiago's feelings had mellowed. He looked at it for a whole minute before deciding what to do, then made his way back to the closet and stuck it in the back of the drawer next to the first.

On the day the next letter arrived, Santiago instinctively stuck it inside his trousers. It had been a year and a half since he'd laid eyes on Miguel. He carried it with him for the whole day, close to his skin. That night he locked himself in the closet, took the envelope from his pocket, exhumed the earlier letters from the drawer, and opened them in the order in which they'd been mailed. By candlelight he discovered that, rather than words, they contained flashes of time, fragments of places far away caught by the lens of his Polaroid.

From that day on, about every six months, Santiago performed the same ritual: he locked himself in the storage closet, opened the latest letter, immersed himself in the journey, followed his brother's trail through landscapes that for him remained out there, in the snapshot of a moment in Miguel's life. As he ran his eyes over each he would inevitably imagine his brother smiling on the other end of the camera, a woman running his fingers through his hair, a different woman every time yet always amused, already in love.

On his walls was laundry hanging from a balcony on a side street in Barceloneta, brightly colored rocks and cacti above the dunes of the Mojave Desert, straw hats lit by sunbeams filtering through market tents in Bangkok, large Irish clouds scuttling across a paddock of sheep with black muzzles, the reflection of a bonfire on the foamy shores of the Whitsundays. Everything was there, with the exception of Miguel, who was in every single fragment and none in particular. Maybe that was why Santiago managed to let himself be swept up by them, accepted the letters, opened them, abandoned himself to their contents. It came to him all of a sudden after being separated for three years. He understood that every single photo taken, fanned in the air, stuck into an envelope with a stamp, then shipped, received, opened, nailed to the wall and contemplated, was something more than another step in the world. It was a step closer to this moment.

Santiago had returned to working on occasion. He needed beer money. One day he walked by the Casa de Guayaberas, entered, dropped his father's name—just that once and for the last time—and procured the job he wanted: bringing in clients for a commission. He didn't haggle over the cut the Casita owner offered. He strode back out into the plaza and convinced Mérida's tourists that a fancy shirt could suit you regardless of if you were Mexican, regardless of if you had a wedding to attend. As always in Plaza Mayor, he caught up on the latest goings-on. One afternoon he noticed Alfonsino Ruiz, big and broad, hugging a girl, a ring on his finger. Ruiz recognized him and smiled. Santiago lifted his chin in greeting. In the plaza he also discovered that Soledad Sanchez had moved to the other side of the city and was engaged to a guy from an affluent family. Santiago appeared to take it in stride, but that evening he anesthetized himself by doubling his regular intake of beer in Camilo Orioles's place, which was where he was holed up now, in the usual pall of smoke and shadows. The bartender wiped off a glass and watched him read, for the fourth time, Miguel's letter.

"He get himself in a bind?" he asked after a while.

"Who?" replied Santiago.

"Your brother," the owner said, pointing to the letter.

"How'd you know it was from him?"

Orioles stared at him intensely and slowly puffed on his Cuban cigar, which he continued to chew with his toothless mouth.

"It's written on your face."

Santiago took a breath. It was out of necessity that he'd wound up under Orioles's watch. In the closet, after reading a few lines, he'd come across the words that he could neither swallow nor stomach. He blew out the candle, let himself be engulfed in darkness, lingered in a black well of memories. Maybe that's how it all ends, he thought: locked in a closet without a light. He felt dead inside, so he left closet and house behind and cut across the neighborhood streets until his path sputtered out at the bar. He had set the letter down on the counter, his mug of beer on the letter. And once he'd drained his beer the letter seemed easier to read. He gave it another go, slowly reached the end, started over, read it again.

"Besides, the last time I saw him he'd gotten himself in a real bind."

"When was that?" asked Santiago.

"Years ago."

Santiago picked up the letter. He drew it close, as if to drown in it, flush out every detail from the pores of a sheet of paper that had the whiff of oceans and regrets. Then he removed the envelope from his pocket. He could just make out the name of the place it came from on the postmark. Slowly, patiently, Santiago unscrambled the name, and finally turned to the bartender, who had an answer for everything.

"Where is Topolobampo?" he asked.

Camilo Orioles sneered disdainfully, as if the question were beneath him. He took one last puff of his cigar, removed it from his mouth, and stubbed it out on the counter next to the black rings of other cigars that he'd smoked and disposed of just like that. He exhaled a cloud of smoke.

"How the hell should I know?"

Santiago's night was like a Cuba Libre with no ice. Alcoholic, dark, warm. He tossed this way and that in his hammock. The quiet rumble of Mérida was unbearable. Maybe he'd had too much beer, too many memories.

"Teresa?"

"Who's that?"

"It's Santiago, Santiago Moya."

"What is it, Santiago?"

When she wasn't working at the stationery store, Teresa Rodríguez was busy raising the four kids she'd given birth to all in a row. They slept with her on the same mattress that in the morning welcomed her husband, a night attendant at a *gasolinera*. As he came down from his shift, Teresa would scramble eggs and leave to open the shop. The runts would scarf down their warm eggs and then go back to bed with their father; out of necessity they had learned to sleep for fifteen, sixteen hours a day, like cats. Meanwhile the woman sold newspapers, read novels, and reshelved hundreds of road maps and world maps.

"Where's Topolobampo, Teresa?"

Teresa Rodriguez knew immediately that underneath Santiago's middle-of-the-night question lay Miguel, just as he had years before.

"Topolobampo is in the state of Sinaloa, Santiago."

"Sinaloa? What part of the world is that?"

"What do you mean what part?"

"I mean what side of the ocean?"

Teresa Rodríguez sighed. She was whispering so as not to wake up her children.

"Sinaloa is in Mexico."

Santiago lowered his voice too. He didn't want his mother, asleep in the room next door, to hear him.

"In Mexico?" he whispered in disbelief.

"Sinaloa borders Chihuahua, Sonora, Durango, Nayarit, and the Gulf of California. The capital is Culiacán. Topolobampo is in the municipality of Ahome, not far from Los Mochis, the municipal seat."

Santiago grew quiet. He'd been picturing Miguel on the opposite end of the planet. He had pictured a whole ocean separating them. Days, months, years, a lifetime of traveling. Instead they were treading the same turf, he and Miguel, their home turf. This discovery came as a surprise but, to his mind, didn't change much; his brother was still far away. Teresa Rodríguez may have traveled by running her fingers across a map, but Santiago had never gotten even that far. He had never left Yucatán, not once. On a couple of occasions, as a boy, he had ridden a donkey half a mile or so beyond the city limits on an errand for Vicente Moya.

The door to his room opened. Maria Serrano had woken up. In her sleep she had heard Santiago whispering on the telephone and it was his whispering that disturbed her most of all. She came out in her nightgown and found him there, cradling the receiver, staring off into space, at a country that he could only try—unsuccessfully—to imagine.

"Santiago, what is going on?"

He looked at her in the dark. Never before had he felt so much like her, the son of an unbeautiful mother, abandoned by Vicente Moya one June night for the skirt of a contortionist. Or else he'd left out of some sense of justice. Santiago looked but couldn't see her; all that emerged from the shadows was her flimsy white gown and the few white tufts in her hair. He had never felt so abandoned—by Miguel.

"It's your brother, isn't it?" asked Maria Serrano, as if she had been expecting that moment all her life, as if that picture of the two of them—Santiago shirtless, clutching the phone to his chest; her barefoot, all dreams expired—had hung in the hallway forever. The same hallway that, like Mérida, silently enclosed them.

Santiago hung up the phone, took a deep breath, then dug up the truth. Maria Serrano read the letter without saying a word. Not till reaching the end did she signal to her son to follow her.

In the kitchen she climbed on top of a chair, reached into the back of the cupboard, extracted a coffee tin, and set it down on the table.

"Your father left it," she said.

She opened it. Inside was the savings Vicente Moya had accumulated during the years of their courtyard parties, rolled into a wad of bills, which he'd forgotten or left behind to clear his conscience.

"Take it. Go find your brother."

S antiago didn't sleep. His brother's letter may have kept
him awake, but his father's pesos had filled him with
dread. Because Vicente Moya's money and Maria
Serrano's blessing meant he had the privilege of deciding. He
wasn't used to that kind of privilege. He curled up in his hammock, his protective cocoon, and tried rocking himself to
sleep, but sleep didn't come. When the sun came up, Santiago
was still awake and felt the urge to go outside, to walk in order
to clear his head, to abandon his thoughts to the night he hadn't
slept through, to the room that was Miguel's, where traces of
him remained. He vaguely remembered having swept his
brother's hammock into a pile on the floor. At some point he
had simply decided to take it down.

"Why did you remove it?" Maria Serrano had asked that
day.

"For more space," Santiago answered, unable to meet
her eye.

But the next moment he knew he had no idea what to do
with that space. And he never did fill the void. Nor the void his
brother had left in the house, in the courtyard outside the
house, in every corner of the city, in the bars, plazas, streets,
nor in himself. He never filled it. He tiptoed outside to avoid
the maternal gaze of Maria Serrano. He didn't need to hear her
to know she was coming out of her room. Santiago walked
Mérida's network of streets, fighting off his hunger when he
got closer to Camilo Orioles's hole in the wall, from which

every morning the aroma of stewed short ribs wafted. He turned down a *calle* to avoid passing by Teresa Rodríguez's stationery store, where inside there was a map of Mexico with a line that ran from Mérida all the way to a place called Topolobampo. For hours he walked the arteries of the city that had seen him grow up and grind to a halt, down the streets he'd once traveled holding little Miguel by the hand and Soledad Sanchez by the same hand, the hand with which he'd hit his brother the last time he'd seen him, over a thousand days ago. He walked all the way to Plaza Mayor where he had once trafficked in hammocks and lies and seen his grandpa take his last breath, then he pressed on past the city. With the same restlessness as when Pan was by his side, he walked to the fields where the prostitute's trailer was now gone. There was still a trace of the love he'd paid for, a silhouette on the ground, like the silhouette that the old Ford left after Miguel stole it for his first journey. He walked all the way to the spot where he and his brother had crammed into Hermenegildo Serrano's car and Miguel taught him how to drive. And once he arrived, he looked out at the horizon beyond Mérida and tried to calculate whether he was capable of reaching that place. As always, it seemed too far away, too great a distance.

When the sun slid behind the low-slung houses of the white city, staining them black, Santiago made his way to Camilo Orioles's bar, despite the fact that the barkeep knew about the letter and, like Maria Serrano, made him feel as if he were faced with a decision, although Miguel had hardly extended an invitation.

The word "time" appeared in his letter. The word "mistake." The word "need." But there was no "reunion." Not even "meet up."

Yet deep down Santiago knew that he had to go, had to leave in search of him, just as his mother had said.

Greasy-palmed Camilo Orioles placed the mug of beer in

front of him. Santiago plunged in as if it were a lake, tried to disappear, to dilute the noise in his head, to water down his vision, to make himself invisible—to others, to himself.

"You get yourself in a bind?" asked Camilo Orioles after a while.

"Who?" answered Santiago.

"You."

It was pointless; he couldn't disappear.

"Why do you say that?"

The bartender stuck a finger in his nose, in search of something.

"Last time I saw you drink like that you were in serious shit."

Santiago tried and failed to remember that time.

"When was that?" he asked.

Camilo Orioles dug a green string of snot out of his nostril, held it out to get a better look, balled it up with his two fingers. As a matter of perspective, Santiago did disappear for a moment.

"Maybe I'm getting you mixed up with your brother," concluded Orioles, distracted, as if he were gauging how many carats his diamond weighed.

Santiago looked at him and felt a sharp disdain for that man, a feeling he may not have sufficiently investigated. In the blink of an eye, he sensed he was capable, given his disgust, of raising his mug and smashing it over his skull. The thought seemed to come from outside himself, as if it weren't his own, and took him aback. By some imperceptible impulse, his right hand was already tightening its grip on the glass handle. It was an energy that mounted inside him, tucked deep inside his stomach, under a solid layer of frustration. He interpreted it with blinding lucidity, a courage of analysis unusual for him, which spooked him, and which he tamped down by lifting the mug to his lips a second time. As soon as he'd taken a final swig

from the *jarra* and set it back down on the counter, he felt a tap
on his shoulder. Behind him was Teresa Rodríguez.

"Teresa, *¿qué pasa?*"

She had something to say but didn't know how; she'd given
it too much thought. She'd wanted to tell him that night on the
phone but hadn't managed.

"There's a ride to Topolobampo," she said. "First thing
tomorrow morning a truck will be stopping at the *gasolinera* to
fill up. It's headed in that exact direction. My husband says it's
no sweat, you just need to be there at six."

Santiago looked at her surprised, tipsy, and defenseless.

"Teresa, I don't want to go to Topolobampo," he whispered. And after that, he felt the need to say it again, only
louder.

"I'm not going anywhere!" he repeated out loud. Too loud.

Camilo Orioles and his handful of patrons turned to look at
him.

Teresa Rodríguez took it so hard that she had no strength to
respond. She looked at him incredulously, trying to understand. And maybe she did. She took a step back, then another.
But before turning around to go, she uttered one last thing.

"It's the same truck Miguel left on."

Santiago was drunk when he got back home. He'd had one
beer then another after Teresa Rodríguez had slipped out of
Camilo Orioles's bar, where the latter continued to serve him
his spotty glasses filled to the brim without passing comment,
eyeing him with a vein of respect.

Maria Serrano was waiting up, her hands in her lap, seated
in front of a cold plate of *sopa de lima*. The boy wasn't hungry
but sat down all the same.

"Should I heat it up?" his mother asked.

Santiago shook his head. He poured a large spoonful down

his throat. He repeated the operation. He was hell-bent on emptying the plate and withdrawing to his room to sleep. But after ingesting the third spoonful he felt an acidic river coursing up from his stomach.

He got up just in time to reach the window and vomit up his beer and *sopa de lima* on the dry ground at the edge of the garden. Doubled over, half inside and half outside the house, he recalled Teresa Rodríguez's words. "There's a ride to Topolobampo." It was as if he had to decide now, once and for all, whether to climb out the window and light out or go back inside and stay there for the rest of his life. Then Maria Serrano came over and ran her cool hand over his forehead, holding his head with maternal tenderness, waiting for it to pass.

Santiago let himself be coddled for a while, welcomed it, let the contact with his mother's skin calm him down. Maybe that was the answer he'd been looking for. This was where he belonged. This was the place. This was where he was protected, looked after, consoled. Here. Where he'd always been.

Then, out of nowhere, Maria Serrano whispered something.

"My baby," she whispered.

Though he couldn't explain why, Santiago had the distinct sensation that his mother wasn't referring to him, that she was caressing his forehead while thinking of the son who wasn't there. Thinking of the beautiful boy. Thinking of Miguel.

He spat out the dregs of saliva and vomit, aggressively straightened up, and wriggled out of her maternal embrace. He trained the same lost eyes on Maria Serrano that he'd trained on Teresa Rodríguez an hour earlier. And again, he felt the need to clean house, to set things straight, to shout, to reject, always to reject, to reject everything, even the evidence, even his blood, even love.

"I'm not your baby," he shouted.

He wiped his mouth with the back of his hand.

"I never was."

Maria Serrano stared at him speechless. Deep down Santiago had a right to his rage and she knew it. Deep down Santiago's rage had always been there, behind his eyes, buried under a layer of silence and distance. Deep down Santiago's rage was life, was truth. And deep down, way deep down, even if it hurt, it was a good thing. That was why Maria Serrano didn't say anything. There were no words to explain, no amount of simple excuses to keep him from drowning.

Santiago left his mother and the kitchen and went to his room. His body was shaking, his throat sore, his tears wouldn't come. He felt sleepy, very sleepy. He quickly undressed, tossed his clothes on the floor. In the dark his gaze fell on a corner of the room lit by the moon, on Miguel's hammock, which he himself had tossed there.

Santiago regarded it the way a trapeze artist regards his net: there it was underneath him; it might serve no purpose or it might save his life. He picked it up, after a painfully long time unfurled it, and hooked it to the nails on the wall, which for years had held up Miguel's body. Before he had time to regret it, Santiago leaped into it. And for just an instant he seemed to catch the sweet scent of his brother. Then he sank into a bitter sleep.

In the letter there appeared the word "remember." The words "because" and "why." The word "regret." Miguel's words flickered under Santiago's eyelids in the dreams he dreamed while flying back in time like a trapeze artist in the air, shielded by his brother's hammock.

Maria Serrrano threw away the leftover soup, closed the shutters, and tidied up the little kitchen. She was about to return to bed when she felt the need to stay. By candlelight she sat down in the seat Santiago had occupied just before, sank her finger into the bottom of the past, and she, too, traveled back in time, in the hopes of retrieving the wrongs that had been committed. When the last candle guttered out, Maria fell asleep where she sat, exhausted, serving her punishment.

Dawn found them like that, asleep in places they never slept. The house was immersed in a profound silence, broken here and there by the creak of Miguel's hammock hanging from the old nails in the wall, where, they would soon discover, destiny was about to direct its gaze. Santiago's sleep was induced by beer and fatigue, tasted of rage and vomit. A deep sleep that could last a lifetime and determine the rest of his life. Instead, with natural inertia, one of the nails came loose from the wall, yielded under the weight Santiago had gained over the years, and Santiago plunged, a trapeze artist without a net, collapsed on the floor like dead weight, hit the ground with a heavy thud, entangled in a web of broken dreams and the ropes of Miguel's hammock.

Maria Serrano woke up when her son did, seated in the kitchen, her hands in her lap, roused by the sudden crash. After a while Santiago appeared in the hallway, breathless and hesitant. He stopped and stared at her from just beyond the doorframe, as if he hadn't the strength to take another step, to think another thought.

"What time is it?" he asked with a kind of desperation.

Maria Serrano looked up at the one clock in the house, which had hung forever next to the sideboard.

"Ten to six," she said.

That was the answer Santiago was looking for, all he needed to make up his mind.

He ran back into his room, quickly dressed, stuck whatever was at hand in his canvas bag, came back out into the hall a few minutes later, only this time he took the steps he needed to take, the steps that separated him from his mother, who had been waiting for him in that spot in that way since she'd watched him disappear into his room, perhaps since the day he was born. Or since the day Miguel had been born.

Santiago entered the kitchen and relented, paused a step away from Maria Serrano, in silence. Every time Miguel had gone away he'd tendered kind words, dispensed smiles and hopes. All Santiago felt was pain, a sense of betrayal, that he was running away. Were he to try to explain, he would risk convincing himself that it was wrong to leave, so he simply knelt, pressed his lips against the back of his mother's hands, kissed them with the tenderness one displays when forgiving others and asking for forgiveness. When he looked up there were two tears running down Maria Serrano's cheeks—one forgiving, the other asking for forgiveness. Two tears unaccompanied by words, because she knew time was running out, Santiago had to leave, had to go look for his brother.

"You're a butterfly," was all Maria Serrano managed to say, thinking back on the day that she'd watched him dance in the courtyard. "Fly."

So, like Vicente Moya and Miguel before him, Santiago left. He flew, took to his heels, so that the wind would dry his tears before they had time to materialize and so that he would catch a truck that wasn't coming back. *That* was the truck he needed; there would be no others passing through town, not for him. He ran breathlessly, without looking back, kicking up dust in the narrow streets of Mérida, crossing the empty city at dawn till he'd reached the last house before the road that led to the *gasolinera*. Just past that house, as the sun bled across the horizon, Santiago watched the truck—which he'd never drawn on any sheet of paper, which was supposed to carry him far from there, which was supposed to bring him to Miguel—pull away from the gas pump, drive off at breakneck speed, and leave him behind, his stride broken, stranded in the middle of the road, a prisoner of the city.

S antiago dropped to his knees before that nothingness, before the usual prospect of giving up, wasting away, staying put, being forsaken in the middle of a now desolate road. His head bowed in prayer, a prayer consisting of curses, his fingers jabbed into the earth that wouldn't let him go, his mind filled with the bitter idea that things would always turn out that way, that he had no hope of achieving something or arriving someplace. The same sensation had come over him the night that he'd touched Soledad Sanchez's naked body but failed to make her his. He thought about how he'd lost her, the lazy way he'd let her go. He thought about Hermenegildo Serrano's dimly-lit house where he'd held her for the last time. And it was just as he was remembering that night that he recovered his strength and saw a solution. Instinct led him back there. He rose to his feet with a courageous and crazy idea that did not come naturally to him. Because the word "courageous" was in Miguel's letter. The word "crazy" too.

He found the key to the house under the vase and the key to the Ford in the kitchen drawer. The car, on the other hand, was out front, right where his brother had parked it years before when he'd come back from San Cristóbal, a place and a journey he hadn't told Santiago about because Santiago had never asked him.

There was a layer of dust on the dashboard, a map of Mexico, a picture of the Virgen de Guadalupe in place of a license, and two photographs. In the first there was a stretch of colorful houses, seen from above, immersed in a wooded valley. In the second, a group of huts clustered around a white church with a jungle in the background. To Santiago they seemed, for some reason, significant clues. In Miguel's letter there was also the word "curiosity." He shut his eyes and turned the key in the ignition, and Hermenegildo Serrano's engine coughed up a clot of oil and rust and fuel that had collected over the years that the car had sat there. But Santiago pressed down hard on the gas and the old Ford began to hum, just like in the old days, as if it had been waiting all that time to hit the road again, for the longest and most improbable journey imaginable. Because to imagine crossing an entire country in a battered old car without a license, you had to be courageous and crazy and curious. Yet Santiago had no misgivings; that was exactly what he was going to do.

The interior of the red Ford shielded him from the outside, and the clouds of Mexico pressed in on the white edges of the sky. Santiago had the sensation of uninterrupted peace, long and quiet as the streets he was driving down. Leaving behind a city and the life he'd lived there was like diving into the silent depths, where there was no one for miles, not a living being.

Around lunchtime he pulled over to the side of the *carretera*, a dusty clearing where some trucks were parked. He got out and took a seat at one of the plastic tables on the beat-up veranda of a bar. He was greeted by a nine-year-old waiter in shorts, his frail chest exposed.

"Today we have *caldo de zopilote*," he said.

Santiago nodded and ordered a beer to go with it. Then he turned to a table nearby where a truck driver, his tank top rolled up to reveal a tattoo of a blue cross on his large belly, was tucking into the same chicken broth, sloppily sucking down every spoonful.

"Excuse me," interrupted Santiago. "Do you happen to

recognize this place?" he asked, extending the photos he'd found in the car. The man looked at the one with the white church and shook his head. Then he looked at the other.

"That's San Cristóbal de las Casas. I'm sure of it."

Santiago thanked him. He stared at the image, trying to see something in it that wasn't there, ate his broth, then climbed back in the car and drove for hours, his thoughts racing without a voice, miles going by without a bend in the road. The *tierra* of Yucatán gave way to the *tierra* of Campache, Tabasco, Chiapas. Late in the night, after a day of traveling forever inside the clouds, he came out into the valley of San Cristóbal, and the temperature suddenly fell while the car slipped past the colonial houses in the dark.

The next day, inquiring in a *posada*, he discovered that the church in the photograph was the Iglesia del Bautista de San Juan Chamula and unwittingly found himself aboard the same shuttle that had taken Miguel there—the van with no roof that Marcelina Fernández Ortiz steered up the slopes of the cordillera. Before getting in, Santiago hesitated, thinking he should move on to Topolobampo to find Miguel. Then he thought, no, he should go to Chamula, since Miguel was to be found also and especially in the echo of his words, the ground he'd tread, the shadows of the people he'd met. In the truck he shut his eyes and felt his brother was close, closer than he'd been in years, in the wind running through his hair, over his body. At the end of their climb, the profile of the church of Bautista, which was the image captured by the camera years before, confirmed his feelings, erased any lingering doubts he had.

Mingling with the other tourists, he walked the tract that ran from the cemetery to the church square all the way to the heart of the miracle revived every day in the Iglesia of Chamula, without mass or priests, only the mystical purr of prayers. Pine needles, darkness, incense, candles. Santiago moved among the wooden saints and thought of Miguel, how he seemed to reside wherever there was mystery and—after years of being thought of as a divinity—traveled the world searching for the divine in order to find something of himself.

Under the statue of Saint Nicholas, a family was absorbed in the ritual. The shaman had his hand on the forehead of a girl, her shiny black hair woven into a long braid held in place with colorful hair ties. He made the sign of the cross on her forehead and offered her a potion that she drank in one gulp. Then the man gathered up a live hen that had been quiet the whole time, lifted it in the air, once, twice, three times, and finally pulled its neck with a clean movement; the animal fluttered and died. The next moment an elderly woman from the family held out a prayer card to the *curandero*, which he took between his fingers, waved about as he had the chicken, and gently ran over the girl's head before tossing it in the air, sending it flying wherever fate or Saint Nicholas or John the Baptist willed it to fly. The card danced in the darkness, cleaved the air of the deconsecrated Iglesia of Chamula, where ancestral animism and modern progress had seeped into the Catholic ritual, and people tore the haloes from the statues of saints that performed no more than a handful of miracles. Not until the card landed, slid across the pine needles, and stopped an inch from Santiago's feet, did he realize that it wasn't just any holy image, but a Polaroid. Not until then did he realize that printed on the photo was not the face of a saint but the face of Miguel.

The girl with the long braid was Yaxté, and if anything her beauty was more savage after all those years—her wide eyes wet from the tears she'd spilled, her hands shaky, as if she had lost something. At the end of the ceremony she withdrew behind her family into one of the few limestone houses.

Santiago searched for Marcelina Fernández Ortiz, made his explanations and inquiries.

"The brother of the *niño hermoso*?" the woman asked, stunned.

Santiago nodded, and when she threw her hands around him to kiss him on the cheeks, he was, as always, unprepared and felt uneasy in Marcelina's Amazonian grip. The woman smelled of rain and tabasco.

"Tell me, how is Miguel?" she continued.

"I haven't—" murmured Santiago, "I haven't heard from him in a long time."

Marcelina studied him curiously to get a better sense of his motives, to understand the meaning of their meeting without having to resort to questions. So, in the end, she asked none.

"The day Miguel was arrested . . . " she began.

The dumbfounded expression on Santiago's face and the surprise it triggered in her were enough for her to decide the story needed to be recounted properly, perhaps even resolved. She gave the tourists a fifteen minute break to visit the town, leaving them to be assailed by peddlers and children. She took Santiago by the arm, firmly yet politely, and began to explain while walking at a good clip toward Yaxté's house.

"The ritual you saw in the *iglesia* has been repeated every morning ever since," she explained. "Her family makes her do it in order to cast out the demon that stole her soul, in order to annihilate the specter of Miguel that to this day torments her and prevents her from taking a husband. Some swear they've seen him running in the forest at night, naked and radiant."

In the yard of Yaxté's house three old women were warping a loom amid starved hens whose fates were already sealed. As soon as Marcelina and Santiago entered, Yaxté's mother barreled toward them like someone determined to defend her turf rather than welcome them in. She had recognized Ortiz, whom she tacitly blamed for having given the devil a lift in her van, for having brought him to Chamula and therefore inside her house. They appeared about to clash when Yaxté leaped out of nowhere and put her agile body between the two, anticipating her mother, planting herself in front of Ortiz.

"*¿K'uxi elan avo'onton?*" asked Ortiz in Tzotzil. How's your heart?

"*Chich'mul Ko'nton,*" responded Yaxté. My heart feels sad.

"Who's he?" interrupted the mother.

Ortiz hesitated, apparently mulling over the impact her answer would have.

"The boy's brother," she finally said.

The woman reacted with disdain. She let out a cry of protest and grabbed her daughter by the shoulders to push her behind her, screaming about their deceit. The old women stopped their weaving; the hens fluttered about in fear.

"Lies! Lies!" she repeated as if possessed.

Yaxté wriggled free of her mother's grip, drew closer, looked Santiago in the eye, ran her hand along his face, and with the end of her finger touched the mole on his right cheek.

"It's his brother," she told her mother and sighed.

The woman finally quieted down, cautiously drew closer to her daughter again, and observed Santiago. If the other boy was the devil, she thought, then this had to be a devilish trick. She quickly mulled over how she might use the situation to her advantage.

"If he's the brother," she said, addressing Marcelina Fernández Ortiz so the woman would translate, "answer me honestly: is he coming back for Yaxté?"

And it was then, at the end of that question in the yard of a house in Chamula, that Santiago sensed things had to happen this way, sensed the meaning of his intuition in Mérida, which had driven him to follow a hunch and surrender to the voice of Marcelina Fernández Ortiz, which had conveyed him, light as pollen, to the flower in front of him, to this intoxicatingly delicate girl whose sadness flew from her dark eyes and scattered in the air around her. Santiago felt it at the bottom of his throat, Yaxté's bitter unhappiness, the dead emotion that nurtured illusions every blessed day for seven springs waiting for Miguel.

So he did what he had to do. What he felt was his duty. He shook his head. No, Miguel was not coming back, Miguel always left, and no one knew why, he abandoned those he loved because he loved the journey of life too much to hang around or turn back. He shook his head to tell her to stop waiting, and in that wordless exchange, not unlike his exchange with his brother, Yaxté responded without speaking; her sadness simply melted all at once, became liquid, ran from her dark eyelashes in large, expectant tears, swollen with a pain that for years she'd locked inside a cage of hope. Yaxté cried, and that ended it. She turned around to find her mother's body, clung to her for deliverance, grabbed hold of her with the instinct of the child she was before meeting Miguel, that she had reverted to being while waiting for him, and it would be the last time she cried before finally becoming a woman. The old Tzotzil trembled as she held her, having found her again after her frantic search. Then she put an end to the affair: she fished the photograph of Miguel from her pocket and handed it to the devil's brother so that he'd take it away.

Two hours later, Santiago was holding the photo like a relic. He didn't immediately leave San Juan Chamula, didn't climb aboard Marcelina Fernández Ortiz's van. He stayed in town to ponder whole chunks of his brother's life that he knew nothing about. He briefly returned to the *iglesia*, and in the mirror that John the Baptist held, his own face reflected back to him seemed like the face of Miguel. In the end he caught a lift with the same Coca-Cola truck that his brother had escaped in years before. Sitting on cases of clear glass bottles, looking out at the dust rising, the sky full of clouds, the photo of Miguel's face

taken the day that Yaxté tried and failed to steal his soul,
Santiago wondered if the Moya family had a soul, if he himself
had one, wracked with the kind of doubt one feels when seeking their destiny far from home, as the road unraveled and the
clink of glass rattled him and made even his thoughts fragile.

Hermoso
BEAUTIFUL

T hinking. The roads of Mexico seemed made for that. For Santiago, thinking was as novel an experience as driving for miles. His brother was to blame for the pain that beset the girl of Chamula, but it also had nothing to do with him. Miguel was hope, mirage, desire. That was what he thought crossing the unspoiled jungle of Chiapas and he decided that from then on, he would travel straight to his destination, to Topolobampo, no more detours. He would only stop when he had to, to fill up on gas and eat. He didn't want to risk stumbling across other ruins Miguel had left in his wake. He pictured an entire country, an entire planet crying over him, waiting for him in vain after having been seduced and abandoned, as if he were a tornado that had ravaged the landscape, ripped things from their roots and flung them elsewhere, broke them beyond repair. But tornadoes weren't to blame; they are part of nature, like the natural world that was then dazzling him on his drive, and the same inherent, destructive power they possessed also contained the seeds of rebirth and followed the cycles and seasons, the sun and the moon, death that became new life. Miguel's beauty was in the nature of things. Only by accepting that idea could you understand it, accept it, respect it, love it for what it created, for what it destroyed, for what it created again.

Santiago's train of thought chugged along the *carretera* through the states of Veracruz, Tlaxcala, Hidalgo. When, looking at the map, he realized that he was passing by Mexico City, he recalled the words Teresa Rodríguez had used to describe it: *It contains the best and worst of our country, the glamour and the gutter.* He felt that Miguel must have been there too, attracted by a mystique so powerful it resembled his own. He wondered in what part of the city, in which apartment, lay a woman still thinking of him, living an existence she struggled to reconstruct. He couldn't have imagined that among them was Rosita Romero, living and working, a mother and wife now, who, over time, had used the pain inflicted on her by Miguel to change, to become something else, though never once fooling herself that she'd forgotten him.

There was the word "solitude" and the word "inability" in the letter. Santiago read it before dozing off for a few hours in the front seat or as he was driving, if he couldn't remember a passage and felt an urgency to mull it over, while the wind from the window riffled the pages in his hands. Then he'd speed up, rush toward the brother he was anxious to find, occasionally carry on a conversation in his head, concoct whole phrases that he'd have liked to have told him and hadn't those nights they lived together. He felt a vague sense of loss that he could only stem by driving faster.

A hundred miles outside the capital, Santiago stopped in a small village off the highway to lunch in the shade of a roadhouse pergola, and at the end of the meal he put his feet up and nodded off, caught up on the sleep he hadn't slept, and let the cool breeze lull him. Shortly after he awoke to a commotion; in the little square outside the *posada* a group of people were pointing at the sky. Santiago would have gone over to see what it was about had he not noticed, on the end of his foot, an orange butterfly. It rested there, slowly opening and closing its wings. He kept looking at it, hypnotized, until, with an almost imperceptible flutter, it flew away. Then Santiago stood up, followed it with his eyes as it rose in the air, and discovered the reason for the fuss outside the roadhouse. There was a bright cloud gliding past the white clouds, hundreds of densely-packed identical butterflies were soaring toward the highlands in the near distance.

"You're a butterfly," Maria Serrano had told him.

"Mariposas monarca," explained an old gray-haired woman who was leaning against the wooden beam of the pergola and had read his thoughts. "They travel thousands of miles to winter here."

Santiago felt he had no choice. A butterfly sticks with his fellow butterflies. He hopped in the car and, forgoing his previous decision, abandoned the road to Topolobampo to follow the *mariposas.* He followed them for miles and miles, entering the state of Michoácan and the park named after them, clambering up the mountain road till the road ended. Then he abandoned the car, headed into the woods on foot, traveled uphill, over rocks, beyond a stream, propelled forward by an inexplicable energy, by a passion that burned in his hands and the soles of his feet and his chest, all the way to an enchanting patch of undergrowth, where immense conifers loomed over red and yellow flowers and purple leaves. When the grass turned gold and he was surrounded by *oyamel,* sacred spruce trees, he knew he'd arrived, though he had to adjust his eyes to the dark forest if he was going to succeed in finding them. After a chase lasting hours he came face to face with the butterfly that had greeted him upon waking, along with millions of others hugging the trees, so that their branches quivered under the weight. the staggering weight of butterflies that painted the forest, the bark, and everything around them orange and black in a majestic, surreal picture. Packed in to warm themselves and signal others to the place that they'd reached and conquered, after journeying three thousand miles from North America to arrive here, in this valley nine thousand feet up in the heart of Mexico, which was simply the place they had chosen. They were everywhere, a carpet that covered the earth and darkened the sky, and suddenly Santiago was a part of it all. With their thousands of weightless wings sounding like a steady drizzle, the butterflies swarmed him, landed in his hair and on his cheeks and shoulders and inside his shirt, stitching together his first tailored shirt, made for him by nature, which he became a part of. Like a butterfly. Like Miguel. Santiago's physical features disappeared; his face and the mole on his face no longer existed. Santiago was a butterfly, which, after all, is nothing more than black caterpillar with colorful wings. And now he had wings, he could sense them, and he felt he could fly far away. They had emerged at a specific moment in time, had sprouted the minute he decided to leave Mérida and go search for his brother. Now he was sure that he'd find him, he'd find Miguel, just as every third generation of monarchs found this place on earth by some kind of miracle. A miracle that pervaded Santiago while tiny butterfly feet brushed his skin, crept over him, and orange wings lined with chocolate-colored striations and white spots fluttered inches from his eyes, from his heart, moved him, made him proud, made him feel part of something immense, which contained Miguel too, Miguel's beauty, which was therefore his beauty. That was how, with his arms open to the sky, to the world, to life, Santiago discovered the beauty of crying, slaking the thirst of the *mariposas* on his face, and he also discovered that Maria Serrano had been right when she called him a butterfly, had been right when, on the hospital bed with a newborn Miguel in her lap, she'd whispered that he too was beautiful. That's how Santiago felt. Beautiful.

Ser hermanos
Being Brothers

When he arrived in Topolobampo, about five days after leaving Mérida, Santiago wasn't the same person. The journey had changed him far more than physically: his life, seen from a distance, appeared minuscule, and Mexico a place less menacing than he had feared. Maybe that was why, when he arrived in Topolobampo, he saw something beautiful in it. Even if it was nothing more than a fishing village facing the Sea of Cortez, a small city like any other. But it was a place to explore and where he would see Miguel again. Santiago was sure of it, he felt he was close, and it took no longer than the time to have a beer to confirm his suspicions. He entered a *posada*, ordered a *cerveza*, and showed the bartender the photograph of his brother in the foreground that the Tzotzil woman had given him. The man pointed to a house on top of a hill at the edge of town overlooking the boats coming in from Baja California Sur. Santiago finished his beer in one gulp. He didn't know it yet, but it was from one of those boats that Miguel had disembarked and, after his endless journey, first stepped foot on Mexican soil with his heart set on returning to Mérida. But a moment later the memory of the pain of Santiago's punch and the fragility he'd felt hit him full in the face. He wouldn't take a step closer to home without being certain that there would be no more hurdles in that house, that he wouldn't be lugging behind more pain. He entered a telephone booth, dialed the Moya number and heard Santiago's voice, but after three years without seeing or talking to him he didn't manage to say anything. He hung up, found a place to rent, allowed some time to pass to reacquaint himself with his native country, hanging in the balance on the edge of the world, a step away from Mexico's escape hatch, and left it to time to somehow give him the answers. He found a job at the docks unloading barrels half the day and the rest of the time threw himself into cultivating a piece of land around the house, even considered staying put. Then, when nostalgia won out, he picked up pen and paper, wrote a letter to Santiago, and buried it in a drawer, thinking he'd never send it, that he'd remain in Topolobampo and grow old far from Mérida, from his family, from his brother.

But here was Hermenegildo Serrano's immortal car climbing the hillside, headed for Miguel's house, where Miguel was busy digging under the sun in a straw hat, his muscles defined from working at the docks and in the field, his fingernails black with dirt, a months-old beard hiding his face—perhaps his reason for letting it grow. He heard the car coming, dried off his sweat, and thought it was a car the same color as his grandpa's. Then he thought: It's a red Ford, like Grandpa's. Finally he became convinced that it really was his grandpa's car and believed he was hallucinating from the heat. He assessed the likelihood of his grandfather in the flesh getting out of the car, because he couldn't imagine anyone else driving it all that way. Which was why, when Santiago climbed out of the car, Miguel couldn't believe it. What was more, he'd never mailed the letter. He stood fixed in the yard, dumbstruck, dropped the spade on the ground, and let his arms hang at his sides.

It was Santiago who took the final steps to reach his brother after traveling miles to reach him. He got a few feet away and as he stared at him, dug up the only words there were to say.

"What are you doing here?" he asked. Then he raised a hand and lightly patted Miguel's head, where he used to hit him as a boy, then slid his hand down to Miguel's cheek, where he'd hit him as a man.

"What am I doing here?" murmured Miguel.

After that, Santiago closed the gap between them once and for all, hugged him with all his strength, squeezed him harder than he'd squeezed anyone, with the exception, twenty years ago, of a two-year-old boy on a street in Mérida—the same person after all. Miguel returned to that street with Santiago, his older brother who punished and forgave him, the brother who protected him, and he felt a profound need to be protected by his brother, who was the best friend he had, perhaps the only friend in a place where men either revered or envied him. So he raised his arms and squeezed his brother back. They held each other tightly for a long time, as Mexicans do, gripping one another firmly so they wouldn't fall, united to resist, like their fathers' fathers, whose Mexico had been invaded and plundered but had managed to keep its soul. And the soul of the Moya brothers joined together contained the contradiction of a country adorned with both beauty and ugliness, with violent and mild contrasts, poetry and magic and a pure love that always triumphed, no matter what.

Then the door to the hut on the hill opened.

Out stepped a dark-skinned girl with Asian features, her smooth hair swaying over her shoulders, an absolute beauty. Santiago saw her and smiled instinctively. And Suchin—that was her name—understood and smiled back. Because she was the one who had sent the letter in secret to the Moya household, extracting it from the dark drawer where it had been hidden. She smiled and then, with the tenderest of gestures, the kind that says everything without saying a word, placed a hand on her stomach, so that one could clearly intuit the child she and Miguel were expecting.

Santiago looked at his brother and saw he was already prepared to hold a baby in his arms. It seemed as though he was training his arms by plowing the hard earth for the child to come, so that he could prop him up, be an example to him, give him a future. And yet again he sensed that, at the very moment he'd gotten Miguel back, had plucked up the courage to travel as he did, had felt as if he were like him, his brother had already moved on, become someone else, had reached the next stage of maturity. And yet this pursuit, begun in a hospital ward, had brought him here, had changed him and would continue to change him over time, and therefore—Santiago now felt it clearly—having a brother, a beautiful brother, had been above all else an opportunity. This awareness allowed him to regard Miguel for the first time without rancor or negative feelings and, after all those years, not since he'd defended and stood up for him by beating up Alfonsino Ruiz perhaps, to feel suddenly like the older brother again. Santiago looked him in the eye and understood the meaning of the letter he had written, the words he had chosen, the land that he was plowing, this house suspended above the nothingness of Topolobampo, far from the one place where he should be, where his child should be born. And he understood that this too was love. Miguel's act of love for him, to defend him from himself, to protect him from the wrong he'd done, that he might do again. Yet Santiago was no longer afraid.

"Let's go home," he said, looking at Miguel.

El tiempo que queda
THE TIME REMAINING

It was Maria Serrano's destiny to wait. A mere few days after Santiago had left, she was convinced he wasn't coming back. Vicente Moya and Miguel weren't coming back. No one was coming back. Something outside Mérida had swallowed them all up. Maybe a monster. Or something inside them, and therefore inside her, had eaten away at the family from within, one bite at a time, until it had left her in this empty house, where she let her thoughts consume her in the kitchen and stared into space, remembering the past, holding herself responsible for things that weren't her fault. One afternoon, strung out by her memories, with no desire to do anything, she dragged herself into her sons' room, where Miguel's hammock lay on the floor in the spot where Santiago had fallen. Maria Serrano collapsed onto the recliner and reflexively switched on the TV. She wound up absorbed in the same telenovelas that he used to watch, in lives completely irrelevant to her own that nevertheless, one episode after another, surpassed it in importance. In a certain light they may have saved her life, given her a reason to continue eating during the commercial breaks, a reason to see how things turned out. That is where she passed the time, even at night, even asleep, nailed to her seat, unwashed, remote in hand, the volume deafeningly high to muffle the voices outside and inside, the echo of her melancholy thoughts. Her trance increased the distance between her and her loved ones and brought her closer to the characters flitting before her, mixing them together in a phosphorescent universe in which pain was divvied up into episodes and dispersed in sentiments recited by others, rendering reality a fiction and fiction a reality in a state of altered sensations.

That was why she didn't hear the door open that night. And that was why, when Santiago and Miguel appeared side by side in the room with a pregnant girl behind them, she mistook them for characters in a telenovela and needed a moment to bring them into focus, to discern that inside that tummy was the gift of a grandchild—a luxury she'd never allowed herself to imagine. She looked back at the screen, then observed them silently observing her, and came to her senses the one way possible: she switched off the TV and came back to life. Finally, with the stately elegance she had inherited from her father, the same elegance with which Hermenegildo Serrano swayed across the dance floor in his youth, she fixed her oily hair in the silent house, after days of artificial noise and actors' voices, and, without even the strength to rise, gave her children and the girl the kindest look, a look that she had lost in the circus tent. And, as in a telenovela, you could say that everything slid back in place. You could say that the Moya household returned to being a family again.

The time remaining was yet another time of expectation, only cheerful now, a brief interlude before the birth of Miguel and Suchin's child. The two had met in the floating village of Tonlé Sap, Cambodia. Miguel was on board a tail boat when he saw her sitting on the dock outside her house made of wood and corrugated metal, her toes in the water and a bowl of shrimp in her hands. As the boat was slipping away, widening the gap between them, he felt he had arrived.

Long afterward, Suchin would ask him what exactly he had felt in that moment.

"Hunger," he answered with a smile, "for shrimp."

When in fact at that moment Miguel had felt that the journey he'd made, every bus, boat, and plane he'd taken, every person he'd met, was a means, a necessary stage along his journey there, and therefore precious. Including Santiago's blow to his face. He also felt that the same freedom he'd discovered as a boy when he fled Mérida in his grandpa's car was at work in the decision of when and where to stop. So he filled his lungs with oxygen and leaped into the murky lake, steadily stroking through the water while people on the tail boat and in the village stood still to take in the spectacle of someone, in an apparently crazy act, seizing life. He reached the floating house, pulled himself out of the water, and sat down next to her, breathless and drenched, hoping that she would be the first to speak.

And, after a long silence, Suchin did speak.

"Do you have any idea what's in the water?" she said.

Miguel was bowled over; her grammar and her English pronunciation were impeccable. He looked at the river, looked at her, looked at the river again.

"What?!" he asked, terrorized.

Suchin burst into joyful, sweet laughter. Then she held the bowl out to him. And Miguel felt that for the first time he was being poked fun of by a woman. He smiled, picked out a shrimp, and burst into laughter too, a cheerful laugh directed at himself.

Now Suchin wielded the same sense of humor, learning Spanish and quickly winning over Maria Serrano, who had already given her credit for returning her two sons to her and was eagerly awaiting the life she'd bear, which would fill the recent silence that had reigned over Casa Moya. They spent a few days there, eating, reminiscing, telling stories. Then the couple moved into the Serrano house, which the girl decorated with lights and cacti. She had fallen in love with cacti, in fact, which didn't exist on the lake, and placed them high on top of the furniture and shelves so that they could watch her son grow without pricking him. Meanwhile Miguel remodeled the house in the levelheaded way he usually approached such matters, just as he'd taken up driving, playing music, and farming the land. Occasionally—he didn't come out unscathed—he would prick himself on one of the cacti and curse Suchin's name, yet he was never able to get really angry at her and always wound up laughing at himself.

One December day, after lunch, when the streets sweltered under the early afternoon sun hanging over Mérida, Miguel and Suchin were married in the Iglesia de Nuestra Señora de Guadalupe, the church where Vicente Moya had once lit an enormous candle for the Virgin after Miguel's resurrection. The prior evening, while he watched Suchin sleeping in the dark, one hand resting on her belly to protect the fruit of their meeting, Miguel had felt short of breath, like that long-ago day when he had plunged into the *cenote*, only this time completely different. Just then, Suchin woke up. Felt a kind of vibration.

"Is this love?" Miguel asked her.

"Is what love?" she replied.

"Like walking around with your stomach full."

"It definitely is for me," said Suchin, smiling, rubbing her belly only to find Miguel's hand there.

So Miguel asked: "Will you marry me one day?"

"Yes," said Suchin without hesitating.

"Tomorrow," he said.

In the empty church, where no one was there to see them, they were married. The priest had agreed to perform the wedding. Present was Suchin's one witness, Maria Serrano, and Miguel's one witness, Santiago, who wore a *guayabera blanca* like Vicente Moya and who at one point stood at the altar and in a broken voice spoke about, among other things, his father. He spoke of his absent father, not once using the word *papà*, not once uttering his name. And then he told a story about a baby whose birth he'd witnessed, whom he had one day hit, and about a journey that had kept them apart, Miguel's journey across the globe, and the journey of their life together. He also spoke about the journey about to begin: the one stirring in Suchin's belly, the journey of a butterfly that wintered in Mexico and in spring would fly away.

In town, news of Miguel's return, marriage, and imminent fatherhood was met more with relief than resentment, since, after that last fateful night in the courtyard, desire for him had been snuffed out by panic, by the awareness that the boy was too much for everyone. Likewise, the different, foreign beauty of the woman who had caught his eye confirmed for them that no one there ever stood a chance, and that fact took the sting out of their resignation. *El hombre perdido*, as many of the women had rechristened him, would remain out of reach. As if he'd never returned at all.

Then, one night just before Christmas, Maria Serrano heard the crunch of dirt under the tires of her father's Ford pulling up to the courtyard, and once again had it all sussed out. She cried out Santiago's name, and mother and son ran out of Casa Moya to the red car where Suchin had already gone into labor and was moaning and whimpering, grabbing hold of whatever she could in the backseat.

"You drive," Miguel said as he climbed out of the car, since Santiago had more experience behind the wheel and his own hands were shaking. They lit out for the hospital. Sitting in back with Suchin, Maria Serrano couldn't help but think back on the night when her father and her husband, sitting in the space now occupied by her two sons, tore through the dark to save Miguel. Then they approached the exact spot, the tallest *tope* in town, where the car had flown in the air and the Moya family with it, only to drop back down on the pavement in a pall of smoke, the spot where Hermenegildo's soul departed while Miguel was departing his body. Maria Serrano, who was assisting Suchin, became distracted for a moment. When she raised her head, the *tope* was right in front of them, like a wall they were about to crash into. She was about to yell at her son to hit the brakes, but Santiago beat her to it, slowed to a stop, and slowly carried them over the hump. Once they had made it across, he looked in the rearview mirror and caught his mother's eye. Their look said all there was to say: it suddenly became clear to Maria Serrano that Santiago, though just a child at the time, recalled everything about that night, recalled everything in his life, had retained every feeling, affliction, and injustice, every wrong he'd done and every wrong he'd been done, in order to become what he was, to grip the steering wheel and deliver them safe and sound, to safely usher in the little creature his brother was expecting.

Two hours later, on one side of the glass window in the hospital corridor, was the face of Isabel—day zero. On the other side, twenty years older, were the faces of Santiago and Miguel, their stunned looks reflected in the glass.

"She's beautiful," murmured Santiago.

"Beautiful," repeated Miguel.

Chillingly so, compared to the five newborns around her, three girls and two boys, some downright ugly, though each one beautiful in their mother's eyes. Little Isabel was simply beautiful, beyond a shadow of a doubt. While they were looking at her, she turned over—where she found the strength was anyone's guess—and rolled onto her side as if she might pick up and leave. Her thin legs peeked out from underneath her pink blanket to reveal a small mole on her ankle. Like the period at the end of a story, the point at which every new story begins.

A Destination

Un destino
A Destination

Miguel knew what was inside the envelope the moment it arrived. He was at Casa Moya with Maria Serrano and Suchin, who was holding Isabel in her arms. A year old and the girl had never cried.

Santiago had left town a few months after the birth of his niece. In springtime, like a monarch butterfly. He had spent the winter nosing through books, consulting maps, and reading Teresa Rodríguez's stock: histories of travel and travelers and essays and short stories about that family of butterfly. Apparently, the monarch possessed a kind of internal GPS based on the earth's magnetic field that led them to their destination.

Of all Santiago's discoveries, that had been the most important.

"I'm going to my *destino*," he announced one day.

"Photograph everything," replied Miguel. "Show me what you see." Then he put the Polaroid Santiago had given him around his neck.

This time Santiago was sure to arrive punctually at the gas station, which was lit up in the morning sky, and he hopped on the same chocolate-scented truck that his brother had ridden years earlier. He crossed Mexico on the road he'd already been down, only now he stopped wherever he felt like for however long he liked. He returned to the monarch sanctuary to watch them emerge from their slumber and fly away. Then he moved on to Topolobampo; the route was circuitous and familiar yet necessary for him to work up the courage to take his leap. After all, his life had followed a circuitous yet necessary route. And once there, he found his courage. He boarded the first ship for Baja California Sur, off to see the United States, off to see the world.

Now the world was laid out on the kitchen table, where Miguel had spread the photos. The Colorado River coursing through the vast expanses of the Grand Canyon; the ruins of Machu Picchu at sunset in a drizzle; the crescent moon over the coast of Copacabana seen from Pan di Zucchero; Route 40 running parallel to the Andes; the enormous frosty outline of Perito Moreno reflected on the surface of Argentino Lake. Everything was there, with the exception of Santiago, who was in every single fragment and none in particular.

Then Miguel set the last photo down on the table under the tearful eyes of Maria Serrano. Gone were the panoramas. With an animated *milonga* in the backdrop—in what must have been the heart of Buenos Aires—and the profile of a woman clasping his trim body, there was Santiago. Black trousers, red shirt open to the chest, standing straight, looking confident, the mole on his cheek front and center, like an artistic flourish. He was performing a move that would have made his grandpa proud of the talent that he'd handed down. They felt as though they were watching him dance, moving sensually, with utter cool and the same natural grace he'd displayed in the Moyas' courtyard, his agile elegance like a butterfly's. It had been right under his nose, his *destino*, and he'd failed to see it. They all looked at him in silence. His face serious, his chin raised, his arms squeezing the ballerina, his eyes on a future that seemed in his sights. Looking at that image, captured thousands of miles from home, you had the distinct impression that, as he stood on tiptoe in his shiny shoes, in the middle of the dance floor, he was about to take flight.

GLOSSARY

Barbacoa: cooking method that originated in the Caribbean, from which the name "barbecue" derives. In Mexico, it traditionally refers to a whole sheep slow-cooked in a hole in the ground and covered with maguey leaves.

Bombas: playful or romantic verses recited by men to their female dancing partners during *la jarana*, a traditional dance in the Yucatán Peninsula. The verses are recited when the music stops.

Botanas: traditional Yucatecan snacks served for free in bars.

Cenote: natural freshwater sinkhole formed by the collapse of one or more limestone cave ceilings. The name, of Mayan origin, means "cave of water."

Chácara: Mexican equivalent of hopscotch.

Champurrado: chocolate version of *atole*, a warm drink made with cinnamon, corn flour, sugar cane, vanilla, and water.

Charangas: ensembles that play traditional Yucatecan music.

Curandero: in indigenous Latin American cultures, a shaman who practices folk medicine using herbs and other natural remedies.

Flores cempasúchil: *Tagetes erecta*, or Mexican marigold, found in coniferous forests in tropical climates in Mexico and Guatemala. As early as prehistoric times they were considered flowers of the dead.

Gasolinera: gas station.

Güiro: percussion instrument made from *güira*, a type of gourd. Notches cut into the upper part are strummed with a drumstick to produce short, sharp notes.

Gusano: commonly known as the worm, a butterfly larva that infests agave plants and is bottled with certain kinds of mezcal to give them flavor. It is believed to possess magical, hallucinogenic, and aphrodisiacal properties.

Huipil: traditional white cotton shirt for women with an embroidered bustier.

Jarabe Tapatío: Mexican folk dance par excellence. It symbolizes a man's courtship of a woman. The latter rejects him at first but ultimately gives in to his advances.

Jarana: literally "revelry," a traditional dance of the Yucatán Peninsula.

Jarra: mug.

Limpia: folk cure to exorcise evil and reverse bad luck by rubbing a person with herbs.

Maquech: Mayan word for beetle, also known as the "Yucatecan beetle." Considered a token of love, it is traditionally decorated to become a "living jewel."

Mariachis: traditional Mexican bands who play at celebrations, parties, and serenades. Since the 20th century they have dressed up as *charros* (traditional Mexican horsemen). They typically include seven or twelve musicians.

Marquesita: crepelike dish stuffed with various fillings.

Michelada: Mexican cocktail made with beer, lime juice, and assorted sauces and spices.

Mukbil pollo: pie made with corn, pork fat, chicken, and assorted condiments wrapped in banana leaves and cooked in an underground oven, per Mayan tradition. It is customarily prepared on All Saints' Day.

Natalicio de Benito Juárez: On March 21st Mexico celebrates the birth of Benito Pablo Juárez García. Considered a national hero, García was the first American Indian on the continent to hold the office of presidency, from 1858–1872.

Nochebuena: Christmas Eve.

Pan de Muertos: sweet bread made with aniseed and placed on gravestones as an offering. The souls are believed to absorb the essence of the food.

Panuchos: Yucatecan dish believed to have originated in Mérida. Tortillas are stuffed with refried beans, then deep fried and topped with shredded cabbage, chicken or turkey, tomato, red onion, avocado, and jalapeno.

Papadzules: traditional Yucatecan dish. In its simplest form, the tortillas are covered with a pumpkinseed sauce, stuffed with hard-boiled eggs, and topped with a spicy tomato sauce.

Papel picado: paper handicraft used as decoration during holidays and special occasions. The paper is cut to form elaborate designs.

Poc chuc: standard Yucatecan dish made with pork marinated in sour orange and grilled.

Puchero: stew that takes its name from the clay receptacle it is cooked in. The three-meat version (beef, chicken, and pork) is the classic Sunday brunch dish in Yucatán.

Ranchera: popular genre of Mexican music. The lyrics range in subject, from family life and horses, to revolution and rural life, to bars and love affairs.

Rebozo: traditional Mexican garment worn by women. A cotton, wool, or silk rectangle, it can be worn as a scarf and is often used to carry newborns or objects.

Sopa de lima: chicken soup with lime.

Tamalitos: corn flour wraps filled with meat, cheese, or fish. Generally enclosed in a corn husk or a banana peel and stewed.

Tzotzil: The Tzotzil Maya from the central highlands of Chiapas are an ethnic group of American Indians directly descended from the Mayans.

Vaquerías: large, traditional festivities in Yucatán, originally associated with branding livestock.

Vihuela: ancient musical instrument in the lute family, similar to a guitar.

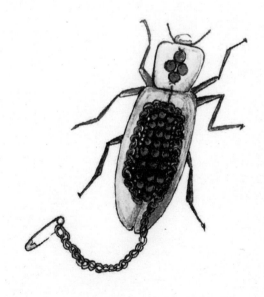

ABOUT THE AUTHOR

Massimo Cuomo was born in Venice in 1974 and lives in the countryside near Portogruaro. He is the author of three novels. *Beautiful* is his first book to appear in English.